Content Advisory: Although this book falls within the young adult genre, it does contain some violence and foul language and is intended for readers 16+.

GAME OF DEATH

THE FERAL SENTENCE – BOOK 1
BEASTS OF PREY – BOOK 2
PRIMAL INSTINCTS – BOOK 3
REIGN OF BLOOD – BOOK 4
GAME OF DEATH – BOOK 5

Shade Owens
www.shadeowens.com

Edited by Nikki Busch
www.nikkibuschediting.com

RED RAVEN PUBLISHING

ISBN: 978-1-7775422-7-6

PART one

PROLOGUE

It's hard to imagine this happened, but it did.

Two years ago, we went to war with our sworn enemies—the Northers. Despite the losses we suffered, we've come out stronger than ever.

Now, I live in a world that can only be described as paradise on Earth. The Village—once a desolate wasteland covered in ash—has been rebuilt from the ground up. A dozen wooden shacks line up the back wall, and hundreds of single tents constructed of finely sanded wood sit flawlessly across the open space. Around the tents, luscious green grass covers the ground like a giant carpet— a result of several days' work transplanting seeds.

I'm still astonished by the amount of work every single woman put into rebuilding our home after the war. Palm seedlings stand tall around the Village's perimeter, and an abundance of vibrant colors remind us that even after death, life can flourish.

While we no longer have beautiful green trees towering around the Village, new life has begun to emerge from the ashes—strong sprouts, vivid flowers, and thick green grass. Around the Village, we've constructed a wooden wall, similar to the gate the Northers had, to protect us from any exterior threat. Two gates have been added to the entrance of the Village for safety and convenience, and an additional gate remains at the back.

For the first time in as long as I can remember, I smile.

Every day, I smile.

No one fights anymore—at least not the way they used to before the war. It's as if I live in an alternate reality. I can't even remember the last time I fantasized about leaving the island.

For the first time since being banished to Kormace Island, I'm happy.

Truly happy.

How is this even possible? Is this the universe's way of apologizing for all the torturous shit I've gone through?

It has to be.

The only question now is, how long will this last?

CHAPTER 1

"Robin, get over here," Ellie said, chasing after Robin.

She looked exactly like her mother—light blond hair, a petite frame, and eyes as blue as the summer sky. While the sight of her warmed my heart, it also pained me.

Robin giggled, squealed some incomprehensible word, and fell flat on her cotton-covered butt.

Then, the crying started.

When Ellie caught me watching them, she shook her head with a sweet smile and scooped little Robin into her arms.

I thought of BluJay's face—the fear, the sadness, the hurt. But the moment her baby girl came out, all of that disappeared, and an indescribable joy lit up her face. Every day, I tried to hold onto this image in my mind—her smile and her tears of joy. It was easier to remember BluJay as a mother filled with love rather than as a corpse.

After that brief heavenly moment, everything had gone to hell. It was as if she knew she was dying. She'd grabbed my wrist as tight as she could and made me promise her I'd take care of her little girl.

Robin, I thought, smiling as Ellie bounced her up and down in her arms. It was the name I'd given her in honor of her mother.

"Is she ever getting big," came Fisher's voice.

I glanced up to catch Fisher looking down at me.

She appeared much healthier now that she'd stopped using her walking stick. Her leg, although still scarred from the crocodile attack, wasn't as gruesome looking as it had once been. It resembled an old tree's bark or a wrinkled blanket. She stretched her back and sat down on the log next to me.

"Still can't believe this is real," she said, gazing throughout the Village.

Today marked the two-year-anniversary of both our losses and our victory. Fisher had held onto a small booklet made of leather and parchment paper. I'd never known her to be an artist, but it turned out she was. She drew faces, mostly using sticks of charcoal and, occasionally, flowers to rub in some color. It was incredible to see how many tools we'd come up with as a mixed society. Our people as a whole were now a combination of the original Village dwellers, Norther slaves, and even a Norther—Iskra, who'd proven herself to be an invaluable part of our society.

Fisher ran her finger along one of the back pages of her book and across countless little drawn sticks that signified a day passed. She'd bundled them in groups of fives, with one mark running horizontally across her sticks. The entire page was full. At the very bottom, she scraped her charcoal stick one more time across the last remaining four, and underneath that wrote 365, 2, which I knew meant *Day 365, year 2 following the war.*

We'd started officially counting days after the war as a way of embracing our new start.

She flipped through her pages to return to the front, and as she did that, I saw text written throughout the book.

"What's that?" I asked, craning my neck. "Poetry? Are you a writer?"

Smirking, she shook her head. "I wish. I don't have that talent. I'm documentin' everything, so one day, if they ever come back for us, they'll know our story, you know?" She looked saddened, her head pulled forward and her shoulders curved inward.

"So, our history," I said.

The corner of her lip pulled up and she glanced sideways at me. "Exactly. I've been goin' around collecting women's stories. All of them. The slaves, everything. It's pretty damn amazing, Brone, to hear everything they've gone through. And to hear about Rainer, about the Northers when they were kids, all of it. If I could write a book, I'd write about Rainer's story. Man, if I ever get off this island, maybe I will and I'll be rich." She nudged me and laughed, something that never got old.

Fisher never used to laugh, so to see her this way lit up my heart in a way I couldn't describe. Aside from Ellie, Fisher was my best friend. During the last two years, I'd told her things I'd never told anyone, like how my mom's boyfriend, Gary, had also hit me a few times when Mom wasn't around.

I'd never voiced that aloud to anyone because I didn't want anyone thinking I'd killed him out of anger or revenge. I'd only hit him with the pan to save my mom—it hadn't been about me. Fisher understood that.

Side by side, Fisher and I watched as the toddlers played together, giggling and throwing sticks. Some were well-balanced on their feet, while a few others stumbled over their chubby thighs before crashing into the grass.

Fisher placed her book on her lap and ran a hand across a clean white sheet. Glaring intently toward the children, she held her charcoal stick in her left hand and started drawing lines.

I didn't dare say anything. When Fisher drew, she disappeared from reality. While she looked pissed off, she was concentrating and loving every second of it. I knew precisely what she was thinking and why she was drawing the children playing—we'd become a big family. Smiling, I watched them play, and every few seconds, I glanced down at Fisher's drawing coming to life.

Eliot came running out from behind one of the tents with a goofy grin on his face and his arms waving like an octopus's tentacles. Beside the mothers, he looked huge, but everyone knew he was as friendly as a golden retriever.

He reached down, and with his tanned, muscular arms, scooped up a boy and a girl, then kissed each one on their foreheads. What I loved most about Eliot was that he treated every child like his own, even though some of them were the biological children of his dead brother, Isaac.

He grinned and his molars made an appearance, resembling white pieces of gum inside his cheeks. I couldn't even imagine what it was like being the father to twenty-three children.

Iliza, the Egyptian beauty he'd fallen in love with, walked to his side with a hand over her round belly and leaned her head on his shoulder.

Fisher brushed the tips of her fingers across her drawing and laughed through her nose.

"What's so funny?" I asked.

"It's crazy," she said.

She didn't have to respond to me to know what she was talking about. Every day, I felt this way.

How had we, hundreds of convicted murderers, managed to create such a peaceful society? Occasionally, women got on each other's nerves, but in comparison to how things used to be, this was remarkable.

Fisher rubbed her thumb beside one of her drawn child's feet to create a shadow. "Honestly, I don't even want to get off this island. Everyone's happy. I don't know how you made this happen, Brone, but you did."

In the distance, I caught a glimpse of Murk frying a fish over the Village's open fire. After the war, she hadn't even tried to reclaim her position as leader. It was as if she'd known her time was up. Now, she enjoyed her freedom—she wasn't burdened by responsibility anymore, and she deserved that. It was a bit like watching someone retire after a lifetime of service.

Every day, her spirits were elevated, and I no longer viewed Murk as some cold, powerful woman—instead, I saw an older woman who wanted nothing more than to live the remainder of her life in serenity.

Some days, I even caught her playing with the children, her grin so wide I barely recognized her.

I turned to Fisher. "I didn't do all of this. Everyone took part."

She nudged me in the shoulder. "You know what I mean."

Our attention turned toward Biggie, Rocket, and Elektra, who came through the Village gates dragging a dead boar. Elektra, now lankier than ever but almost as tall as Biggie, smiled smugly as she tugged on the rope. What she didn't realize was that behind her, Biggie was doing most of the heavy lifting.

It was extraordinary to see my Hunters come back from each hunt with food for our people. We were still surrounded by the Dead Zone, after all. They were no doubt traveling incredible distances to find food. Slowly, life had begun to return following the burning of our Village and a large portion of the jungle.

What blew my mind most of all was the fine work of two women in particular—Clarisse and Matilde. Having once been slaves, both of these two beautiful souls were part of the group I'd initially rescued from the Northers. Clarisse, a former nutritionist from Colorado, knew absolutely everything about the importance of a healthy, balanced diet full of plant-based protein. Matilde, on the other hand, had grown up in Portugal before migrating to the United States, where she studied hydroponics and marine biology.

With her mind-blowing knowledge, we'd managed to repopulate the Working Ground's bay of water with an array of fish to be consumed.

Every day, she went diving into the water to care for the bay, her slick black hair combed back on her head when she resurfaced.

The rule was simple: women could use the bay to bathe, but urinating was to occur on land. I'd found this to be a bit silly at first, seeing as the bay was so big. But then, Matilde explained to me that human urine is essentially full of nitrogen, potassium, and phosphorus—nutrients that help plants grow. She'd said something about fertilizer containing those three ingredients and that our pee was basically fertilizer. Long story short, she said that if everyone were to urinate in the bay— and realistically, we were several hundred women—we would be filling it with fertilizer, in a sense, which would feed the algae. Algae was a big oxygen sucker, so the more algae there was, the less oxygen remained for the fish underwater.

She'd explained all of this to the people of the Village during one of our weekly classes, something I'd initiated to help promote constant learning and growth. Anyone who'd once held a specialty was asked to give educational sessions to help share some of their knowledge. Proxy, with that encyclopedia-like brain of hers, had volunteered each week and had even asked if I could implement daily sessions. While her knowledge was invaluable, I didn't want to stress the women out by forcing them into anything.

Instead, I'd decided to take it slow until the women began to show more interest.

It was important to establish some sort of educational program because as the children started growing older, they would need some form of education. Unlike Rainer, these kids weren't going to become mindless soldiers; they were going to have a life worth living.

"Real meat tonight!" one woman shouted, pointing at the dead boar.

At once, several women came running toward the Hunters to help carry the animal. One woman patted Elektra on the back—a gesture that meant something along the lines of, *Well done*—and Elektra stiffened her posture pridefully.

Walking toward Fisher and me, Rocket wrapped an arm around Elektra. "Her first kill."

"You shoulda seen it," Elektra said, her long orange hair swaying behind her back as she jumped up and down. She crouched, whipped out an arrow from her quiver, and loaded her bow.

"Whoa," Rocket said, pushing her weapon down. "We talked about this."

Elektra cleared her throat. "Sorry." She put her arrow away, and with an invisible one, started reenacting the hunting scene.

Behind her, Rocket smiled like a tired mother, rolled her eyes, and threw a thumb out at Elektra. "It was all her."

Biggie stomped her way toward us, her legs jiggling with every step. "Girl did damn good." She slapped Elektra on the back, causing her to drop her bow.

Elektra swung around with a scowl, and I couldn't help but laugh. "Get used to it, Elektra. Biggie here once had me hanging inches away from a school of piranhas."

Elektra wrinkled her nose. "School?"

"Girl, you got a lot to learn," Biggie said. "It means a bunch o' fish that swim together."

Elektra paused, then without warning, burst out laughing. "You did that to *Brone*?"

Biggie smacked a hand over her belly, her deep laugh spreading across the city. "She din't think it was funny then."

I smirked, remembering how angry I'd been. How could I have reacted any other way? She'd scared the crap out of me and I was also still processing the fact that I was never going to see home again. I remembered jumping on top of her, prepared to bash her face in.

God, I didn't miss that rage.

Ever since we'd defeated the Northers, all of my anger had dissipated. It was like a giant weight had been lifted off my shoulders, and at last, I could breathe again.

"Come on," Rocket said, tugging on the bottom of Elektra's bloody shirt. "Let's get this cleaned up."

She threw her chin out at me. "See you at the Working Grounds?"

I smiled at the thought of sunbathing next to the Working Grounds' waterfall. I parted my lips, prepared to tell her I'd see her soon, when a subtle rumbling shook the earth beneath my feet.

An earthquake?

It couldn't be; it wasn't powerful enough. What I was feeling were vibrations coming from somewhere else. What was that? And why did it sound so familiar? I wasn't the only one hearing it. Everyone exchanged a look that translated to, *What the hell is that?*

Closing my eyes, I listened.

It was coming from above. But from where? Craning my neck, I searched the sky, unable to see anything.

It couldn't be, could it? I searched the others for validation, but their faces mirrored what I was thinking: *impossible.*

"What the hell is that?" Elektra finally said, breaking the silence.

Rocket didn't even bother telling her to watch her mouth. Her eyes, bright green balls, widened at me as if to say, *It can't be.*

She had every reason to look so awestruck. That sound wasn't an earthquake, and it most definitely wasn't anything natural. Although I hadn't heard that sound in as long as I could remember, I knew exactly what it was—a plane.

CHAPTER 2

For a moment, it was as if I'd traveled back in time to when every day, our lives were at risk.

Women circled me, yammering away as if trying to buy tickets to some sold-out show.

"What if it's a rescue plane?" one woman shouted. "We have to go see!"

"Are you an idiot?" came another woman's voice. "We have no idea who's on that plane!"

"Well, we won't know until we check, will we?" the other woman snapped.

They were freaking out, and with good reason. I'd come to learn that these women needed certainty above all else. It was the fear of the unknown that spread like an airborne illness, sending even the kindest women into a fit of anger. For the first time since the war, women looked at each other with hatred and animosity.

In the middle of the crowd, women divided themselves: one side demanded we go see the plane, while the other argued that it was too dangerous. I'd fought relentlessly to bring our people together. I wasn't about to let some plane get in the way of that.

I breathed in, conscious of the air expanding my lungs, and breathed out. Suddenly, everyone stopped talking as if my breath alone had been an order for silence. The only sound to be heard across the Village were children giggling, some crying, and Eliot stomping around trying to keep the kids close by.

From within the crowd, I caught a glimpse of my closest friends—at least, those who remained: Biggie, Rocket, Coin, Hammer, Fisher, and Quinn. The look in their eyes expressed precisely what I was thinking—we had to find out more.

They didn't vocalize those thoughts, though, no doubt out of respect for my position as their leader.

"Well the longer we stand here, the less chance we'll have—"

"Oh shut your pie hole, Yasmin."

"The fuck did you say?"

"Enough!" I shouted, and everyone went quiet again.

Finally, standing up on the old log under me, I straightened my back. "The Hunters will go investigate the situation."

"Hunters? What if it isn't a threat? I mean, this plane would be a rescue," one woman said. "Why are we sending the Hunters?" Her bristly brows were so slanted they changed the shape of her face. "And, what? We're supposed to stand around here while the Hunters go check it out? Shouldn't we all be going? What if the Hunters leave us behind? I mean, maybe we're finally getting off this goddamn—"

The moment I raised a hand, she sucked in a sharp breath and held it. "I'll be joining the Hunters."

The bickering blew up again.

"You're the leader, you can't go!"

"What if something happens to you?"

Everyone started talking over one another so loudly that they sounded like a flock of seagulls.

I realized it was unconventional for me, the leader, to venture out into the jungle. It was breaking the very foundation of our society—stability. Without their leader, who would make decisions? Who would maintain order?

But I couldn't *not* go. These women were afraid of being betrayed by the Hunters, and the one person they truly trusted was me. If this were, in fact, part of a rescue mission, I needed to be present on behalf of my people.

Raising a solid fist in the air, I scanned the crowd until one by one, the women stopped talking. "Murk will be in charge until I return."

Lips began to part in the crowd, but no one dared say anything. How could they? Murk had been the original leader. If anyone was fit to lead, it was her. At the back of the crowd, Murk nodded, the cool look on her face never fading. Although she no longer wanted to lead, I knew I could count on her to step up if the occasion required it.

"There's absolutely nothing to worry about," I said. "Stay close to each other, and as always, stay in the Village or within the Working Grounds until I get back."

Although hesitant, the women of the Village nodded, their gazes shifting between me and Murk, who did her best to exude confidence.

Throwing my chin out at my friends, I said, "You guys ready?"

Aside from Fisher, who no longer ventured outside of the Village, and Quinn, who I only later discovered suffered from chronic bronchitis, everyone nodded like armed soldiers.

"Hammer," I said, "you got any weapons?"

Grinning, she widened her stance and crossed her arms. "Have you not been inside my tent?"

Ever since I'd reimplemented the monetary system, Hammer had spent her days whistling to unfamiliar tunes and hopping around the Village like she owned the place. Every day, she'd spend hours building all sorts of tools, gadgets, and weapons. As Hammer had described it, collecting various metals from our enemies had been equivalent to spending the day at a hardware store with a limitless credit card.

She'd created axes, clubs, boomerangs, knives, crossbows, spears, and even nunchucks.

At first, I hadn't wanted any weapon inside the Village given the violent past many of us had lived through, but after having spoken with Murk, I'd decided being prepared for potential enemies wasn't necessarily a bad thing.

The rule was simple—no one could actually *buy* a weapon; they were reserved for exterior threats. Hammer had agreed to use locking compartments pulled off the crashed plane. They weren't fancy, but they served their purpose.

"Can I come?" Elektra asked, fighting to catch her breath.

Where had she come from? That kid never stopped running.

Before I could say anything, I caught a glimpse of Ellie coming up behind her. In her arms, she held little Robin and bounced her on her hip— something she did every time Robin started getting cranky. Although I wanted nothing more than to hug them both, the look in her eyes made my stomach sink. It was obvious she was angry, and Ellie rarely ever got angry. It was a gaze that translated to, *Are you seriously going to leave us again?*

Ever since Robin had come into the picture and I'd adopted my leadership role, I stopped leaving the Village altogether. In a strange and wonderful way, Robin and Ellie had become my family. It was understandable that Ellie would be upset that I was heading out into the wild and putting my life in danger.

Beside me, Elektra rolled back and forth on her heels, waiting. Without looking at her, I said, "You can come."

She'd spent the last year hunting by Rocket's side. I had to stop thinking of her as a helpless child and instead appreciate how valuable she'd become to our society.

With a grin, she hopped in the air, extended her lanky legs, and kicked the heels of her feet together.

"Rocket, Biggie, and Coin," I said, "you guys come too. Get your weapons ready."

I deliberately decided to exclude Hammer because she controlled the Tools tent, which meant it was her responsibility to ensure all weapons remained locked. Admittedly, the other reason I no longer sent her out on hunting missions was that she wasn't as limber as she had been before we rebuilt the Village and probably wouldn't be able to keep up. I often caught her rubbing her knees and wincing in pain when she sat down to eat, and I didn't want to make it any harder for her.

Still feeling Ellie's intimidating stare aimed at me, I jerked my head sideways to say, *Can we talk?*

As she approached me, she sighed with Robin still bouncing in her arms. When we came face-to-face, Robin giggled and reached for my hair.

"Listen, I won't be long," I said.

"It doesn't matter," she cut me off. "Things have been great for a long time. Why are you going out there and putting your life at risk? You're in charge now. Send someone else. We're happy, Brone. Why the hell—" She brushed Robin's thin blond hair back and kissed her forehead. "Why the heck are you doing this?"

"Because this is a big deal," I said. "It's a plane, Ellie." I beamed, suddenly envisioning all the possibilities. "What if this is it? What if they're searching for us?"

She bit her bottom lip and turned her head away. Deep down, she was likely thinking the exact same thing. Why else would a small plane land on Kormace Island? What if they were reporters? What if all of Mr. Milas's corruption had been uncovered at last and a new government was sending a team to search for survivors?

"I promise, I'll be careful," I said.

She sucked in a long breath and raised her chin. "You better come back in one piece."

I smiled at her. While no one else in the Village had any right to boss me around, Ellie was the one person who dared talk to me like that. Admittedly, I liked it, and it made me want to kiss her hard on the lips.

So, I did, and the pink spreading across her cheeks told me she wouldn't be holding onto any anger. As I pulled away, Rocket, Elektra, Biggie, and Coin came marching my way with bows and quivers fastened to their backs. Around their waists, belts were loaded with knives, ropes, and water bladders.

"I'll be back before you know it," I said, planting a soft peck on Ellie's cheek. Gently, I rested a hand on Robin's soft fuzzy head and kissed the tip of her nose.

Walking away was harder than I had anticipated. I hadn't left Robin or Ellie's side since the war had ended, but, being the leader of the Village, I felt it was my responsibility to see to this myself.

If negotiations were going to take place, I wanted to be the one to discuss them.

"All right, let's go," I said, pointing toward the Village's opening.

"Just like old times," Rocket said.

A moment of silence followed Rocket's words. Sure, it was like old times, only it wasn't. Flander was no longer with us, and neither was Trim, Eagle, Arenas, Franklin, or Johnson. How were we supposed to simply forget about them?

Things would never be the same.

CHAPTER 3

We walked in silence for hours, listening to the sound of our breathing and our feet crushing vegetation, fungi, and insects on the jungle floor.

While there was no telling where the plane had landed—or if it had landed at all—I knew one thing for certain: any pilot intending to land a plane would land it onshore. The island's jungle was far too dense.

"My feet hurt," Elektra complained.

Rocket gave her the stink eye and Elektra sucked her lips until they formed a small dot on her face.

"We talked about this," Rocket said.

Suddenly, Elektra was back to being a prepubescent teen. She scowled at Rocket the way a young girl would after being told to stop playing on her phone in class.

Biggie smacked her round belly and laughed. "Talked about what?"

Without smiling, Rocket said, "Complaining."

"Man, if Trim were here," Biggie said, snapping her fingers in the air, "you'd be gettin' way more than a talk."

No one said anything, so Biggie cleared her throat, no doubt realizing Trim's name had dampened the mood.

It didn't help that we were walking through the Dead Zone surrounded by leafless trees and dirt. Every few feet, we'd find a blooming flower sticking out like a parrot in a crowd of penguins. How long would it take for the forest to return to the way it had once been? Would it ever?

I stepped over a log that resembled a rotten limb when Coin let out a sharp whistle. Everyone froze, waiting for Coin to say something. But instead, she lit up, her dark cheeks forming little balloons under her eyes, and pointed up into one of the dead trees.

Following her finger, I stretched my neck and stared upward.

On a thick, curved branch sat a beautiful toucan, its orange and yellow beak reaching far from its face. It peered down at us with its small black and blue eyes that resembled doll eyes, then threw its head back. "Craw, craw!"

"Is that—" Rocket said, her head tilted so far back her mouth hung wide open.

"Molly," I breathed.

"Who's Molly?" Elektra asked.

The sight of Molly hit me a bit harder than I'd have expected. Swallowing hard, I turned my attention to Elektra and pointed up at the bird. "See its feet?"

"Yeah," Elektra said, bouncing in one spot. "The blue ones? I see them! I see them! Hey, what's wrong with that one? She's missing part of her foot."

"Not sure," I said. "Trim's the one who named her. She said she always recognized her in the jungle because of her foot."

"That's so sad," Elektra said.

While Elektra felt sorry for the bird, all I could think of was Trim, and how she was no longer with us. And, I thought of everyone else and wondered what they might have said had they been standing here with us, looking up at Molly. Although I should have felt sadness at the thought of my dead friends, all I felt was a sense of calm. I couldn't quite put my finger on it, but it was almost as if they were standing right next to us, telling us that they were okay.

I'd never known what to believe in regarding the whole afterlife thing, but I wanted to believe that death was only the end of life on Earth.

Rocket shivered and rubbed her arms. "You feel that?"

Biggie turned in circles as if searching for Trim and the others. "What? What is it? You feelin' somethin'?"

"Oh, stop it," Coin said. "You're gonna freak the

kid out. Ghosts ain't real. When you die, you die. That's it. You're gone forever. That's why you gotta appreciate every single day." She pointed at all of us and twirled a finger around her ear. "Whatever you're feelin' is all in your head."

"You take that back!" Elektra snapped.

Rocket rubbed Elektra's back the way a mother does a sick child. "Whoa, kid, easy."

But this did nothing to calm her. Instead, Elektra pulled way, clenched her fists, and with a cracking voice, shouted, "Now!"

Why was she so upset about this? It wasn't like she'd known Trim or the others all that well. Did she care more deeply than we knew? Or, was she defending Rocket?

Coin scrunched her nose, one nostril rising higher than the other. "Take what back? The truth? Kid, I wasn't trying to offend—"

Without warning, Elektra threw herself at Coin, sending them both flying into the dirt. With her lanky arms and sharp-knuckled fists, she started swinging for Coin's face.

"Yo, what the hell!" Coin shouted. "Get her off me!"

Coin wasn't weak by any means—she was stocky and carried the kind of muscle you'd find in a lightweight bodybuilder. So when she didn't hit back, it was likely out of not wanting to hurt Elektra.

In a swooping motion, Biggie scooped Elektra up, forced her arms down at her sides, and held her tightly in that position. Elektra kicked her legs and rolled her head in every direction imaginable, almost as if possessed by some demonic force.

"Let go of me!"

"Calm," Biggie said soothingly.

This wasn't the first time someone held Elektra as hard as they could until she calmed down. But she was getting taller, and now, the only person able to do it without struggling was Biggie or Eliot.

"You don't know anything!" Elektra shouted.

She was being so loud I wanted to tell her to zip it, but the pain in her eyes told me that this was about something much more than coming to Rocket's defense.

"She's always with me! She promised me she would be! And she told me I'd see her again!" Elektra cried out.

Her face was swollen and plum in color, making me wonder if Biggie was squeezing too tight. But, behind Elektra, Biggie stood calmly without showing any signs of exertion and kept whispering, "Calm down, kiddo. It's okay."

The fight lasted a few minutes longer until finally, Elektra went limp and burst into tears. At once, Rocket came running by Biggie's side.

"Let her go, let her go," she said.

Slowly, Biggie brought her back to the ground

and unlocked her fingers from around Elektra's waist. With tears glistening off her cheeks and a contorted mouth, Elektra threw her arms around Rocket's neck.

"Hey, it's okay," Rocket said, brushing Elektra's frizzy hair back. "You're okay. I'm right here."

I'd never seen Elektra cry so much. I'd witnessed countless fits of rage but never anything like this. Typically, her fits lasted a few minutes with intervention, and often, she'd come out of it and go about her normal business. She'd even apologize at times, seemingly ashamed. But not once had I ever seen her break down like this. These tears were the result of a deep pain none of us knew anything about.

"What's going on, sweetheart?" Rocket asked.

Wiping her eyes with the back of her arm, she sucked in a glob of mucus and fought to catch her breath.

"You can talk to us, you know," Rocket said. "We're your family now."

This seemed to upset Elektra even more. Sniffling, she dug her head into Rocket's neck. It was a sad thing to see, especially being that Elektra surpassed Rocket by at least a foot in height. She trembled as she cried, her back hunched and her long arms wrapped around Rocket

"You don't have to talk about it if you don't want to," Rocket said. "But I want you to know that we've all lost people we care deeply about. It's so hard. It hurts." She pulled Elektra back and patted her heart. "In here, it hurts. Are you hurting?"

Elektra nodded, her slobbery bottom lip trembling.

"She... she took care of me," Elektra said.

"Who did, honey?" Rocket asked.

"Leah, my big sister. Mom was... Mom was always too fuzzy."

Rocket forced a playful smirk, no doubt trying to make Elektra feel safe. "Fuzzy?"

"That's what Leah called it. Mom took lots of pills and drank strong stuff all the time. I... I was too young to know what it was then, but I guess it was like that moon stuff you guys drink sometimes."

"Alcohol?" Rocket asked.

Elektra nodded and with her arm, wiped her eyes. "One night, Mom got so bad she hurt me. I don't remember all of it, but I remember my face and my wrists hurting a lot. Leah came running downstairs when she heard us. She was sixteen, older than I am now, and bigger than Mom. So she tried to stop her." She swallowed hard, cleared her throat, and gazed up at the sky as if watching her memory form in the clouds. "Mom had a gun in the kitchen drawer. I don't know why she reached for it when Leah came running down, but she did. I guess Leah's footsteps scared her, or something, and she... she shot her. It was so loud it hurt my ears. I remember thinking they blew up and I'd never hear again. I was only a kid. Five or six, I think. I didn't know what was going on." Elektra pulled in a long, quivering breath. "Then, Leah fell against the wall and there was blood everywhere. I started screaming so much that Mom pointed the gun at me. But she didn't use it. Instead, her hands started shaking. I think that's when she realized what she'd done, and she put the gun in her mouth and pulled the trigger."

Everyone remained silent, including Rocket, whose eyes were bulging so far out of her skull they looked like they were on the verge of drying and falling out. How had we not known about this? The poor kid had seen something no child should ever witness. No wonder she had issues.

"Oh my God, Elektra," Rocket said. "I-I didn't know. I'm so sorry you went through that."

Elektra shrugged as if trying to brush away her feelings. "After Mom shot herself, I ran to Leah. She was still breathing, and she grabbed my hand and told me, 'No matter what happens, I'll always be with you, sis, and I promise I'll see you again soon.' I knew she was leaving. I'm not sure how, but I knew. So I hugged her until I fell asleep. When I woke up, my shirt was covered in blood, Leah was under a black plastic tarp, and people in uniforms were everywhere."

Swallowing hard, I averted my gaze.

"Is that why you ended up in foster care?" Rocket asked.

"Yeah," Elektra said. "But no one wanted me. They kept saying I was nothing but trouble."

Rocket grabbed Elektra by the face, and with her thumbs, wiped away the tears sliding down her cheeks. She planted a firm kiss on Elektra's forehead. "We want you, you understand? I know we can't replace your big sister, but we're your family now and we want you."

Smiling sweetly, Elektra's big watery eyes rolled toward the rest of us.

"That's right," Biggie said.

Coin, having no doubt forgiven Elektra's attack after that story, stepped forward. "We aren't goin' anywhere, kid. And don't worry about what I said. I'm scared o' ghosts so I like to pretend they don't exist. Anyone who thinks ghosts aren't real is an idiot, you hear me?"

Elektra chuckled and wiped her bloodshot eyes again.

When her gaze fell on me, I winked at her. "Once a Hunter, always a Hunter. You're part of the pack now."

"Come on," Rocket said, grabbing her hand. "Let's go find that plane and figure out how to get off this island. When we're outta here, I'll buy a big fancy house and we can all live together. All of us.

We'll be a big Hunter family."

Coin scoffed but quickly changed her tune when Rocket shot her a death glare. "Y-yeah! Rocket's right."

We all laughed, cleansing the dreadful atmosphere. Around us, everything had begun to darken, and through the trees, the sun was setting over the ocean water's horizon, looking like a giant ball of fire.

"Sun's going down," Coin pointed out.

Despite my pain, I didn't want to stop moving. If the plane had landed, there was no telling how long the visitors would be staying. What if this was it? What if this was our chance to escape the island? This plane—the pilot, and whoever sat inside—was our link to the outside world, and therefore, our ticket off this island.

If only the plane had flown above us earlier during the day, we wouldn't have been forced to camp out for the night. Traveling in the dark was an incredibly stupid thing to do. If we didn't somehow end up on Ogre territory, we risked running into a wild animal without even knowing it. Jaguars, I'd learned, were most active around dawn and dusk.

I'd never forgotten this because Rocket and Fisher had gotten into a heated argument about it.

* * *

"You think I don't know anything about them?"

Fisher snapped at Rocket. "One of them ate my fuckin' girlfriend. You think I'm an idiot? Those motherfuckers are nocturnal. That shit should've never happened. We were hunting in the middle of the day!"

No one else dared get involved in the argument. Instead, we all stood staring as if watching some championship wrestling match.

Rocket stood in front of Fisher with crossed arms and an overly elevated chin to stare at her opponent. "Fisher, I'm not trying to start a fight. I'm only telling you what I saw on Jill Norman's Discovery Channel."

Fisher scoffed. "Fucking geek. Don't believe all the bullshit you hear. Maybe if you'd pull your head outta your fuckin' ass—"

"Whoa, okay," Flander cut in. "Ain't no need to get rude, ladies."

"Mind your fuckin' business, Flander," Fisher said.

She was so angry her face seemed warped. I didn't blame Fisher for getting so upset—any time the topic of jaguars came up, she blew up. Who wouldn't? She'd watched her girlfriend get dragged up into a tree and munched on by one.

"Okay," Rocket responded. "Well, Jill knows her stuff, and she—"

"I don't give a flyin' fuck what she said!" Fisher snapped.

She swung around, jabbed her spear into the jungle's moist earth, and stormed off.

Trim gave Rocket a look that translated to, *Was that necessary?*

Rocket shrugged and made her bright eyes go big. "What? It's a misconception people have. They think jaguars are nocturnal. Apparently, they aren't. They're more active at dawn and dusk. Did you know they're also good swimmers? Who would have thought?"

Trim shook her frizzy-haired head and pinched the bridge of her nose. "I don't care what the truth is, Rocket. You know how Fish is. Don't bring this up again, okay?"

CHAPTER 4

"Man, this is bullshit," Biggie said, jabbing her spear into the crackling fire. "We ain't got no idea where that damn thing landed. How long are we supposed to keep walkin'?"

Elektra peeled open a banana and took a bite out of its tip, her right cheek ballooned as she chewed. "You think they came back for us? You think we're going home?"

It was nice to hear Elektra refer to the real world as *home*. Up until today, all I'd known about her was that she' been in the foster system before being dropped off on the island. I hadn't known anything about her real family, and now that I did, I felt more compelled to include her in everything we did.

I thought of my mother and wondered if she still thought about me. How long had it been? Three or four years now? Were riots being held? Were people coming to their senses and realizing that prisoners weren't returning? The sentence I'd been given was three years, which had now passed. Was my mother searching for me? Was she putting up a fight? Or, was she drowning herself into oblivion, having lost the only two people she cared about?

How was she holding up, anyway? She'd already had a difficult time taking care of herself with her fibromyalgia, I didn't want to imagine how much worse her condition had become with the added stress of me murdering her boyfriend, and me being sentenced to serve time on a remote island.

What about the others? As I searched my friends around the fire, I wondered if any of them would be returning to a life of homelessness should we ever return. Who would want to hire a felon who'd spent years of their life living in the jungle? Maybe the host of a reality TV show.

"We could be walking for a while," Rocket said. "Hopefully we actually find the plane. I mean, it could be anywhere. It could also be anything. What'd you guys think it is?"

"Could be a drop," Coin said. "But what kinda drop?"

Biggie shook her thick-haired head. "Naw, man. I doubt it's a drop. Why would the plane land on the island?"

"What makes you think it landed?" Rocket asked.

Biggie made her eyes go big as if to say, *Weren't we listening to the same thing?*

"The damn thing was loud, and then it wasn't," Biggie said. "It was obviously descending. That's what you do. You reduce the throttle. Engine slows down, you start gettin' more drag. So, like I said, it was landing. I'd be willin' to bet you bitches twenty pearls on that one. The only thing I'm wonderin' is, who is it? 'Cause no one flies that close to the island. It ain't allowed. Y'all know that."

Everyone stared at her, likely thinking the same thing as me—how did Biggie know so much about planes?

"What?" Biggie said, staring back at us. "My grandpapa had his own Cessna. He let me fly it a couple o' times."

Elektra finished her banana and threw the peel it the dead forest. She then stuck her head inside her little suede bag, nodded, and came back up for air.

"Still got three left," she said.

She was likely referring to her bananas. I'd warned everyone that traveling through the Dead Zone meant that food would be scarce.

Biggie sighed. "Man, I wanna go home."

I inched closer to the fire. "We have to keep exploring. You guys all agree the sound was coming this way, right? So we'll find it. We have to keep moving forward, that's all."

Everyone nodded, and Rocket bowed her head, the fire's orange glow making her cheekbones seem more prominent than they were. "Well," she said, lowering her voice, "a plane would only land on the island for one reason—to search for us, or to drop off a big load. If it were anything else, like an emergency landing, it would've been shot down."

Elektra swallowed so hard I heard the gulp.

Coin sucked on her gold tooth that looked brown in this darkness, stared into the fire, and didn't say anything.

As much as I didn't want to believe it, Rocket was right. Every other one of the island's drops had taken place over the ocean water. Women were tossed out of a helicopter and forced to swim to shore. The idea of a plane landing on the island didn't sit well with me.

If they were dropping something, it likely wasn't people. So what could it be? A poisonous gas? Oh God, why was my mind jumping to the worst-case scenario?

As much as I didn't want to admit it to myself, the idea of a plane coming to our rescue wasn't exactly plausible. If that was the case, why only bring one plane? Why not have media coverage during the event? Something was wrong, and until we uncovered the truth, I had to prepare for the worst.

The fire's heat warmed the tip of my nose. "Are your weapons sharpened?"

Everyone nodded.

A cool humid breeze swept through the jungle, sending shivers up my arms and down my back. How far could the plane have landed? How long would we be walking? We'd already spent several traveling and my feet were aching. I wasn't used to trekking long distances anymore. Ever since I'd stopped going out for hunts, I'd lost a great deal of endurance.

Taking a gulp of water from my water bladder, I stood up and climbed into the temporary, lightweight hammock Coin had constructed. It was smooth against the skin and stretchy like a giant elastic band.

I should have thanked her for building us beds out of the few vines she managed to find, but I was too preoccupied thinking about our survival in the Dead Zone to say anything. So instead, I ordered them to put out the fire. The last thing we needed in a forest with barely any leaves was to make ourselves an obvious target by sitting next to a bright orange dot in the middle of absolute darkness.

Closing my eyes, I breathed in the smell of burning wood and became hypnotized by the eerie silence of the Dead Zone—insects hummed, but nothing more.

CHAPTER 5

"Brone! Brone!"

My body shook from side to side and I jolted upright. Elektra stood beside my hammock with eyes bulging and her mouth wide open. I jumped so fast out of my hammock that I almost fell to the ground. At the same time, I snatched my bow and loaded an arrow.

Biggie and Coin were still sleeping, but Rocket had heard the commotion and was now climbing out of her hammock and reaching for her knife.

Elektra slapped a finger over her mouth, grinned, and pointed toward shore.

What had she found? And why had she gone off venturing on her own?

"What?" I mouthed.

By the excited look on her face, I knew we weren't being attacked. So why the hell did she wake me up like that?

She scooped the air to say, *Come on*, and darted toward shore. Rocket and I exchanged a glance and at the same time, chased after Elektra. I clapped twice as loud as I could to wake Coin and

Biggie so that they could catch up.

Morning dew licked my ankles, and I shivered as I brushed past leaves covered in cold water droplets.

The moment we stepped out onto the beach, Elektra pointed toward the water. "Look!"

With gentle waves crashing, I couldn't see what she was pointing at. But then, the broken raft came into view—long planks of wood and frayed rope spread messily across-shore. Beside it was a body with sun-tanned skin, countless black-ink tattoos, and well-defined though not overly large muscles.

"Is that—" Rocket said.

"A man," came Biggie's voice.

"What the f—" Coin mumbled.

With my loaded bow, I moved forward, aiming my arrow's point at the man's chest. He lay in the sand with broken pieces of wood around him as the ocean's water slid up and down his body.

"Why ain't he movin'?" Biggie asked, rubbing her tired eyes.

"Maybe he's dead," Coin said.

I rushed closer to the body. "Come on."

When we reached the man, it was obvious he wasn't from the real world. His dark brown hair was short, tangled, and covered in powdered salt and wet seaweed. His jaw, an oval shape, was masked behind a short scruff full of hairless scars. It was almost as if he'd cut himself time and time again trying to shave with a dull knife.

His skin was so tanned that it had taken on a leathery look. He appeared to be several years older than Eliot, maybe in his early thirties. Across his chest were two intricately detailed angel wings; they ran all the way to the sides of his pectoral muscles and disappeared under his armpits. Dozens more tattoos ran down his arms, around his wrists, and over his knuckles. I could tell they'd once been black, but they'd faded to a dark gray— no doubt the result of so much sun exposure.

"Is he alive?" Elektra asked.

Coin stretched a leg out, extended her big toe, and picked his shoulder.

At the same time, Rocket nudged her away. "Don't touch him."

Clearing my throat, I leaned forward, my arrow still aimed at him. "Who are you?"

No answer.

Clearly, he was unconscious. Yet I saw something. His lips, both heavily cracked, had turned a cloudy blue.

"Shit," Rocket muttered. "He's either dead or he's about to be."

Dropping my bow, I rushed to his side. At that moment, this man wasn't the enemy or a threat— he was a human being who needed help. I pressed two fingers under his jawline and waited.

"I can barely feel his pulse, but he's warm. He

must've drowned." I pulled hard on his shoulders and grunted. "Help me."

Everyone rushed around him, grabbed him by his limbs, and dragged him away from the cold water.

"All right, back up," I ordered.

Climbing on top of him like a horse, I tilted his head back, opened up his mouth, and placed my ear next to it.

Nothing was coming out.

Without wasting any time, I placed two flat hands on his chest and started compressions fast, and hard. "One, two, three," I whispered.

Pinching his nose, I pressed my mouth against his and breathed in until his chest ballooned.

While I didn't have any sort of real-world certification, Iskra had taught me how to perform CPR, and I'd since made it a mandatory training for everyone in the Village.

I kept at it, cycling between compressions and breaths until my arms became sore.

Why wasn't he waking up?

A gentle hand touched my shoulder. "Brone, he's gone," Rocket said.

I shrugged hard, pulling away from her touch, and continued compressions. Why did I care so much? I didn't even know the guy. For all I knew, he was a monster. But, after the number of people we'd lost to the war and the number of dead bodies

I'd seen over the last few years, death was something I wanted to avoid at all costs.

"Girl," Biggie tried.

"Shut up," I hissed, moving toward his mouth again.

"Why is she still going?" I heard Elektra ask.

"She's trying—" Rocket said, and just then, the man coughed hard, and I pulled away with two hands on either side of my face. He turned his head sideways, squinted, and coughed again until water came pouring out of his mouth.

Without hesitating, I lunged to my feet, picked up my bow, and aimed my arrow's head at his tattooed chest.

Clawing at his chest, which was likely burning, he looked up at me with tired eyes.

I may have saved his life, but if this man proved himself to be a threat to my people, I wouldn't hesitate to strip him of his second chance and kill him myself.

CHAPTER 6

"Who are you?" I asked.

He grimaced, raising a hand over his brows to block the bright morning sun. "Wh-wh-where..."

"Great," Coin said. "The man probably doesn't even speak English."

Slowly, he rolled onto his hands and knees, coughed up again with a rounded back, and tried to stand. Too weak to do so, he fell back onto his knees. "Where—" he tried again.

"Kormace Island," I said.

Sighing, he gave up trying to stand, sat down, and pulled his knees up to his chest. "Kormace Island?"

I nodded.

"You've gotta to be kiddin' me."

The words came out of his mouth with a broken accent.

"So he speaks English," Coin said.

Biggie stepped forward with a knife in one hand and a balled fist. "Who da fuck are you?"

"Biggie," I said, giving her a look meant to tell her to tone it down.

"I—I'm Number 73," he said, refusing to make eye contact.

Number 73? Was this some sort of joke? I wasn't sure how to feel about this guy. There was something off about him—both with his demeanor and his appearance. His skin, calloused and scarred, looked like he'd spent years living in the wild.

"Where'd you come from?" I asked.

As if suddenly remembering what had happened, he searched the sand in a panic. "What... What happened? Son of a bitch." He ran two hands through his salty hair and breathed out. "It's ruined. How... How did this happen? It wasn't supposed to be like this... Man. The guys warned me. I shoulda listened."

His voice was deep and rugged, even more masculine than Eliot's. Every time he moved sideways, resting his body weight on one arm, his tricep bulged.

"Hey," he said. "I don't want any trouble, okay? I was only lookin' to get out. I didn't think I'd end up *here*."

His last word made it sound as if he either despised Kormace Island or feared it.

What wasn't he telling us?

"Get out of what?" I asked.

He hesitated, running the back of his hand against the scruff of his patchy beard. "I—I'm from

Grohen Island."

What the hell was Grohen Island?

"You don't know what that is?" he said, sounding relieved. Quickly, he cleared his throat. "Well, it ain't no place important and the sooner I forget about it, the better."

Biggie planted a hand on her waist and swayed her head from side to side. "Man, I don't think so. You ain't gettin' off that easy. Spit it out. Don't be you be keepin' secrets from us if you wanna live."

Stepping a bit closer, I jerked my loaded bow in the air. "You heard the woman. Tell us."

"All right, I'll tell ya," he said. "But you gotta promise you ain't gonna kill me."

I didn't like the sound of that. What secret was so big it warranted his death?

"Grohen Island's the third penal island for male murderers."

CHAPTER 7

"Third?" Rocket asked.

I knew what he was talking about before he even opened his mouth to explained—Mr. Milas, Attorney General of the Department of Justice, had publicly announced that four islands were being reserved for convicts, one of them being Kormace Island. I didn't know much about the male islands, and I certainly didn't know anything about Grohen Island.

"So you're a fuckin' killer," Coin said, clenching her teeth.

"Easy," I said. "Let him talk."

While I didn't much like the idea of having a male convict around, I was curious to know more. How had he ended up here? How far away was the island? Did he know in which direction to go to make it back to the real world? Obviously, he knew more than we did about our geographical location, and I couldn't ignore that.

He licked his pale cracked lips. "I waited years... Spent most of my life on that damn place. You have any idea how hard it is to survive that island?"

Although I wanted to say, *You're preaching to the choir, buddy,* I kept my mouth shut so he could keep going.

"Men playin' their fuckin' lottery game."

Rocket scoffed. "Lottery? Sounds like a party to me."

The way he looked up at her—with a hatred so raw and primal—made me see the criminal inside of him. "It wasn't. Not a single man has a name on that island. We're all numbers. Each month, they pick two numbers"—he raised two fingers in the air, gangster-style—"and the guys gotta fight to the death."

For a moment, I felt sorry for him. Sure, he seemed like the kind of guy who'd spent a lifetime in prison before being banished, and like he belonged to some notorious gang, but who was I to judge? Who were any of us to judge?

"Why would they do that?" Rocket asked.

"Population control," he said, staring at the sand between his toes.

It was obvious by the solemn look on his face that he'd lost a friend or two to this barbaric lottery game.

"Who's they?" Elektra asked.

Number 73's eyes rolled up to meet Elektra's, and his features immediately softened. Maybe it was her age that made him want to tone down his aggression.

He forced a smile, and it appeared foreign on his face. "The Council."

Clearly, there was nothing to smile about, but it was almost as if he were trying to be sweet with her, which was a bit unexpected given his badass appearance.

"What's that?" Elektra asked.

"The men in charge on the island. They control everythin', and anyone who stands up to them gets cut to pieces. I mean—" his eyes shot toward us, the adults, and Rocket shrugged one shoulder.

"It's okay," she said. "This kid's tougher than she looks. She can handle anything you have to say."

He nodded, looking relieved.

"What's your crime?" I asked, standing stiff with shoulders drawn back.

The last thing I wanted was for this man to think he had any sort of advantage over us due to his size. We were the ones with the weapons, and this was our land. He had to understand that leaving his island didn't make him a free man—we were in charge here.

He scoffed. "Which one?"

"If you expect us to let you live," I said, "you'd better tell us about who you are and why you got sent to the island in the first place."

He rounded his shoulders and twirled his thumbs. "Dumb gang shit, ya know? I was young. Shot up some kids from another gang. Spendin' years on an island changes a guy."

He averted his gaze and waited for me to say something. What had I done, saving this man's life? We knew nothing about him.

His stare made its way from my lips to my chest to my hips, and I became uncomfortable.

"The fuck you lookin' at?" Biggie snapped, stomping toward him.

His hands bounced up by his face like springs. "I—I'm sorry. I mean no disrespect. You gotta understand. I haven't seen a woman in years."

Rocket side-glanced me. "This is a bad idea, Brone."

"I mean no harm, I swear," he said. "I ain't gonna stir any trouble. I'm not a bad guy, okay? I made a mistake. I'm not that guy anymore. Ain't that why y'all are here? 'Cause of some dumb shit you did in your younger days?"

Everyone exchanged a look. That was exactly why most of us were here, but there were also many other criminals on this island who didn't feel any remorse for what they'd done.

So, was it true? Had this man changed since he'd been convicted? Was he a dangerous gang man, but a harmless guy outside of the gang life? I wanted to believe he was a decent guy—I truly did. The last thing I wanted to think about was some male criminal raping my women to satisfy years-worth of fantasies discussed on an all-male island.

"Listen," he said, hands still floating in the air. "I can be useful, okay? I'm real good with my hands. I can build you anythin' you want—"

"We already have the area covered," Coin said sharply.

With arms crossed over her chest, she squeezed her fists to make her muscles bulge out intentionally, then sucked hard on her golden tooth.

I jerked my chin out at him. "What else you got?"

He hesitated, and then as if being struck over the head with a newspaper, he stiffened his back. "What 'bout that plane that came this way? Did it land? I saw it before I crashed against that damn rock. I'm real good with engines if anything's wrong with it. If you got someone who can fly it, it could be our ticket outta here." He then gave me a full up-and-down look. "But I'd also be willin' to bet you can persuade the pilot to take us home with that bow of yours."

His dark eyes lit up and he smiled, revealing two canine teeth that stuck out over his other crooked teeth. Somehow, they suited him, giving him a vampiric appearance.

"You're talking about stealing a plane from someone," I said plainly.

He hesitated, then shrugged.

"Yeah," he said, matter-of-factly. "If me

stealing some government employee's plane's what I gotta do to get my ass off this island, I'm gonna do it."

CHAPTER 8

"This is insane," Rocket hissed, glancing back at Biggie and her new puppy.

Number 73 walked with his head bowed and rope fastened around his neck and wrists. At the other end, Biggie held onto the rope like a leash, tugging hard every time he slowed his pace.

Did I like the idea of stealing from someone? At this point, I didn't care anymore. This guy, whoever he was, was right. The plane likely belonged to some government agency, and if that was the case, I wouldn't hesitate to take it. My one concern was for my people.

A few years ago, I'd have taken the Hunters and Ellie with me, and left everyone to rot on the island. But ever since the war had ended, I'd developed relationships with my women, and no way was I abandoning them on this island in exchange for freedom. If freedom was even a possibility, I'd have to find a way to make sure everyone got off the island safely.

"Ya know," Number 73 said, "if the plane thing doesn't work out, I can build you all a boat.

Couldn't do it on Grohen 'cause men kept tearing it down. Seems like this island's pretty calm."

I searched Coin, who appeared to be as uncertain as I was.

It wouldn't have been the first time we'd contemplated building some sort of ship and sailing out to sea, but where would we go? Who was to say we wouldn't die traveling across the ocean? We had no idea where we were, or how to reach land. Furthermore, what if patrol boats sat nearby, waiting to take out any prisoner attempting to sail away?

"How'd you know you'd reach land with that raft of yours?" Coin asked, glancing back at the man.

He shrugged, an arrogant look on his face. "Went based on information I got from Number 109. The dude was one of America's baddest hackers."

I stopped walking and turned around. "What does hacking have to do with murder?"

He scoffed. "Lady, you must be delusional if you think the government ain't all corrupted and shit. This guy was responsible for stealin' millions of dollars and breaking through government firewalls. The government didn't want to keep him around, so they said he was responsible for some guy's death and shit."

"I'm aware of the corruption," I said coldly.

"Anyways, he told me he got a hold of the penal island maps. No one listened to him, but I did. Everyone thought he was a weirdo. I mean, he was. Talkin' to himself and shit all the time." He shook his head and laughed, likely seeing this hacker's face in his mind. "He'd talk real fast, too, like he was on dope. Told me how we ain't as far as we think we are, and the islands ain't all that far from each other, either. I mean, the last thing I wanted was to end up on another island, but hey, this one beats an island full of men."

He smirked at his own comment but didn't look up.

"You must be real happy," Coin said, her eyes narrowing. "You landed the jackpot, didn't you? An island full of women."

It was obvious she hated the guy, and she wasn't shy about making it known.

He clicked his tongue. "Well, I ain't complainin' about that."

Biggie tugged so aggressively on his leash that he tripped forward, but caught himself in a run. "Chill out, I'm only playing!"

"You'd better learn some respect, boy," Biggie said, her voice deepening. "You have no idea what we've been through on this island. You hear me? This ain't some fuckin' fantasy island full of women for you to pick from. We clear?"

He nodded quickly, eyes aimed at the jungle

floor. Biggie was quite a bit taller and thicker than him. With her at our sides, I felt safe. If he tried to pull anything, she'd knock him out in a heartbeat.

We continued walking in silence, with Number 73 breathing heavily behind us. It sounded like he either had a sinus infection or a deviated septum. Although I knew it wasn't his fault, I couldn't help but get annoyed at the sound.

"Can you breathe through your mouth?" I said at last.

He looked up at me, shocked, and parted his lips.

When I faced forward again, I caught Rocket smirking beside me.

"What's so funny?" I asked.

"You okay?" she asked, still smirking. "You seem a little... tense."

I *was* tense. Not only were we searching for some plane, we now had a male murderer with us who had every intention of stealing that plane. For all we knew, he'd try to force us to take off the moment we found it, and I'd be forced to kill him. No way was I leaving my people behind, and it was doubtful that if we found a plane, he'd be willing to turn the other way and return to our Village with us.

Besides, how could we be certain that our return home wouldn't result in us being shot down from the sky? If it was a government plane, certainly, there was some sort of communication protocol before flying in unauthorized airspace. And to top that off, how could we even go home, anyway? We were convicted murderers. If we were found roaming America, we'd be thrown back in prison or sent back to the island.

Was it at all possible that the plane was, in fact, private? That it had somehow managed to land by fluke? With that thought in mind, something hit me. What if the plane had landed due to insufficient fuel? Not only would we be left without a functional plane, but people from the outside world would be stuck on the island.

There were so many possibilities, and the decisions fell on me.

I've been through far worse.

"I'm fine," I said, staring straight ahead. "I'm in my head, trying to prepare for different scenarios."

"I get it," Rocket said. "It's a lot on one person. Even a badass like you." This time, she nudged me and playfully dropped her head on my shoulder.

I parted my lips, not knowing what to say, when Number 73's husky voice blew up behind us.

"Stop!"

CHAPTER 9

Biggie's face contorted so severely that she resembled an alien. "Yo, what the f—"

"Biggie," I hissed, staring at Number 73.

His eyes, two huge brown balls, searched the ground at my feet. He hadn't shouted out of anger—something was wrong.

"What is it?" I asked.

With his wrists still tied in front of him, he pointed his patchy chin toward my ankles. Slowly, my gaze fell toward the ground.

A mere inch away from the skin of my legs was a thin metal wire stretching from one tree to another. Before I could open my mouth, Number 73 lowered his voice and cut in. "Tripwire. Did your leg touch it?"

Checking one more time to be safe, I shook my head.

He raised his hands in front of his chest and shook them gently. "Back away slowly."

I moved away, wincing. What if I had touched it and didn't know? Was something about to explode? What the hell was this thing? In a panic, I followed the wire to the tree on the left, where it twirled around its bark several times.

Coin stepped forward, knees bent as if prepared to jump ten feet into the air. "Where'd this come from? It looks like... it looks like metal."

"Maybe an old Norther trap," I said. "They were hunting for us in the Dead Zone, remember?"

"Norther?" Number 73 asked.

No one answered him.

Coin rubbed her chin, seemingly unconvinced. "We aren't in the Dead Zone anymore."

"No," I said, "but they were all around us. It wouldn't have stopped them from placing traps around the Dead Zone's perimeter."

"I don't know," Rocket said. "You're telling me this thing's survived over two years without being tripped on?"

"Well," I said, trying to understand it myself, "the Dead Zone isn't far back from us, and we all know how barely anything goes through there. So, yeah, maybe it's been sitting here with nothing to disturb it."

"Or it's an Ogre trap," Elektra said. "Right? Aren't Ogres the crazy ones? Maybe they did this."

"Ogres?" Number 73 quirked a brow.

Again, we ignored him and I shook my head. "Ogres are too primal for this. They don't work with metal."

"Metal?" Number 73 said. "How do you guys

have metal on this island?"

Biggie tugged on his rope. "Shut up."

At the same time, Coin scowled at the wire, following it to the other side. She moved carefully through long grass and flower bushes, probably afraid of making something go off. Crouching forward, she pushed the tall grass out of the way to inspect the trap.

"Um, Brone," she said.

As I approached, she pushed aside a dozen yellow flowers and a handful of honeybees flew up into the air. While bees didn't bother me, the sight of them was bittersweet; they signified life, but at the same time reminded me of death. Twice in the last two years, one of my women had died due to anaphylaxis.

I was fortunate enough to not have any allergies.

"You seeing this?" Coin asked.

I had to move closer because I couldn't believe what I was looking at. "Are those batteries?"

"Batteries?" Rocket said, rushing to meet us around the trap's base. "What for? And where the hell did a battery come from?"

How was this possible? Could a battery have survived the Russian plane crash? Had there been devices on that plane containing batteries? It was a DDC battery—I'd have recognized that thing anywhere. DDC batteries looked somewhat like the old-school AA batteries, but apparently, lasted longer. Everyone I knew from my old life hated these batteries. Not only were they shaped differently, which meant older electronics couldn't use them, they were also crazy expensive.

Coin and I stared at each other, and I was willing to bet she was thinking the same thing as me.

"Can those batteries even last that long?" I asked. "I mean, didn't that plane crash over twenty years ago? What's the shelf life on those things?"

"It appears to be exactly that—twenty years," Coin said, inspecting the gadget. "So, it's hard to say."

"Um, excuse me," Number 73 said, but Coin and I kept talking.

"So, it's probably a Norther trap," I said. "But what does it do? Is it an electrical current? A bomb? And for all we know, the batteries don't even work anymore."

Coin bit her bottom lip, then turned toward the gadget again. "Nah, it's working. See this light?" Without touching it, she ran her finger over it, muttering to herself. "This connects to this. And this... Okay. Yeah. Hmmm. What the hell?"

"What is it?" Rocket asked.

Elektra jumped over a tree stump like a grasshopper, but Rocket caught her midair by her shirt. "Don't fucking do that!"

That was the first time I'd ever heard Rocket swear at Elektra, and I was willing to bet it had been out of fear.

Clearing her throat, Rocket said, "Elektra, you can't be moving fast like that around a tripwire. We have no idea what it does yet, and there could be other traps we don't see. Are you trying to get yourself, or all of us, killed?"

Without saying a word, Elektra lowered her head shamefully. "S-sorry."

Rocket clenched her fists, made her eyes go big, and growled out of frustration. "Don't do it again."

"So weird," Coin said. "I suppose this could have come from the plane, too."

"What?" I asked.

Coin pointed at something. "This gadget here."

It was hard to tell what it was. From where I was standing, it appeared to be a small plastic box with a wooden clamp holding wires together.

"What is that?" I asked.

"I'm not sure," Coin admitted. "I've never seen this before."

"Um, ladies," Number 73 said.

"What will happen if we pull the batteries out? Will it shut down whatever the weapon is?" I asked. "Maybe we can get a better idea of what it is if we open up the box."

Being totally out of my element, I felt like an

idiot. I knew nothing about tripwires or electrical gadgets, so all I could do was ask questions and hope that somebody else had an answer.

"I think it's safe to take it out," Coin said, but it came out sounding like more of a question.

"Hello?" Number 73 said.

"I wouldn't do it with your fingers, though," I said. "Use a piece of wood. It's non-conductive. Make sure it's a dry piece and not a damp one."

Coin stood up, reached for a branch overhead, and snapped off the driest one she could find.

"You guys seriously ignorin' me?" Number 73 cut in.

"What the hell do you want?" Coin said, squeezing her branch so hard it snapped in two.

I wanted to tell Coin to tone down her hatred for the man being that he was the reason I hadn't walked right into the wire, but he started talking before I could say anything.

"That box right there," he said, pointing with his tied hands, "is an alarm. It either emits a loud sound, or it alerts someone nearby."

Coin scoffed. "Alerts someone? Like a communication device? That's not possible. I get that the Northers were pretty resourceful, but ain't no way did they figure out how to rewire some electrical box and use it to receive signals."

"I don't know what to tell you," he said matter-of-factly. "I'm only telling you what I see, and I've seen lots of these before. You got a question about weapons and shit, I'm your guy. That's what I did before things got outta hand. Arms traffickin'."

Coin didn't say anything.

How could she? This guy obviously knew what he was talking about. But had the Northers been that smart? Had they seriously rewired something and made it their own?

"I mean, all it takes is one electrician," I said. "Maybe they had one."

"Who are these Northers?" he asked.

"The enemy," I said plainly. "But they're dead now."

"They were convicts, too?" he asked.

I nodded. What was he getting at? Why was he asking so many questions?

"Well, unless one of them smuggled a battery on this island, those Northers ain't the ones who built this."

I parted my lips, but nothing came out.

"When did they die?" he said.

"About two years ago."

"What about that plane you're talkin' about?" he asked. "When did that crash?"

I was getting annoyed with his questions, but it was obvious by how curious he was that he was only trying to figure it out.

"I don't know," I said, searching the others. "Twenty, thirty years ago."

A smug smile spread across his face and he clicked his tongue. "Man, then you got some other enemy on this island, 'cause them Northers ain't the ones who built this."

"How do you know?" I asked.

My words came out cold and defensive. The last thing I wanted was another enemy, especially one capable of setting up advanced tripwires.

"See that battery right there?" He pointed at the DDC batteries—four red and black cylinders the size of my pinky. On them were the letters LR in bold font.

"Those right there are of the latest models that came out for that battery. The LR model came out in 2072, so this battery didn't come from that plane."

"Okay," Rocket said. "But like you said, someone could have smuggled it in."

He elevated his chin, almost as if amused. He already knew the answer to all of this, and he was taking his time revealing it. "You said they died two years ago."

"What's your point?" Rocket asked, sounding as impatient as me. "Maybe this trap has been sitting here for years."

For the first time, Number 73 laughed. "I'm sorry to break it to you, but shelf life don't mean shit in this heat and humidity. You'd be lucky to get a year out of those batteries in this nasty ass weather. And you see that wooden clip? It's clean. No mold, no moisture, nothin'. This trap looks brand fuckin' new to me."

CHAPTER 10

"You don't believe him, do you?" Rocket asked.

How was I supposed to answer? Of course, I believed him. What reason did he have to lie? It was clear none of us wanted to believe him. That's probably why Rocket kept pestering me about it. Maybe she wanted to believe the trap was an old Norther trap so badly that she kept asking me the same question over and over again, hoping I'd answer differently.

She peered back at Number 73 and rolled her eyes. "The guy's some low-life gang member. Maybe he's trying to get something out—"

I didn't have to say anything for Rocket to understand my glare. We were all here for the same reason—because we'd made a mistake at one point in our lives. Who was she to judge him? Most of my friends on this island had done stupid things, but not once had I thought them to be *lowlifes*.

Besides, he'd saved us; there was no telling who that alarm signaled.

"Well, you know what I mean," she said, trying to correct herself. "Plus, he's a dude. He's probably trying to scare us."

I turned my head sideways. "Scare us? What for? Look, Rocket, I get that you're freaked out, but you trying to blame the new guy isn't doing you any favors. If you think about it, he's right. The thing looked pretty new to me, too. He stopped me from stepping on the tripwire. He didn't have to do that."

"She's in denial," came Elektra's voice.

Appearing beside Rocket, she offered a hotshot smile. "When she gets scared, I mean. Rocket starts talking a lot. Like, more than me."

"I don't get scared," Rocket growled.

Forcing a smile, I reached for Rocket's shoulder. "It's okay to get freaked out, you know. You don't think I'm panicking inside?"

Her flat features made it obvious she didn't think that whatsoever. "You're always so composed, Brone, like everything's gonna work out no matter what."

"Well, everyone has their way of dealing with stress," I said. "You talk a lot... I go quiet."

When she didn't say anything, I cleared my throat. "Listen, even if the trap's new, it doesn't matter. We took out the fucking Northers, you hear me?"

This made her smile. She nodded, reminding me of a preteen trying to regain confidence after losing an athletic championship.

"You're sure we killed them all, right?" Rocket

asked. "I don't remember seeing Zsasz's body after the fight."

I stopped walking and Coin bumped into me.

"Whoa," Coin said, unsticking her clammy skin from mine.

The frightened look on Rocket's face made me want to projectile vomit. I parted my lips, but nothing came out. Although I hadn't killed Zsasz, I'd cut her in numerous places and left her to bleed to death. This, in my mind, was far better than being merciful and ending her life with a single blow.

And what was Rocket trying to say? Did this trap belong to Zsasz? Did she have enough intelligence to make something like this? Even if she did, where the hell had she gotten the battery from? It didn't make any sense.

My heart skipped a beat and I swallowed hard, freaking out inside. My cheeks felt so hot it was like I was standing next to a fire.

Without warning, Rocket threw her arms up in the air. "See, nothing! You stand there like a goddamn statue."

"What—" I said.

Rocket slapped her forehead and let out a childish chuckle. "I'm messing with you, Brone."

Clenching my teeth, I stared at her. "That was your idea of a joke?"

Rocket tried to say something, but it came out

like a squeal. She was laughing so much that her eyes disappeared entirely, and tears started slipping out at the corners. Elektra, standing tall behind her, laughed until her eyes watered, too.

Slowly, a smile crept on my face. How could I stay serious when these two were laughing their heads off? Even Biggie and Coin, who hadn't heard any of what Rocket had said, joined in on the laughter.

Still smiling, I let out a frustrated growl and pretended to strangle Rocket by the throat. "I can't believe you!"

"What's so funny?" Number 73 asked.

I shook my head as if to say, It isn't important, and kept walking.

Behind me, Elektra kept whispering something in Rocket's ear, and the two of them would start laughing again. She was no doubt making comments about the whole Zsasz joke.

Although I didn't want to dampen the mood, we needed to remain quiet and vigilant. We'd already come across a tripwire—what other traps had been laid out?

"I need you guys to watch everywhere," I said.

Like a soldier, Rocket cleared her throat and gave me a brisk nod.

I'd contemplated moving to shore and traveling outside of the jungle, but we had no idea what other enemies lived on Kormace Island. If Number

73 was right about the trap being brand new, it meant someone else was out there.

All I could hope for was that the trap had been placed simply for hunting purposes. For all we knew, some Rogue was surviving this island by using advanced tactics.

It was the feeling of not knowing that bothered me.

We continued our path, glancing through the trees every so often to inspect the shoreline.

Across the shore, the afternoon sun beamed down on the ocean water, making it teasingly inviting. My shirt, cool and damp, stuck to my sweaty back. I wiped the back of my neck, feeling dirt and grime roll up into little bits.

What if this was all for nothing? What if Biggie was wrong and the plane hadn't even landed?

If we didn't find anything soon, I'd have to give up and order everyone to return home. We couldn't travel the entire island for something we weren't even certain about.

As if reading my thoughts, Coin whispered, "Are we even sure it landed?"

Shaking my head, I squinted out toward the shore.

"You guys talkin' about that plane?" Number 73 said.

When I turned around, Biggie held his rope tightly in her fist, and with her eyes, threatened to tug at it as a way of telling him to shut up. But when she caught me watching her, she loosened her grip.

"It landed," he said smugly.

Biggie arched an eyebrow and leaned her body back to give him a feisty up-and-down look. "How da hell do you know that for sure?"

He threw his chin out toward the breaks in the trees, where bright yellow light shone in.

"'Cause," he said. "See those wheel lines?"

At the same time, everyone rushed closer to the edge of the forest.

I couldn't believe it.

He was right—again.

In the sand were two lines that ran all the way down the beach and around a rocky bend.

"Bet you he landed somewhere around there and taxied around that cliff," he said.

"Taxi?" Elektra asked.

"He?" Coin said, slapping two hands on her waist. "The hell makes you think the pilot's a man? See, this is why I didn't want you to save this guy, Brone. Sexist fuckin' prick."

"Who you callin' sexist?" Number 73 grimaced.

For the first time, his anger came out. His brows, dark and unevenly shaped, came so close together they cast a shadow over his eyes. "You don't know nothin' about me, so keep your damn opinions to yourself."

"What?" Coin asked, puffing out her chest. "Now I'm not allowed to have an opinion? You're the man, right? So we should be listenin' to you."

Scoffing, he rolled his eyes, but it was obvious he was fuming inside. "The fuck is wrong with you? I ain't got nothin' but respect for women. You're treatin' me like I'm some goddamn rapist 'cause I'm a man." Saliva sprinkled off his pale, peeling lips, and he wiped it with his tied hands. "Like I came here on purpose to take advantage o' you all. It ain't like that. Like you, all I want is to go back home. I got a wife and a little girl waitin' for me."

"Sure, that's the perfect—" Coin started.

"Both of you, shut the fuck up," I said. "Enough of this battle of the sexes bullshit."

Before Coin could keep arguing, I jabbed a finger in the air at her. "You've obviously had some shitty experiences with men, and I get that." Redirecting my pointed finger at Number 73, I added, "But all this guy's done for us is help us. So, you need to tone it down and stop picking fights for nothing."

"And you," I said, now glaring at Number 73, "you'd better get your anger under control."

He nodded, almost expressionless.

Still glaring at him, Coin crossed her arms and tightened her lips.

Out of nowhere, Number 73 smiled sweetly and nodded at Elektra. "Hey, kid. Taxiing means drivin' the plane on land. Usually to get ready for takeoff, or to get out of the way after landing."

Elektra beamed. "Let's go find the taxi plane!"

CHAPTER 11

Although not well-versed in airplane terminology, I knew it was a private jet by its size and slick appearance. It reminded me of the type of plane you'd see in the movies—the type men and women wearing fancy suits and matching sunglasses—typically presidential staff—would walk toward on the runway.

Two red streaks were drawn on either side of its body, and its wings were positioned overtop of the plane. Its body, which was unlike anything I'd ever seen before, reminded me of a whale. Its belly was curved and fat, which wasn't at all what I remembered planes looking like. Four propellers sat at the front of the wings—two on each side. Unlike large passenger planes I'd seen before, these weren't hidden inside of large cylinders; they were open, like mini helicopter blades. Along the side of its tail was written E905—or at least that's what it looked like from this distance.

"Holy shit," Coin said, slapping a hand on Biggie's chest.

Biggie grimaced and peeled her fingers off.

"Don't you be touchin' my titties."

"Sorry—" Coin mumbled, staring at the plane. "I don't see anyone, do you?"

Rocket turned to me. "It's like they just left it there."

"You're right," I said.

"The pilot," Number 73 said, "man or woman... could be sittin' inside. And that thing is probably a Cyclone."

Was there anything this guy didn't know?

When he caught me staring at him, he added, "Bluecraft Cyclone plane. It's amphibious. Like I said before, I was in the business of transportation before gettin' sentenced."

"Amphibious?" Elektra asked.

Smirking, he added, "It can land and take off on land and water. See that belly? That's how it floats. They likely landed in the water and climbed up on shore. Ain't nobody wanna land in the sand. That shit gets stuck in your landin' gear and the plane's nose can crash."

"What do we do?" Rocket asked. "Go check it out?"

Just as she said that, Elektra lunged forward as she'd done earlier, and Rocket quickly grabbed her by the back of her shirt. It was a strange thing to see—with Elektra's most recent growth spurt, Rocket had to stand on the tips of her toes to reach her.

Glaring at Elektra, I said, "You need to learn impulse control. If you can't do that, being a Hunter isn't the right fit for you and I'll assign you something else."

Normally, I didn't comment on Elektra's behaviors; Rocket was the one in charge of that. But I hoped that coming from me—the leader of the Village—she'd take it a bit more seriously. For the last two years, Elektra had been going out with the Hunters every time they went hunting.

This wasn't the first time Elektra started running out of nowhere since we'd left the Village. Had I not been friends with Rocket, I'd have never allowed Elektra to become a Hunter.

Was this what she was like every time they left the Village?

If Elektra's behavior was going to put the Hunters' lives at risk, I wouldn't hesitate to disallow her from going hunting.

Elektra cast her eyes to the ground and nodded, no doubt realizing how serious I was.

"We don't know who that plane belongs to," I said.

Biggie slammed two hands on her round waist. "Well, it ain't military."

Coin nodded fast. "Biggie's right. Can't be that much of a threat."

I locked eyes with Rocket. Although she appeared to share my uncertainty, she seemed to be leaning more toward the idea that the plane was not a threat. Unconsciously, I swept my gaze sideways, my eyes landing on Number 73.

Although I didn't know the guy, he'd proven himself rather useful in situations like these and I was curious to hear what his thoughts were.

"Well, your friend here is right," he said, tilting his head toward Biggie. "It ain't military, and I highly doubt it's government."

"Why do you say that?" Biggie asked. "For all we know, a new president took over, hopefully a woman this time, and is comin' to apologize—"

Coin scoffed. "Please, ain't no way a woman is in power. The day a drag queen tries to run for office—"

"What the hell do you have against drag queens?" Rocket cut in.

Coin shook her head and smirked. "Man, that shit freaks me out, that's all I'm sayin'." She chuckled, her golden tooth reflecting the sun. "No woman should ever be bigger than Biggie."

Biggie laughed, but Rocket didn't seem impressed.

"Well grow up," Rocket said. "It's art, it's entertaining, and it's downright awesome. Who the hell are you to judge? You're probably bitter 'cause with those muscles of yours, you got mistook for a queen with a real good tuck. Either that or you're secretly a drag king."

Coin's jaw dropped and her eyes doubled in size, but nothing came out.

"What's a drag queen?" Elektra asked, breaking the tension. "And what's a tuck?"

Pinching the bridge of my nose, I sighed. Were they seriously talking about this when we were standing in plain view of an airplane? Was it that difficult to stay focused on the present moment? No doubt feeling my frustration, Rocket and Coin stopped bickering about drag queens, and Elektra stood there, her head turning from side to side, waiting for an answer.

Number 73 let out an amused laugh. "No disrespect, but the president wouldn't be flying in a plane like that. He, or she... would be flyin' in something way more expensive. What don't make sense to me, though, is that the plane is private. Everyone knows that the airspace around the islands is unauthorized. So how'd they get in?"

"They?" Rocket asked. "You think there are several people in there?"

Stretching his neck, he said, "For sure. Who flies a private jet like that without any passengers? That shit's expensive on fuel."

Everyone paused, and an uncomfortable silence weighed down on us. Although I'd grown accustomed to making decisions on behalf of several hundred women, I wasn't prepared for this. A plane? How the hell was I supposed to handle this one?

Was it better to hide out and observe from a distance? Or, was it better walk right up to it? If we hid and observed, we risked the plane taking off before ever getting our answers. The hungry curiosity in everyone's eyes made me believe they were all thinking the exact same thing I was.

This was a potential ticket off the island. We couldn't stand around and *hope* to figure everything out from this far away.

"Come on," Coin said, breaking the silence. "If it's a private jet, it ain't a drop, which means it's probably some rich folks. Besides, we have weapons—"

"You're right," I cut her off. "Everyone, put your weapons down."

They all stared at me as if I'd recently been released from a psychiatric unit.

"We don't know who's out there," I added. "They could have a gun on them."

Coin scoffed. "Yeah, they could, which is why we should have our weapons, too."

"That's my point," I said. "If we walk out there looking like a bunch of savages—" I stopped myself and took a moment to study everyone. For the first time, I realized that was exactly what we looked like—savages. Our faces were covered in dirt and grime, our fingernails were black, most of us had scars or scabs on our bodies, our clothes were torn and stained in blood, and in our hands, we held weapons constructed of bone, wood, metal, and rope.

Had I seen this version of myself several years ago, I'd have likely lost consciousness.

We were primitive, and to anyone coming from the outside world, we would come off as feral, uncivilized women incapable of even speaking a word of English.

"If we look like a threat, we're going to be treated like a threat," I said.

Slowly, everyone unclipped their belts, slid off their bows and quivers, and lowered their weapons into the dirt.

Biggie threw her head sideways. "What're we doing about him?"

Stepping toward a plane with a man tied around his wrists wouldn't do us any favors, either. And it wasn't like we could tie him up to a tree. The guy wasn't dumb—no matter how strong of a knot we'd tie, he'd manage to get out of it. Furthermore, he'd then have access to our weapons.

"Cut his ropes." My voice remained firm. "And keep your concealed weapons on you." Pointing at Number 73, I added, "I'm in charge here. Do you understand? You don't do anything unless I say you do. And don't try anything funny, because I swear to God, I *will* kill you."

With slanted eyebrows, he nodded and drew a

cross over his chest.

Biggie raised her shirt and pulled out a short metal blade. He stared at the knife longer than I liked, but it didn't feel malicious—it was as if he were inspecting the craftmanship.

In one quick motion, Biggie sliced her knife through his restraints. The second he was free, he rubbed at his irritated wrists and extended his fingers over and over, no doubt trying to regain blood flow.

"All right, let's move," I ordered.

A soft breeze swept over the ocean and toward us, making my short hairs wiggle on top of my head. After it had grown out, I'd allowed it to stay short—I'd never been a short hair type of girl, but what was the point of having long hair on this island? It was dirtier, messier, and way more difficult to manage.

"Whatever you do," I said, turning around, "stay calm and smile."

Everyone forced a smile, including Coin, whose lip twitched on one end as if being yanked by a fishing hook.

As I moved forward, I focused on the sand's warmth around my toes.

It's going to be okay. It's going to be okay. It's going to be okay.

Although I couldn't see through the plane's dark windows, I wondered if anyone was sitting inside. If there were people inside, were they watching us approach? And why were they here in the first place? Had it actually been an emergency landing? Were these innocent people who knew nothing about the island? Would they panic when they saw us coming?

It still didn't make any sense to me. Everyone knew that Kormace Island was protected by the federal government—no unauthorized planes were allowed to come into contact with the island or even fly above it. The only way a plane landed on this island was in pieces or in a ball of fire.

Even the military helicopters—the ones used for drops—never touched down. That thought alone made my stomach feel tight and queasy.

As we moved closer, the plane felt much larger and grandiose than it had from a distance. I couldn't remember the last time I'd seen a vehicle up close in person. The metal, clean and shiny, made it seem as though I was staring at some alien ship. Everything from the outside world felt like such a distant dream now.

"Hello?" I called out. "Is anyone here? Do you need help?"

I figured it was best to approach the situation speaking clean English, first and foremost, and by offering help. If the pilot and passengers weren't aware that this was Kormace Island—the Island of Killers—it was far better to present ourselves as natives to the island rather than wait for them to figure out we were convicted felons.

"Hello?" I called out again.

Why wasn't anyone answering? Was it possible that the pilot and the passengers had left the plane to venture off into the jungle? On the other side of the plane, a small ramp-like staircase floated next to the pilot's window, though from where I was standing, I could only see the very bottom of it.

Was this the boarding staircase? It was open, which meant someone had gotten out.

Without saying a word, Number 73 cleared his throat and pointed at the sand around the plane.

Footprints.

It was difficult to tell in which direction they were going. They formed a chaotic mess around the plane as if a crowd had been dancing, and then several of them headed off toward the jungle. Why on Earth would anyone want to go into Kormace Island's jungle?

Cautiously, I made my way around the plane and toward the open door holding two hands up by my face to show we had no ill intentions.

"Hello?" I tried again. "We're here to help."

My voice carried across the shore, making me feel infinitely small beside this jet. Placing a hand on the staircase's cool railing, I gazed inside the darkness of the plane.

"Hello?"

Behind me, Coin moved slowly, her hand near her waist, prepared to pull out her knife if necessary. I looked back at her, then up into the airplane, and stepped on the first stair. It made the plane move slightly, but overall, everything felt sturdy.

I raised my knee, prepared to take another step when someone's warm hand grabbed me by the ankle. I swung around so fast I nearly kicked Coin in the mouth. But the spooked looked on her face told me she hadn't done it to be funny—something was clearly wrong.

"What is it?" I mouthed.

Her rounded eyes darted toward the jungle. She'd heard something, and it hadn't come from inside the plane.

CHAPTER 12

Although dying to see inside the plane, I couldn't ignore what Coin had heard.

"What was it?" I whispered.

Everyone huddled around us like football players, with Number 73 craning his neck to see inside the plane.

"Something's on the other side. Over there." Coin pointed through the plane as if we all possessed X-ray vision.

Number 73 brushed past me so roughly that I stumbled backward. "Fuck this. I ain't lettin' some noise stop me from headin' home." He grabbed the stair's railing and pulled himself inside the plane in one jump, making the wings move from side to side.

"Hey!" I hissed, but he'd already disappeared into the darkness. "Bastard."

"What'd you hear?" Rocket whispered.

"Someone's out there," Coin said.

Biggie swatted at a mosquito hovering by her face. "Yeah, and now they're prolly wonderin' why a bunch of crazies are tryin' to get inside their plane. What're we doin', Brone? We can't just sit here."

Once again, everyone stared at me, waiting for a command to be given.

But before I could say anything, a loud rumbling exploded in the air around us, and the plane's propellers started spinning.

"What the hell is he doing?" Coin snapped.

Without thinking it through, I pulled myself up into the plane and, quickly glancing sideways, noted it was empty of any passengers. I turned left and joined Number 73 inside the cockpit.

He sat in the pilot's seat, his hands hovering over a bunch of lights and switches as if trying to play an arcade game.

"What the hell are you doing?" I snapped. "Do you have any idea how fucking dumb that was? Now they're going to think we're stealing their plane!"

My voice barely carried over the sound of the propellers. I was fuming inside. I'd specifically told him not to try anything, and there he was, revving up the plane's engine.

He turned sideways, offered a dignified smile, and flipped on a switch. A high-pitched noise filled the space around me, and the plane's dashboard lit up even more.

What was he doing? It was clear the engines were working, so what more did he need to know?

Wasn't that why he'd followed us here? To ensure the engines were running smoothly? Now that we had confirmation, why wasn't he shutting them down? All of this noise was drawing unnecessary attention to us.

"Shut it off! You're going to get us killed!" I shouted over the sound of the propellers.

"Sorry, can't do that!" he shouted back. He slipped on a pair of green headphones and realigned the microphone near his jaw.

What was happening?

"You're a moron!" I shouted.

Shaking his head, he tapped his headphone. "Noise cancelin'. Here." He tossed me a matching headset and wiggled his finger as if to say, *You got something to say, put it on.*

This wasn't happening. My heart pounded so hard I could feel it over the vibrations of the plane.

At once, Coin appeared beside me holding a knife at her waist, a hateful gaze aimed at the back of Number 73's head.

I slipped on the headphones and brought the microphone up to my lips. "What's your plan, smart guy?" My voice echoed in my ears and I flinched. "You gonna fly this thing? See how far you can make it before crashing into the ocean? This isn't a car. You can't flip a switch and hope for the best. Now shut off the fucking engines and get off the plane."

When he didn't listen, I pulled out my knife and pointed it at him.

He casually glanced at the knife but didn't seem too bothered by the fact that I was threatening him. "Listen, I know this ain't what you had in mind, but you don't understand. I can't leave my family behind. My girls need me. I gotta get back home to them."

Grinding my teeth, I fought the urge to stab him in the throat. As much as I was prepared to kill him, I didn't enjoy taking a life. I'd have much preferred to end this simply by threatening him.

"We all have families at home," I said. "Not only are you going to get yourself killed, you're also going to abandon innocent people on this island by taking their plane."

What had I been thinking, bringing him along with us? What did I possibly think would happen? That we'd find the plane, make a deal with its passengers, and find a way back home for all of my people?

The truth was, I'd been too blinded by the idea of getting off this island and by my curiosity to think this through. For years, I'd held on to the idea that one day, I'd return home. Deep down, however, I'd never believed it. In my mind, beneath the desperation and delusional hope, I always envisioned growing old on Kormace Island.

And then, a plane showed up, throwing me

entirely off my game.

"Turn off the engine," I said slowly, squeezing the blade of my knife. "You don't even know how to fly a goddamn plane."

"Listen, I'm sorry. I really am."

He seemed genuinely sorry, and although at first, I couldn't understand what he was apologizing for specifically, the way he stared at me with hard features and a thin line for lips, it became obvious—he *did* know how to fly a plane.

CHAPTER 13

The power was like nothing I'd ever felt before. The vibrations, deep and strong, tickled my feet. The sound, however, was what I found most intimidating. The helicopter that had dropped me off in the water had also felt powerful, but nothing like this.

Number 73 reached for some buttons, hesitated over a switch, and then hit another button.

Did he honestly know what he was doing?

And why couldn't I move? Why wasn't I stopping him? My knife felt hot against my palm, but I couldn't bring myself to attack him. It was as if someone had nailed my feet to the airplane's floor. I was so in awe at being on a plane, especially after all these years without any form of technology, that I couldn't even speak.

Within seconds, we started moving. Slowly, I managed to move my head sideways to find Coin standing next to me, resembling a statue with flared nostrils, an open mouth, and a hand pressed firmly over her chest. Through the passenger windows on one side, Biggie, Rocket, and Elektra ran after us, their arms swaying over their heads.

On the other side, the only thing in sight was deep blue. The same scenery remained fixed through the front windshield; he was taking us into the ocean.

Suddenly, the plane jerked and felt unstable under my feet. Were we now floating in the water? Through the side windows, my friends tried to chase after us with seawater up to their waists.

Number 73 held his hand firmly on what appeared to be the throttle and pushed it forward, causing the plane to get even louder. We started moving fast enough for water to splash into the air beside us and for my friends to become smaller, and smaller. Holding the wall of the cockpit, I glanced at Coin who stared back, unable to speak.

With a peppy cheer in his microphone, Number 73 pushed the throttle as far as it could go and I stumbled backward. He turned his head sideways to look at us from the corner of his eye and smirked. "Preparin' for takeoff, ladies. Sit back, relax, and enjoy the ride."

PART TWO

PROLOGUE

At first, the people resembled toy figurines. They were small and so perfectly shaped they appeared to be made of plastic.

But as the plane flew in nearer, faces began to take form. Men, women, and children waved at us with grins on their faces. There were hundreds of them, if not thousands, waiting to be reunited with loved ones.

Would they be disappointed when they realized only Coin and I were on the plane?

Leaning over Coin's lap, I stuck my face against the small circular window and my breath fogged it up.

"Can you believe this?" I said.

Coin's lips stretched wide, her gold tooth looking shinier than ever inside the plane. "Not really. Man, this feels so surreal."

Then, as if being carried by a flock of birds, the plane landed so gracefully I found myself moving from window to window, trying to soak it all up. This was America—my home. How was this even possible? How had I made it back safely?

The moment we landed, Number 73 cut the engines and a crowd formed around us, gazing through the windows, their eyes wide.

Were they not afraid of us? Why weren't there any police officers waiting to arrest us for escaping?

"Holy shit... We're home," Coin breathed.

"Home," I repeated.

The second Number 73 unlatched the door, the plane filled up with air so crisp that I found myself sucking in as much as I could. No humidity or excessive heat floated around us.

Without wasting any time, I rushed to the plane's door and stepped out, feeling like a celebrity. I raised a protective hand as cameras flashed, microphones appeared in front of my face, and voices buzzed all around.

I almost shouted at them to stop when something else caught my eye—someone else.

Mom.

"Mom!" I shouted.

She beamed, her mouth wide open, and ran toward me with flailing arms. "Oh, Brone!"

The second time she called my name, however, her voice deepened an octave.

"Brone!"

CHAPTER 1

"Brone!"

When I didn't snap out of it, Coin shoved me out of the way with her sharp elbow and charged straight into the cockpit. She pressed her knife into Number 73's throat, forcing him to raise his chin. "Cut the engines, now!"

In an instant, I was back inside the stolen plane that was on the verge of leaving Kormace Island.

Number 73 laughed through his nose but didn't let go of the throttle. "Sorry, no can do."

We were gaining so much speed across the surface of the ocean that any second now, the plane would begin to rise out of the water. Around us, the scenery blurred like a multitude of paints pouring down a slanted canvas.

Why wasn't he afraid? Coin was threatening him at knifepoint, and yet he sat there, looking as arrogant as ever with his green headphones, a sly smirk on his scarred face, and aviator sunglasses he'd plucked off the copilot's seat.

That's when I realized he was the only one capable of flying the plane. He knew deep down, we wanted off this island. In his mind, we weren't going anywhere without his expertise, which made him indispensable.

Fuck that. I wasn't about to leave my people behind.

Gripping my knife as hard as I could, I flipped it upside down and moved toward him. The second he turned toward me with that cocky look on his face, I stabbed him clean through his forearm. He let out a scream so loud into his microphone that I instinctively tore off my headphones. As he pulled away from the throttle, I ripped the knife out, grabbed the throttle's lever, and brought it back to its original position.

At once, the engine's loud rumbling became a deep humming sound, and the plane started losing its speed.

"Crazy bitch!"

Pointing the bloody knife in his face, I said, "Try anything like that again and next time, it'll be your dick, you hear me? Now, bring this goddamn plane back to shore before I lose my patience."

With his hand wrapped around his puncture wound, his dark eyes rolled up at me—a gaze so intense I found myself stepping backward. His nostrils flared to twice their size, and his breath came out heavy.

There was no time to prepare myself. In one swift move, he lunged toward me. Coin tried to come to my defense, but he'd already anticipated her attack and threw an elbow out, knocking her square in the mouth. The blow had been so hard that her golden tooth disappeared behind a wall of dark blood, and she fell on her back, unconscious.

With his good hand, he grabbed my wrist, making me feel like a fragile mannequin constructed of dry twigs.

He squeezed so tight that I felt a snap and a radiating pain shot through my wrist, forcing me to drop my knife.

"Didn't want it to be this way," he growled through clenched teeth, "but you give me no choice." Forcing the weight of his body on top of me, I fell into the copilot's seat. My body contorted, my head squishing against the glass window.

The plane jerked from side to side as he fought to climb on top.

"Get... get off me," I tried, but he was too heavy. I couldn't breathe. His knee, pressed under my rib, made it impossible for me to squirm. If I moved even a bit, there was a chance one or several of my ribs would fracture.

He grabbed me by the throat and squeezed until I found my face swelling up like a balloon being filled with water. In desperation, I tried to make him stop and slapped his wrist over and over again, but it was no use.

The pain became so intense I thought my head

might explode.

In a panic, I kicked out despite his knee in my ribs and felt something displace. But I didn't care anymore. He was killing me. It was better to break a few ribs than to die. The move shifted his balance, but only a bit, and not enough for me to escape. Then, I reached for his face, trying to claw at his eyes, but no matter how hard I tried to get out of it, it wasn't working. He was way too strong, and by the devilish look on his face, far too deep in a state of rage to stop.

He wanted me dead, and he wouldn't let go until my body shut down.

Who was this man? This wasn't the guy I thought I'd saved—everything about him exuded evil. Or, was he simply that desperate to return home? Desperate enough to kill me if it meant a safe return to his wife and child?

Did he even have a wife and child?

Everything blurred, and for a moment, I forgot where I was. Through the blurriness, his narrow eyes appeared. They were glazed over, almost as if he'd consumed drugs. But he wasn't high, at least not on substances—he was intoxicated with anger.

His face, a sweaty contortion that started to lose meaning to me, no longer looked human. He breathed hard through clenched teeth, saliva dripping off his bottom lip and landing on my face.

He let out an animallike growl and pressed

down even harder until my back cracked against the plane's steel door.

"F—fucking bitch," he said. "Trying to take away my freedom."

With the little strength I had left, I scratched at the skin of his arm, my fingers slipping across warm blood. Whether the blood belonged to him or me, I wasn't certain. All I could hope for now was that he'd come to his senses and realize killing me wasn't necessary. But he wasn't calming down—he wanted me dead more than anything.

I should have let him fly the plane. At least then, I'd still be alive.

I blinked once, then twice, as his face started to blacken.

Then, out of nowhere, Number 73 threw his head back and screamed out in pain—a husky growl that vibrated through my entire body. Pushing himself off me, he turned around, and as he did so, I caught a fuzzy glimpse of Coin standing behind him with a bloody knife in her fist.

She came at him again, stabbing him in the shoulder this time. "Son of a bitch!"

She raised her knife once more, prepared to bring it down into his chest. But she didn't get him—as her knife came down, he caught her wrist, lunged off me, and stumbled toward her.

This was it. This was my chance to attack him from behind.

Why couldn't I get up? Out of nowhere, a loud, high-pitched sound entered my left ear, making everything around me spin in circles.

Get up, Brone. Get up.

Was it shock? Had my body already shut down? Was I dying?

When I blinked again, Number 73 was straddled on top of Coin, prying the knife from her, but she wasn't having it. She kicked and squirmed from side to side, holding onto her blade as if it were the last diamond on Earth.

If you don't get up now, he'll kill her.

She needs you. Ellie needs you. Get the fuck up.

Blinking as hard as I could to regain a bit of my vision, I reached for the side of the copilot's seat, and with as much energy as I could find within me, pulled myself up. I swayed from side to side, my hand resting against the seat's leather for balance. In front of me was Number 73, his rounded back moving so aggressively I couldn't tell if he was already killing her.

My left ear was still ringing, but I couldn't focus on that.

At once, Number 73's back straightened and in his hand was Coin's knife.

This was it.

There was no time to waste.

Screaming as loud as I could—which was painful and came out more like a hiss than anything else—I grabbed him by his entire head and threw him backward, right into the plane's control panels.

I wasn't even sure how I'd managed to do that—I felt weaker than I'd ever felt in my life.

With a confused look on his face, his head rolled back, smashing into the top of the dashboard where a strip of metal ran along the width of the plane.

He pulled back and slowly reached for the back of his head, no doubt to see if he was bleeding.

There was no time to waste.

I stumbled toward him, almost falling over, and grabbed him by the face, my thumbnails digging into the skin underneath his eyes. With bulged biceps and trembling legs, I threw him sideways into the steering column.

Something cracked—whether it was the plane's equipment or something in his skull, I wasn't sure, but I didn't waste any time trying to figure it out. When his head bounced back toward me, I smashed it again, and again, and again. Blood splattered across the leather seat and the cockpit's display screens.

At last, his eyes rolled back and his head fell forward, but I couldn't stop myself. I grabbed him by the ear for a better grip, pulled his head toward me, and smashed it into the steering wheel again. There was so much blood that his ear kept slipping out of my palm, so I grabbed at the collar of his shirt and kept yanking until I found myself barely able to move his limp body at all.

"Brone."

The control wheel's handle was covered in blood and slimy gunk, but that wasn't enough for me. This son of a bitch had almost killed me and taken everything away from me.

Punching him in the face, I shouted as loud as I could, but nothing more than a painful whisper came out.

"Brone!"

I wasn't sure how many times she called out my name before everything went quiet, but I didn't stop until my arms went numb, and by that point, his face was nothing more than a bloody mess of missing teeth, a broken nose, and fractured cheeks.

Sighing, I fell into the copilot's seat, feeling like I weighed a thousand pounds. As the adrenaline began to leave my body, the pain in my throat intensified. When I swallowed, it felt like nails were traveling down into my esophagus.

Where had Coin gone?

"C—" I tried, but nothing else came out.

I cleared my throat, but all it did was hurt so bad it made me jump. It was probably better I didn't talk at all. Dragging myself up from the floor, I inched my way to the back of the plane.

The plane had stopped moving, and we were now floating on the ocean's surface, far away from shore.

I wanted to call out for Coin, but I couldn't. So instead, I knocked against the plane's walls as I moved toward the passenger area, hoping the noise might draw her out.

Where the hell was she?

And then, I heard it. Although muffled, it was obvious she was crying. The plane's cabin was dim, making it difficult to see anything. The only light coming through entered the small circular windows, so I didn't see her at first. But then, I caught a glimpse of her short woolly hair bouncing up and down in the farthest seat at the back.

Was she injured? Why was she crying? Not once had I ever seen Coin cry.

I wanted to ask her what was wrong, but even the thought of speaking hurt my throat. So instead, I moved toward her, rested a hand on the headrest in front of her, and leaned in.

The second I saw her, I knew what was wrong. In her hands was a small circular mirror, and she stared into it with watery eyes and trembling lips.

"I know we've got metal to see our reflection," she said, "but it ain't the same. I'm... I'm right here. That's me."

Her desperate eyes rolled up toward me, and at the same time, she reached for her cheek—a graze so delicate it looked like she was petting the light fuzz of her face.

Poor Coin.

How long had it been since she'd last seen herself in a mirror's reflection? It was one thing to try to see your face in a sheet of metal, on a sword's blade, or across the surface of the water, but to gaze into a mirror and to see yourself so perfectly must have been difficult.

"I... I barely recognize myself," she said, turning from side to side, inspecting every inch of her face. Flaring her nostrils, she grabbed the tip of her nose and raised it to peek inside, then ran a finger along her tangled eyebrows. "It's me, but it isn't, you know? I haven't changed on the inside, but this face isn't what I remember. And... these wrinkles around my eyes. What the hell is that? I ain't old."

Finally, she lowered the mirror onto her lap and rested her head against the window, looking defeated. Staring ahead with a blank expression, she stretched her arm and gave me the mirror. "Here."

Although terrified, I reached for it.

Its metallic back was cool to the touch, but holding it in my hands felt like I'd plucked a piping hot plate right out of the oven. Inside, I was freaking out. Was I even ready for this? So much had happened since I'd landed on the island that I feared I might not recognize myself.

But I had to know.

Slowly, I raised the mirror, my heart beating so hard my fingertips pulsated against its little frame.

The moment I saw myself, I stopped breathing.

It was like looking at a monster.

What had happened to me? My left eye, bright blood red, looked like something out of a vampire movie. Was this Number 73's doing? Around my throat were red marks, and up my cheek, little speckles to match. Around the blotchiness were squiggly red lines of various sizes. Burst blood vessels?

Near my collar bone was fresh blood sprinkled like paint thrown off a paintbrush. My hair, short and unkempt, looked like it had been cut by a toddler with a pair of plastic scissors.

Who are you?

Gently, I ran a finger across my cheek where Hawkins had sliced my face open. The scar had healed, but it was big and ugly.

Pulling my lips up, I inspected my teeth. Although not rotten like some women's teeth on this island, they'd started to yellow and were covered in plaque.

"We should bring that with us," Coin said.

Lowering the mirror, I shook my head. "It—it." I struggled, my voice coming out like rocks being ground together. "It'll only spread heartache," I whispered.

And with that, I chucked the mirror onto one of the leather seats beside me and jerked my head sideways, signaling Coin that it was time to go.

CHAPTER 2

"Push harder on that," Coin said. "I saw him doing it. I think it controls the way you turn. No, stop turning the wheel. No, Brone, not like—okay, yeah, you got it. Holy shit, we're moving."

Driving the plane across the ocean water was the strangest and most exhilarating feeling in the world. If only I knew how to fly it, I thought. But as we moved across the water, the plane's engine rumbling loudly, I couldn't help but smile.

Despite the dead body behind me, this was the most fun I'd had in years.

"You're flyin' a goddamn plane!" Coin said.

I smirked sideways at her and rolled my eyes as if to say, I'm not flying it.

She smacked my back. "You know what I mean."

We moved at a gradual pace, similar to the speed of a pedal bike. As we approached shore, I realized I had no idea how to climb back onto land. Were there wheels inside this thing? Were they out? Or could I simply drive up into the sand without any landing gear?

Coin must have been thinking the same thing as me. She hovered over all the buttons and screens as if trying to decipher some complex puzzle. In front of us, Biggie, Rocket, and Elektra waved at us, their arms above their heads and grins taking up half their faces.

Biggie clapped over and over again, no doubt mind-blown that we'd not only managed to prevent the takeoff but that we were controlling the plane.

"Number 73 didn't push any buttons, I don't think," Coin said. "We should be fine. Put some power into it." She pointed at the beach. "Who cares where we park it, as long as it climbs up on shore."

I did as instructed, pushing the throttle forward to gain a bit of speed. To my surprise, we didn't crash into the sand, but instead rolled up as if driving a car.

Everyone rushed around the plane, waving at us to turn it off. It took a bit of searching to figure out how to do so, but I managed to locate the key and shut it down.

Why had they left the key in the plane to begin with, anyway?

It didn't matter.

What mattered was that we were back on Kormace Island with our friends and that Number 73—the traitorous bastard—was dead.

As soon as the propellers died down, someone started banging on the side door.

"Come on," Coin said.

She stepped over Number 73's dead body, moved toward the door's latch, and opened it.

Both Biggie and Rocket grabbed the staircase as it came down, even though it appeared to open on its own.

"What the fuck happened?" Rocket said.

Smacking two hands on her head, she paced from side to side. "Did this really happen? I mean... You guys were about to take off. What happened in there? Where's the dude? Holy shit, Brone—"

Reaching for my throat, I shook my head as if to say, It's been dealt with.

Biggie craned her neck to peek inside the plane. "Is he dead?"

"Yeah," Coin said. "Son of a bitch attacked us." Then, searching the empty shore, she added, "Has anyone come out? I mean, there were obviously passengers on this plane. So where are they? Why didn't they come running when they heard the propellers?"

"I—I don't know," I whispered.

Rocket winced at me.

"Maybe we should search"—I swallowed hard and grimaced, feeling like someone took a cheese grater to the inside of my throat—"the plane."

"So we can figure out who these people are?"

Elektra said. "Like a spy game! Maybe they left clues!"

Ignoring Elektra, Rocket looked at me. "Brone, maybe you should sit down. You don't look so good. We'll go inside and search the plane. You and Coin stay out here and if you see or hear anything, let us know."

Rocket was right—I needed to sit down. As she and Elektra climbed the staircase, I leaned the weight of my body against the plane's exterior and slid down into the sand.

Had Coin been a few seconds later in her attack, I'd have suffocated to death. I couldn't shake that feeling... I'd come so close to being gone forever. Yet, here I was, alive and filling my lungs with air. Bringing my knees up, I lowered my head and rested it in my bloody palms.

What the hell were we supposed to do now? It was clear someone owned this plane, but who? And why didn't they come out? Were they afraid of us? Were they dead? What came next?

I considered searching for the survivors, but again, we had no idea who they were. And if we went back to the Village, we risked losing the plane forever. The ideas swarming through my head ignited the beginning of a migraine, so I dug the tips of my fingers against my eyebrows' pressure points—right above the bridge of my nose.

Tegan had been the one to teach me this, and

while it hurt like hell, it often helped with headaches.

"What're we gonna do?" Coin asked.

Biggie clicked her tongue. "Girl, can't you see Brone's takin' a break? Give her a damn minute."

Although I didn't look up, it was easy to imagine Biggie's scrunched face full of attitude. Coin didn't say anything, no doubt a bit intimidated by Biggie. The two of them both had strong personalities; only Biggie was more outspoken and way bigger than Coin, which was enough to encourage anyone to keep their opinions to themselves.

Without a word, Coin sat down beside me, crossed her legs, and started pinching the sand next to her thigh. She sprinkled it across the dark skin of her leg, then brushed it off. I watched as the sand particles slid down her skin and landed back on the ground.

Was I even alive?

Was I still in shock?

With eyes wide open, I stared into nothingness as the sound around me faded—the seagulls crying overhead, the gentle waves crashing on the shore, and the muffled voices of Rocket and Elektra as they stormed through the plane.

"Stop looking at him," Rocket said.

"But I want—" Elektra tried.

"I said no. Now, get over here."

The plane shook from side to side as Elektra's

footsteps echoed behind me.

"Um, Brone," came Rocket's voice.

I jolted upright at the sound of my name.

Out through the plane's door was Rocket's head. "You might wanna see this."

I climbed up the railing and made my way back inside, following her toward the passenger area. Without saying anything, she stared between two of the seats, her eyes wide.

What was it? Moving closer, I peered around the passenger seat. A flat screen was attached to the back of the seat, similar to something you'd see in a commercial plane, but this thing wasn't a television screen—or at least, it wasn't being used for television viewing.

The screen was black, but it was turned on. Bright green writing scrolled across, most of it numerical.

I cocked an eyebrow at it.

Rocket shook her head. "Yeah, I don't know what it is, either. But look at this."

She ran her finger along the top right-hand corner of the screen, where it read:

BID: $52,899,145.97

I grimaced at her, which was meant to translate to, I still don't get it.

"Is that fifty-two million dollars?"

Rocket pursed her lips. "Fifty-two million big ones. I have no idea what it is, but that's a lot of fuckin' money. Who are these people? And look." She pointed to the left corner. "What's the rest of this?"

On the other side, it read:

Members: 9,641

None of it made any sense. Who were these people? And what did they have to do with members, or with loads of money? Was this plane carrying money? Rocket must have had the same thought. She turned around and started tearing wildly through the overhead storage compartments.

"Don't... don't do that," I said. "You'll give them a reason to hate us."

She scoffed. "Please. We almost took off with their plane. Whoever they are, they already hate us."

"If they saw us," I pointed out.

"Well, if they didn't, they definitely heard us," she said.

"Look," came Elektra's voice. In her hands were red and blue wires dangling from a little black box.

"Where'd you get that?" Rocket asked.

Elektra pointed to a box she'd pulled out from beside one of the seats. "From in there."

In it, several more wires stuck out, along with other gadgets I was unfamiliar with.

"Who *are* these people?" Rocket asked.

Elektra reached inside the box again, and this

time, she pulled out a grenade.

"Shit!" Rocket shouted. "Elektra!"

With a dark green grenade held in her palm, Elektra froze, her eyes bulging.

CHAPTER 3

Rocket raised two hands, holding them stiffly in front of her face. "Okay, listen to me. I want you to put it back down. Slowly! Don't pull out that pin, you hear me?"

"This pin?" Elektra asked, pinching the silver ring around the top of the grenade.

"Yes!" Rocket shouted. She was so freaked out that her voice cracked. "Do you have any idea what that is?"

Elektra shook her head. "It kinda looks like a bug. Or maybe a bug nest."

Then, grinning, she looked up at us, no doubt waiting for us to laugh at her joke. But this wasn't a laughing matter, and by the way Rocket inched her way over, Elektra must have sensed that.

"Give it to me," Rocket said.

Elektra did as she was told and gently placed the grenade in Rocket's hand. The moment Elektra let it go, Rocket sighed and slowly put it back into the box.

"Um, shouldn't we keep that?" came Coin's voice.

With only her head sticking inside the plane, she pointed her nose at the box full of wires Rocket had slipped the grenade back into.

"Could be useful," Coin added.

"We aren't bringing back a weapon capable of blowing up a bunch of people," Rocket said.

Coin looked to me for guidance.

"Rocket's right," I said. It's not like we need it."

Coin scoffed. "Hey, we're standing in a plane with a grenade in it. Ain't no tellin' what else there is in here. These people, whoever they are, are fuckin' dangerous."

"A grenade?" came Biggie's voice.

The moment she stepped onto the plane's stairs, the plane slanted a bit.

"Guys, you need to stay outside and stay on the lookout," I said.

As Coin turned around, preparing to climb off the plane, she shot her head sideways and peered through one of the passenger windows, toward the jungle.

"What is it?" I said.

Without saying anything, her eyes popped wide open and she pointed toward the forest.

"What? What is it?" Rocket asked, stomping through the narrow aisle to catch a glimpse of whatever it was Coin was pointing at.

"Someone's out there," Coin said.

"How do you know?" Elektra asked. "That's

really far to hear something."

It didn't matter how far away we were from the jungle—Coin had ears like an owl. If she said she heard something, it meant someone, or something, was out there.

"How many?" I asked, looking at Coin.

Still squinting through the circular window, she shook her head. "Can't say for sure, but someone's there."

While I didn't want to leave the plane, we didn't have much of a choice. Someone had to have seen us, and standing in here like a bunch of sitting ducks wasn't exactly the smart thing to do. Our best bet was to disappear into the jungle and observe from a distance.

"If there's anything important you found, bring it with you," I said, pointing at the gadgets around the plane.

Rocket moved closer to me. "To be honest, there's almost nothing in here we can use." Then, raising the mirror Coin had found earlier, said, "Well, other than–"

I plucked it out of her hand and threw it back onto the same seat as earlier, attracting a ferocious scowl.

"Why'd you do that?" Rocket hissed.

"We aren't bringing that. Do you guys see anyone in the trees?" I asked.

Rocket squinted toward the thick greenery and

shook her head. "Nothing." Then, she turned her attention to Coin. "You sure you heard someone? I mean, it could have been an animal—"

Coin stared at Rocket and rubbed at her jaw—something she did every time she pondered. "I mean, yeah... maybe. I guess it could have been. But I don't know, man... I got a weird feeling. This doesn't feel right."

"Well," Rocket said, "you know what Trim used to say about instinct—"

"Don't overthink it." Biggie spoke quickly. "Listen to your gut."

"My gut's tellin' me to get the fuck outta here," Coin said.

Elektra rubbed at her forearm, almost nervously. "Me too."

Hesitating, I gave Rocket a look, then threw my chin at the box full of wires. "Grab the grenade."

I rushed off the plane, urging everyone to follow close behind me. As we moved under the airplane's wing, I searched the forest but didn't see anything.

I hoped to God that Coin had mistaken the sound—maybe it had been an animal. But then I remembered everything that had happened. From an observer's perspective, we'd attempted to steal the plane, and now, we were looting it.

If someone was watching, we'd likely made an enemy.

"Let's get back to our weapons," I whispered, darting toward the jungle.

But as we moved away from the plane, an explosive sound spread across the entire beach. Right next to Biggie's foot, a pile of sand shot up into the air like popcorn in a microwave.

She hopped up as if having been electrocuted. "Holy fuck!"

After the initial second of confusion, reality set back in and I understood exactly what was happening—we were being shot at with a gun. At once, everyone bolted away from the plane and ran faster than I'd ever seen them run before.

"Go, go, go!" I said, wincing and pointing toward where we'd come from earlier.

Another gunshot.

This time, sand exploded hard against my leg and I jumped two feet high.

Between my legs and around my groin, muscles tore, but I didn't care. Everything around me blurred, and all I could feel was the sand under the pads of my feet, the warm air sweeping past my face, and my heart pounding so hard that with every beat, I worried I'd been shot.

Almost there, I thought, eyes fixated on the jungle's darkness.

A piercing cry erupted beside me and my heart almost stopped. I spun around to find Coin lying in the sand, her upper lip pulled back over her golden tooth and two hands clasped around her ankle.

Instinctively, I stopped running, my feet sliding in the sand. Was she hit? There was no blood.

"Coin!" I said.

Everyone except for Elektra—who'd already reached the jungle and was standing under a tree, waving at us to hurry up—stopped running and grabbed Coin.

Biggie grabbed her under the arms and held her up.

"My ankle—" Coin said. "It—it gave out."

"It's okay," I said, my voice choppy between heavy breaths.

With Biggie's help, Coin hopped on one leg, her jumps few and far between.

Another gunshot.

This time, Rocket flinched and gave me a terrified look that said, *That was way too close for comfort.*

The moment we entered the jungle, I grabbed my bow off the jungle floor and swung around.

"What're you—" Rocket said.

"Keep going!" I shouted.

Preparing my bow, I swung around and aimed my arrowhead at our attacker.

That was when I saw him.

A man wearing cargo pants, hiking boots, a forest green vest, and a ball cap to match marched toward me with an expression of detestable arrogance. A short beard sat at the bottom half of his face, though it looked like the kind of beard that grew out from lack of hygiene rather than style. In his hands was a black rifle with a slick wooden stock held up against his shoulder.

With an amused smile, one eye closed, and his barrel pointed straight at me, he aimed and fired another shot. The bullet came at lightning speed, snapping the bark of the tree beside my face. I flinched so hard I lost my grip and my arrow fell out of its position.

Fuck.

I couldn't compete with a rifle. Not like this—not head-on. There was only way I'd get a clear shot—if he was distracted or aiming at someone else.

As I swung back around, his next bullet skimmed my shoulder. It burned, almost as if I'd been cut by a giant piece of cardboard. Wincing, I reached for my shoulder and ran toward the others.

When I caught up to the them, Coin was running in an awkward fashion on her injured ankle without Biggie's help.

"You okay?" I asked.

She shook her head but didn't stop moving. "I stepped on a rock and twisted it bad. But I don't think it's broken. I'll deal with it later."

"Come on," I said. "We have to keep moving.

This guy isn't giving up."

"What about the grenade?" Elektra asked.

Biting my bottom lip, I stared at the grenade in Rocket's hand. Was it that bad of an idea? It was easier than trying to take aim with my bow, wasn't it? All we had to do was time it right. But then again, I knew nothing about grenades. My knowledge was limited to watching action-packed movies in which army men threw grenades over their shoulders before shouting, "Hit the deck!"

Was it easy to detonate a grenade? How long would it take to go off? What if I messed it up and it detonated too close to us? I knew knives, bows, and spears, but grenades?

It didn't matter—I didn't have the time to make a decision. Suddenly, Biggie let out a whimper, threw her arms up into the air, and fell flat on her face.

Rolling onto her back, she reached for her ankles. "Shit."

This couldn't be happening. What were the odds of two of my women spraining their ankles in a life-or-death situation? But when Biggie removed her hands, I realized she hadn't sprained her ankles. Across her shins were two ruler-straight gashes that could only have been caused by one thing—a trip wire.

CHAPTER 4

When nothing happened, everyone started breathing again.

"Check it out." Coin pointed at a gadget fastened to a tree trunk on our left. "Same thing as before."

"Another trap," Rocket said.

Biggie, keeping a straight face despite her injury, stood up and shook her legs as if trying to kick the pain off.

"It didn't make a sound," Coin said.

Although I hated Number 73 for what he'd done, I was thankful for the information he'd given us about the trip wires. He'd specifically said that the intent of the trap we'd run into was to notify someone nearby—either by emitting a loud sound or by some electronic transmission.

If it hadn't made a sound, it meant whoever had built the trap had been discreetly alerted somehow, and I was willing to bet the person responsible for these traps was the man with the gun.

"That means—" I started, but was interrupted

by another gunshot. This time, the bullet tore through a dense bush, splitting leaves in half and landing right into the trip wire's battery pack.

The battery exploded into hundreds of pieces, and Elektra turned around with hands over her ears, her messy orange hair catching most of the fragments.

Without saying a word, I slapped the air in front of me—a signal that meant, *Let's get the hell out of here.*

We continued our run, Coin hopping awkwardly. I was impressed with how well she was managing her injury. She likely knew that if she couldn't handle the run, one of us would be forced to help her, which meant we'd have to slow our pace. The slower we ran, the more at risk of being shot we became.

The farther we ran, the safer I felt. This man, whoever he was, wasn't native to the land—we were. I knew better than anyone that traveling through this jungle without getting lost wasn't an easy feat. There was a reason Trim always advised us to remain on certain paths without ever straying too far from familiar territory.

Everything looked the same—dense green bushes, large crooked trees, giant leaves, and hanging vines.

This guy, whoever he was, didn't know the island like I did.

At long last, I stopped running, leaned forward, and placed two hands on my knees. Droplets of sweat slid from my hairline, down the bridge of my nose, and off my lips.

"Think we lost him?" Coin whispered.

Swallowing hard, I nodded. "Coin, do you hear anything?"

She closed her eyes and elevated her chin as if trying to catch a scent. "No."

We hadn't heard a shot fired in quite some time, which likely meant he'd either given up the chase, or he'd lost us.

Biggie scooped a handful of sweat off her dark, glistening chest and stared into the trees behind us. "Who the fuck was that?"

Planting two firm hands on my waist, I stared at the jungle floor. None of this made any sense. Why the hell was some guy chasing after us with a rifle? If it was his plane he was trying to protect, he'd succeeded. Why continue to run after us?

It was almost as if killing us had been his plan all along. There had been no hesitation in his walk; the man had clearly been on a mission to hunt us down. Was it anger? Had we enraged him by almost taking off with his plane?

"Did he look military to you?" I asked, straightening my back.

Rocket tightened the knot in her dreadlocked hair at the base of her skull. "We didn't see him,

Brone. Only you did. What did he look like?"

Aiming my eyes at the sky to draw out the memory, I said, "Cargo pants, green clothes, a ball cap. I mean, it looked like he was dressed for camouflaging."

"So he's a hunter," Coin said.

Chewing on the inside of my cheek, I said, "Hunters don't hunt people."

"Some do," Biggie said.

We locked eyes and I felt sick to my stomach. "No, this is something else. I mean, the guy obviously has some pretty heavy-duty weapons." I pointed at the grenade in Rocket's hand, something that made me uneasy. What if it detonated for no reason and killed us all? "Maybe he's military and we really pissed him off."

"Then why set traps?" Coin asked.

For the first time in a long time, my anxiety crept in.

Something about this was eerily unsettling.

"Do you think he's here to bring some prisoners back?" Elektra asked, no doubt wanting to believe the best-case scenario.

"Again," Coin said, "why set the traps?"

"To keep people like us from getting too close to the plane," Elektra said.

For a preteen, the kid was pretty smart. I supposed that explanation did make some sense.

"Maybe Elektra's right," I said. "We were never

supposed to get that close to the plane, and it scared the hell out of him. I mean—" I swallowed hard, saliva coating the inside of my bruised throat. "This is Kormace Island, the Island of Killers. If I came here on some mission, I'd probably shoot people too if they came too close to my one way off the island. And then I'd keep shooting to scare the living hell out of them."

Biggie, not looking too convinced by my farfetched rationalization, breathed out threw her wide nostrils and crossed her arms. "Man, it don't matter why he's here. How're we gonna go back to the Village and tell everyone some guy with a gun is walkin' around on the island? Oh, and also, we can't use the damn plane 'cause he's guarding it."

"We don't need the plane," I said. "Right now, what matters is that everyone in the Village remains safe. Before this guy landed, no one talked about getting off the island."

"Okay," Rocket said, "but it did land. Now the women have hope. They're probably all talking about what they're gonna do when they get back to America, or wherever they came from."

While I understood what Rocket meant, it was far better to crush false hope than to drag my women into a deadly situation.

When no one said anything, Coin said, "What if we come back?"

Biggie scoffed. "Pfft, girl. Are you insane? Why

the hell would we come back? Ain't you payin' any attention to the situation at hand? We're runnin' from the son of a bitch."

"Yeah, I get that," Coin said. "But if we come back prepared, we could take him out."

Her eyes shot between Biggie, who was looking at her like she was dumber than an empty tin can, and me, who stared back at her pensively, trying to generate potential outcomes in my head.

Was the idea all that stupid? What if we did manage to take him out? What if the plane could be ours? Maybe one of my women knew a thing or two about flying a plane.

"Brone!" Biggie said, scowling at me. "You ain't seriously considering this ludicrous bullshit, are you?"

Shrugging, I said, "It's our one option out of this whole mess."

Biggie clicked her tongue and gave me a fierce look. "You're talkin' about goin' up against a guy wit a gun. And who's to say he ain't got friends runnin' around out there with him? What makes you think he's alone?"

"He probably isn't," Rocket pointed out. "There was a lot on that plane. I doubt he was flying alone." She turned her attention to me. "I know you don't want to let your people down, Brone, but it's not like they have to know the plane landed. We can say we never found it."

Although I didn't like the idea of lying to my women, Rocket was right. Sometimes withholding information to protect someone isn't necessarily a bad thing.

She wiggled her finger at my bruised throat. "And for that, well, you can tell them about Number 73."

I rolled my eyes. "Right, because that's gonna go over well. Now there's a new threat—men from nearby penal islands."

Coin curled her fingers and then ran them through her hair. "Ugh. Brone's right. We can't do that either. We'll have to say we found a drop."

"And what?" Rocket asked. "She turned on us?"

When no one said anything, it was obvious we were all in agreement.

"Come on, let's keep moving," I said, pushing aside a wall of leaves.

But as I raised my foot to step into a clear opening, I froze at the sight in front of me.

CHAPTER 5

"Holy shit," Coin breathed, slapping a hand across Biggie's chest.

Biggie peeled Coin's fingers off and gave her a look that said, *This ain't free.*

"Is she dead?" Rocket asked.

It was impossible to tell. Up in the trees, trapped inside a giant net constructed of thinly sliced vines, was a woman wearing all black, some sort of electronic chest plate, and thick leather boots to match her outfit.

She lay still with her eyes closed as blood dripped from the base of the net.

"Is she one of them?" Rocket asked.

By *them*, I knew she was referring to the man with the gun. We'd already assumed there was more than one of them. On the ground beneath her, a circle was drawn out in the dirt. Around the circle, animal fur was spread here and there and wooden sticks were planted firmly in the earth. Rotting teeth and bone fragments hung from the tips of the sticks.

A sacrificial ritual? This was obviously Ogre

territory, so where was the Ogre? Or the Ogres? And how long had this woman been trapped by them? I scanned the area, catching glimpses of blood smears, skulls, and what appeared to be dried patches of human skin.

At the far back, against a sharp-edged and moss-covered boulder, sat a black rifle similar to the one the man had been carrying. It was placed against the rock, which either meant the captured woman had set her gun aside to inspect the Ogre territory—an unlikely scenario—or that she'd dropped it after stepping on the trap, and the Ogre living here had set it aside, not quite certain of its purpose.

I stared at the blood dripping from the woman's body. I couldn't quite tell where it was coming from. Her chest? Her legs? The mesh netting underneath her had turned a rusty red, almost brown. A set of dirty fingers dangled through the net's holes, along with strands of long blond hair.

"Should we help her down?" Rocket asked.

After what had happened today, I was a bit reluctant to help anyone, especially a woman who'd traveled on the same plane as the man with the gun. He'd chased us as if enjoying the hunt. How could I trust that this woman was any different? I wanted nothing more than to be a merciful and fair leader, but I also understood that surviving this island was about making difficult decisions—it wasn't about making friends.

I thought of Number 73 and how strongly I'd felt about giving him a second chance at life. And what had he done? He'd betrayed us. But, he'd also saved us from stepping into a trap. Some days, I wished that my moral compass didn't exist. Being a leader would have been much easier if my heart and my brain weren't constantly arguing over right from wrong.

What if this woman decided to help us for saving her life? What if she convinced the other man that we weren't a threat? These were all possibilities, but that's all they were—possibilities. It was quite likely this woman was as dangerous as the man who'd chased after us, which meant saving her was a huge gamble.

For all we knew, she had a communication device on her bodysuit and she'd already called for help.

When I didn't say anything, Rocket nudged me, and at the same time, Coin slapped my other shoulder, a loud smacking sound resonating around us.

On instinct, I turned toward her with a tight fist, but she quickly lowered herself into a crouched position and pointed straight ahead. Everyone followed suit, hiding behind thick leaves and prickly bushes.

Then, out from behind two oversized tree trunks came an Ogre.

Her posture was poor and round; her arms were thin, meatless, and covered in blue veins; her dark blond hair was full of leaf bits, insects, and webbing and was matted in unusual places, making her head look deformed; her eyes were so sunken in that she looked like a skeleton wearing a skin suit; and the way she walked with her arms dangling on either side of her made me wonder if she'd been raised by apes.

She let out a deep moaning sound and rolled her eyes up at her prize. Then, without warning, she reached for a spear on the ground and jabbed it into the air as hard as she could.

The trapped woman let out a pained holler and moved in a wild manner, the entire trap swaying from side to side. The Ogre lowered her spear, inspected the bloody tip, then shot it up again, this time, stabbing the woman right through the hand.

She let out a scream so loud that a dozen birds overhead flew away.

At the same time, Rocket and Coin tore out their knives, no doubt thinking the same thing as me—we couldn't sit here and watch someone get tortured by an Ogre. They both stared at me with large eyes, waiting for my command.

Little by little, and as quietly as possible, I pulled an arrow out of my quiver and prepared my bow. I was about to pull on the elastic and aim my arrow at the Ogre, when something caught me by surprise. Another Ogre appeared, looking quite a bit older than the first one. I hadn't seen her at first because she'd come running into the circle on four legs.

The two of them started making weird sounds at each other, scratching their heads, and pointing up at their new toy. Did they even understand each other?

The older one stood up on two legs, and with bowlegs, made her way over to the gun. She snatched it from the rock, sniffed the metal, and knocked on the barrel with her knuckles.

"No, please," said the woman overhead. "You— you don't want to play with that."

She sounded tired. How long had she been bleeding up there? Was she afraid they'd shoot her? Did they even know how to use it? Unlikely.

The older Ogre laughed, revealing a gummy, toothless smile, and shook the gun in the air while stomping her feet.

The younger Ogre dropped her spear and moved toward the gun, swaying her head from side to side with feline-like curiosity. The two of them bickered back and forth, seemingly trying to figure out how to use their new stolen toy.

Then, the curious young Ogre pointed at the gun's tip, stuck her finger inside, and let out a choppy cry that reminded me of a monkey. She pulled her finger out, grabbed the gun by the barrel, and stuck her eye over the hole.

Looking irritated, she pulled away, yelled something, and put her face back up against the tip of the gun, trying to see inside the darkness.

Without warning, the gun went off with a powerful bang, making me want to slap my hands over my ears. The young Ogre's head—or at least what remained of it—shot back, brain matter and skull fragments exploding in every direction. As her body fell to the ground with a loud thump, the old Ogre shrieked, her toothless mouth wide open. She threw the gun into the dirt and dropped onto her four legs, sniffing the air around the gun. Stretching her neck, she looked at her dead friend's mutilated body. Then, without warning, she cried out and ran in the opposite direction on all fours, straight into the denseness of the jungle.

"Come on," I said, stepping out with my loaded bow. "Keep your eyes peeled in case there's more of them. And let's do this fast—that gunshot must have drawn some unwanted attention."

While I hadn't wanted to save the women, the least I could do was give her a fighting chance in case the Ogre came back. Aiming my arrow at the trap's thick rope overhead, I stretched the elastic of my bow. I'd been about to let go when I saw a set of eyes on me.

From inside the hanging trap, the woman's face was pressed against blood meshing, her eyes wide and her dry lips parted. At first, she looked terrified, no doubt wondering if I was about to shoot an arrow through her chest. But there was something doll-like about her; she didn't blink, move, or make a sound.

"Um, Brone," Biggie said, walking around the dead Ogre's brainless body. With her thick finger, she pointed up at the trap, where part of the meshing had been torn apart. Part of the woman's black suit had also been ripped, revealing bloody skin around a dark puncture hole.

There was no use trying to get her down—the bullet had gone straight through the Ogre's head and into this woman's chest.

CHAPTER 6

"Do any of you even know how to use this thing?" I asked, twirling the rifle in my hands.

"Don't point it!" Coin said, shielding her face with her hands. "That's the number one rule."

What was she freaking out about? "My finger isn't even on the trigger."

"It doesn't matter," she said. "Give me that."

Had it been anyone else ordering me to hand them something, I'd have whipped out my menacing look. But, Coin was my friend, and more often than not, I didn't think about rank around my friends.

Pulling it out of my hands, she reached for something near the middle of the gun and pressed down.

"What'd you do?" I asked.

She handed me back the gun. "I put on the safety."

It sounded so simple that I felt like an idiot. What did I know about guns? I'd never seen one in real life. The closest I'd ever come to a gun was in fifth grade when two police officers came to our school to deliver a speech about being street smart. Although they never unclipped the guns from their belts, it was all I could stare at, wondering how such a small thing could cause so much damage.

It was only later, in seventh grade, that I found out about how easy it was to get a gun. Every time I talked about it, though, Mom gave me a speech about how America was falling apart because of guns and how every other month, some kid was shooting up a school.

"You know how to shoot it?" I asked Coin.

She nodded. "Scouts."

Handing it back to her, I said, "Don't go shooting it every time you hear something."

She made her eyelids go flat as if to say, *Do I look like an idiot?*

I'd contemplated cutting the woman's body loose to inspect her for identification and other items we might find useful, but after that gunshot had gone off, I wasn't confident we were safe.

"Let's go home," I said, walking past a dozen frogs impaled on a sharp stick.

Over the last two years, I hadn't seen a single Ogre. We'd reclaimed our territory, and no one other than a handful of new drops had dared step foot on our land. Whether other tribes were out there on Kormace Island was beyond me, and in all honesty, I didn't care. So long as they didn't prove themselves to be a threat to my people, it made no difference to me who ruled what part of the island. I wasn't Rainer or Hawkins, and living on Kormace Island wasn't about ruling over everyone—it was about living amicably and surviving as a society.

As we walked through the jungle, Coin inspected every inch of the gun, looking like a kid in a Halloween costume shop.

Every few minutes, she'd mumble something to herself, like, "Who the hell are these people?"

The rest of us were too busy watching out for traps that we ignored her comments.

"There!" Elektra said, pointing at the ground up ahead.

"What?" Rocket said. "What're we looking at?"

"Oh, never mind," Elektra said. "I thought I saw a wire."

Biggie clicked her tongue. "Girl, how da hell do you *think* you saw a wire? Givin' us a scare like that."

"Well, it looked like—"

"Doesn't matter," Rocket said. "Do you seriously think they came all the way out here to set traps? I mean, we're getting close to the Dead Zone."

Although I agreed with her, we couldn't be too safe. So far, we'd crossed paths with two people from the outside world—both were carrying a rifle and seemed to have advanced equipment attached to their bodies.

"Keep moving," I said, "and let's focus on getting back to the Village. We'll figure out what to do once we're there."

Turning my head sideways, I observed Coin as she played with the gun one last time. Finally, she gripped it with confidence as if she'd practiced for years in a firing range with that precise model.

Out of nowhere, Elektra stopped walking and everyone turned to face her.

"We have that now," she said, pointing at Coin's new weapon. "Can't we go back and kill that guy?"

Rocket scowled and slapped two hands on her waist—something she did every time Elektra talked about *killing* someone.

"You say that like it's as easy as making a peanut butter sandwich," Rocket said.

"How should I know? I've never made one," Elektra said.

Rocket slapped her forehead and rolled her eyes like an irritated preschool teacher. "Killing isn't a game, Elektra. Does it not bother you at all? Do you not feel any kind of guilt or remorse at the thought of killing someone?"

Watching Elektra's reaction made my stomach sink—there was none. She stared back at Rocket as if trying to decide between a glass of juice or milk.

"Well?" Rocket snapped.

"Not if it's a bad guy," Elektra said.

Had we taught her this? Had she spent part of her most impactful years of life learning that war, chaos, and violence were okay? I thought back to when we'd first found Elektra. She'd been living alone in Trim's old treehouse. She'd never told us how long she'd lived there or how she'd managed to survive. Had she killed people? There was no question she'd killed animals to feed herself.

When no one said anything, Elektra forced a laugh. "Why're you all standing there staring at me? You guys are all killers. So why's it so wrong when I talk about it?"

Pinching the bridge of her nose, Rocket moved toward Elektra and laid a hand on her shoulder. "We've all killed, yeah, and I think I speak for all of us when I say we regret the things we've done." She paused, searched us for validation, and returned her attention to Elektra. "On this island, you have to do things you don't want to do to survive. Does that make sense?"

No doubt uncomfortable in front of Rocket's intense, narrow-eyed gaze, Elektra looked away. "Yeah, I get it, Rock. But that guy tried to kill us. So why can't we go back and kill him?"

How was Rocket supposed to explain that even though we went about killing our enemies, it didn't make it right? How did you explain to a child that it was okay to kill someone if it meant saving your own life, but at the same time, it wasn't okay at all?

In my mind, I'd adopted the kill or be killed mentality, and it had taken me quite a bit of time to do it. If the day ever came where we returned home to the real world, I'd be haunted for the rest of my life by everything I'd done on this island.

I wasn't proud of myself for ending lives; nor did I feel apathetic about it. Deep down, I felt dirty and evil, in a sense. But most days, as I watched little Robin bounce in Ellie's arms, or as my friends danced around the evening fire, I reminded myself that everything I'd done was to save my people and to live a semblance of a normal life.

In a disturbing sense, it was less difficult to kill someone when driven by both an inherent need to survive and the knowledge that the person was a monster. Humanizing an enemy by imagining what their life might have been like if they'd chosen a better path in life made it almost impossible to fight back.

If I started thinking about my enemies and overanalyzing why they'd turned out the way they did, I'd never forgive myself for taking their lives. Some days, I wished Iskra had never told me about Zsasz and about how Rainer had abused her as a child. Every now and then, I imagined Zsasz as a child the way Iskra had described her—clownish and playful—and wondered who she might have become had she not ended up on this island or under Rainer's reign. Had her biology dictated that she'd become a soulless killer? Or, were trauma, abuse, and misguided mentoring to blame?

* * *

Mrs. Dawson turned around, an e-pen in one hand and a plain wooden ruler in the other. She pointed at the e-board at the front of the class, where she'd spelled out *Nature vs. Nurture*.

"Can anyone tell me what that means?" she asked, tilting her orange-haired head to one side.

She was so spunky in the way she spoke, and although she taught the new PPS class—psychology, philosophy, and sociology—she reminded me of an old cartoon character my mom had introduced me to: Mrs. Frizzle, the science teacher on *The Magic School Bus*.

With a wide, red-lipped grin, she said, "Well?" and pointed her ruler at Rylen at the back of the class.

He pulled his face back as if he'd been caught looking up a girl's skirt, cleared his throat, and said, "Um, I don't know. Forests versus babies, or something."

Beside him, Alexa rolled her eyes, pushed her purple-rimmed glasses high up on her face, and shot her arm up like a flagpole.

"Yes, Alexa?"

"Nature means that people are prewired to behave or think in a certain way due to their biology or genetics, while nurture dictates their behaviors and actions are the results of exterior influences: the way they were raised, social interactions, education…" She bit the back of her e-pen and waited, a proud smirk on her face.

In an exaggerated motion, Mrs. Dawson threw both arms out, her red and white polka-dot dress expanding to twice its size, and said, "Exactly!"

Making her way behind her desk, she bent forward in front of her computer and tapped the screen a few times. On our desk screens, a new notification popped up: 1 New Assignment.

"I want you all to write a three-page essay about this old debate," she said. "Tell me which one you think is right and why."

She clapped her hands so hard together that my shoulders jerked. With ticking heels, she made her way over to her personal coffee maker, made herself a cup of coffee, and sat down in her leather lounge chair with a book in her hands. When no one moved, she peered at us from behind her coffee cup and said, "You can do your research anywhere online. Oh, and I want it sent to my inbox by the end of class."

As I stared at my screen, I couldn't help but wonder: was my mom's boyfriend Gary an asshole because someone else had been an asshole to him when he was young? Or, had he always been a bad person? I thought of the times he'd yelled at me when I'd tried to defend my mom and how shaken up I'd been afterward. I'd never been a violent person by nature, but every time Gary smashed a beer bottle into the wall or yelled at my mom, all I could think about was pushing him off our apartment balcony.

I opened the assignment, and at the top of the page, typed: *Nature vs. Nurture: a 50/50 Recipe.*

* * *

"You have to respect life," Rocket said, now shaking Elektra's shoulders.

Gently, I pulled Rocket away, realizing that this argument had become more about her than about Elektra. I was willing to bet Rocket, too, was haunted by everything she'd done.

"It's not like she's getting in fights and trying to kill people," I whispered to Rocket. "This is all she knows now. You can't change that. If someone tries to kill her, her automatic response is to kill them."

"Well, it shouldn't be," Rocket hissed.

Fighting the urge to smile, I said, "Shouldn't it be? Wouldn't we all do the same thing on this island?"

Frowning, Rocket offered a one-shouldered shrug. "I guess."

"So let her be," I said. "If anything, you know she'll be safe. She knows how to protect herself and she isn't afraid to do it."

Rocket turned to Elektra, who was now

hopping up and down beside Coin, begging her to let her hold the gun. Like an annoyed toddler not wanting to share her toys, Coin pulled away and told Elektra to back off.

But right when she did that, a loud bang went off, and Coin fell to the ground.

CHAPTER 7

Coin threw her head back and bellowed in pain. Wincing, she clawed at her bloody thigh.

Elektra, looking confused by what had happened, backed away with two open hands as if to say, I *didn't do it.*

It was obvious she hadn't done it—Coin had been holding the gun with its barrel facing up, and the gunshot had punctured her thigh.

The son of a bitch had caught up to us, no doubt having been alerted by the trip wire and the sound of the Ogre's gunshot.

"Grab her!" I shouted, rushing behind Coin.

With as much strength as I could gather, I scooped her up underneath the arms and started dragging her away from the opening in which we were standing. Biggie rushed to grab her legs, as did Rocket, and together, we tore through dense bushes and prickly leaves. We even broke through a bush so dry its branches snapped into pieces.

"Keep going," I hissed.

We ran awkwardly together as Coin moaned in our arms.

"Elektra," I said, and Elektra came running at me with her lanky legs making her look like a daddy long-leg. "Take Rocket's place. I'll take Biggie's."

With sweat pouring out of us, we kept swapping positions every few minutes to give everyone a break.

When it was my turn to jog alongside everyone, Coin moaned like she was trying to say something, so I rubbed the back of my hand along her grimy forehead. "Hey, relax, okay? We'll get you home safe and we'll give you something for the pain."

She nodded fast, her brown skin turning a deep shade of gray.

"We have to hurry," I said. "She's losing a lot of blood."

Inching near Biggie, I grabbed Coin underneath the arms. She was heavy with all her muscle mass, but I couldn't focus on how difficult the task was. What option did we have? No way was I leaving Coin out here to die, even if it killed me.

I'd have to push through it.

The more turns I took carrying her, the more my muscles started to shake—so much so that I feared I might lose my grip and drop her. This was, by far, the most physically demanding thing I'd ever done in my life.

"We got this," I said, barely able to catch my breath.

The more we ran, the dryer my throat became,

and the more it hurt.

But this was Coin—I couldn't give up. We continued until at last, Biggie stopped, bent forward, and waved a hand in the air.

"I—I—I can't."

She was so burned out that she stood with her mouth wide open as if this would somehow help her breathe more easily. She breathed in hard, a line of saliva dangling off her bottom lip.

The rest of us lowered Coin to the jungle floor with care.

I raised a fist, which was meant to order everyone to remain silent, and closed my eyes. No leaves were crunching, no branches were cracking, nothing.

"All right," I whispered. "Let's take a few minutes... I think we lost him. This gives us time to wrap her leg up."

We all fell to the ground, our shirts soaked in sweat and our breaths so heavy I kept telling everyone to keep it down. The last thing I wanted was for this psycho to hear us.

"Coin, you hanging in there?" I whispered.

When she didn't answer me, I poked her shoulder with my toe. "Coin?"

Biggie shook her head, still trying to breathe. "She's—she's out, man. Prolly the pain."

At the same time, Rocket and I shot upright.

"It's not just the pain," Rocket said before I

could get a word in. "She's fuckin' going white." She tore a piece of her pant leg off and started wrapping it around Coin's wound as tight as she could. "Goddamn it... I couldn't tell how bad it was while we were running. Guys, she's bleeding out."

There was no time to waste.

I climbed back up onto my throbbing feet when my back spasmed.

Shit.

How was I supposed to keep carrying her like this?

"We need to get back, now," I ordered. "But we'll never make it like this. We have to carry her differently."

Elektra wrinkled her nose. "How?"

"Like a rolled-up carpet," Biggie said. "We line up and wrap our arms around her."

Rocket's bright eyes shifted to where we'd come from—an array of thick bushes and giant vines. "You sure we lost him?"

I followed her gaze. "No, I'm not, but we all know how easy it is to lose a target in this jungle. Besides, we haven't heard any shots since we started running. If he were nearby, he'd have tried to hit us."

"Why'd he only shoot one bullet?" Rocket asked.

I'd been wondering the same thing, but I hadn't vocalized it. He'd had a clear shot, and yet, he'd shot Coin in the leg. How come? Why not go for the kill? What the hell was he planning?

Elektra bit her bottom lip. "I don't know... I used to play this computer game where I had to build armies and stuff—" She zoned out for a moment as if replaying it in her mind. "It was all a bunch of little characters. Like, a society you'd take care of."

"What's your point?" I said, my tone a bit harsher than I'd intended.

"I used to follow enemies so that I could find out where their city was. I'd be real quiet about it. Well, you know what I mean. Like, I wouldn't attack their characters. The point was to—"

Rocket scoffed. "Why kill a few wasps when you can follow them and take out the nest?"

CHAPTER 8

"Man, what the hell are we supposed to do?" Biggie said. "Ain't like we got a choice. Our girl's dyin'"

"Biggie's right," Rocket said. "If we don't head back to the Village, Coin dies."

Without looking at either one of them, I said, "And if we do go back to the Village, we're risking everyone's lives."

Everyone went silent.

I didn't like this any more than they did, but what were we supposed to do? As Coin's friend, I wanted nothing more than to take the risk and return to the Village. As the leader of my people, however, the right decision was to protect the majority.

Finally, Elektra broke the silence. "Doesn't he already know where the Village is?"

Everyone craned their necks to look at her.

"The plane flew right over us," she said.

I locked eyes with Rocket.

Why hadn't we thought about this?

"That's fucking great," Rocket said. "The dude might not even be following us anymore. He could be going straight to the Village."

"Ain't like he's got GPS," Biggie said. "I'm sure he'll find it eventually, but he doesn't know where he's goin'."

"He does if he's following us," I said.

"We're all talking what-ifs," Rocket said. "We have to make a decision. Either we don't go back to the Village and risk him finding his way there based on the direction we've been heading this whole time, or we go to the Village and risk him following us straight to it. Or, best-case scenario, he never finds the Village."

Without giving it much thought, I said, "We're going to the Village."

* * *

By the time we arrived, the sun had set. Although traveling in the dark went against everything I believed in as a Hunter, we'd had no other choice. Coin had fallen in and out of consciousness several times, and while Rocket's tightly-wrapped shirt around her leg had stopped most of the bleeding, it was obvious she was in excruciating pain.

"We're here," Rocket whispered, pointing at the orange glow surrounding the Village.

The outside view of the Village at night was a fascinating thing to see. With its enormous wooden gates closed, the Village remained hidden from view, resembling a kingdom pulled out of the Middle Ages. The only things missing on the inside were additional cabins with hay rooftops. Instead of adding more four-wall cabins, Coin had insisted we build tent-shaped shelters as they were not only easier to construct, but they were more solid. They weren't quite as large as the cabins she'd rebuilt at the back of the Village, but they were large enough to fit a twin-sized bed, a toilet-like hole that connected to a removable bucket underneath the tent—something I was still mind-blown over—and a few chairs for those rainy days.

Although I hadn't like the idea of women defecating inside the Village, everyone had agreed to empty their buckets every single morning outside the Village, through a small gate at the back. The last thing I'd wanted was women passing through the main gates with buckets filled with urine and feces.

Every time one of these buckets was emptied, women were obligated to wash their hands at one of the Village's water pumps—a creation by one of the Northers' slaves designed to pull water out from deep within the ground. She'd created them using materials from the crashed plane, and alongside them were soap-like dispensers that were constantly refilled by Tegan.

If Coin hadn't been on the verge of dying, I would have smiled at the sight of the Village—my home.

In an instant, one of the Night Watchers

clicked her fingers and the sound of bowstrings stretching filled the air around us. It wasn't hard to imagine them squinting at the darkness, loaded bows swaying from side to side, prepared to kill intruders.

Bringing my lips tight together, I let out a rhythmic whistle—two high notes and a long low note.

In the distance, a similar whistle was returned; only this time, there were two low notes and one high note.

To conclude the wordless message, I finished with a dozen high notes back to back, letting the sound flutter out of my mouth.

"It's Brone," one of them whispered.

The moment we stepped out from the darkness, the Night Watchers and the Tower Guards lowered their weapons. Exhausted, we lowered Coin to the ground as delicately as possible, but dropped her a few inches too early.

Fortunately, she was out cold.

Close to collapsing, I groaned in pain. Although I couldn't be certain, it felt like the insides of my suede shoes were covered in blood. The night we'd camped out in the jungle—the day before we found Number 73—my feet had already begun to form blisters. Being that I didn't hunt anymore, it was rare that I wore shoes around the Village or the Working Grounds. I could only imagine how bad my feet were now. My hands shook violently every time I raised my arm even in the slightest. How had we managed to carry her all the way back? My back was so tight and hurting so much that with one wrong move, it would give out—this had happened before when I'd helped my people construct the wooden cabins, and I'd ended up bedridden for two days. I'd never been one to have back problems, but ever since the Northers had enslaved me, my body had changed.

Leaves crunched and twigs snapped as the two Night Watchers outside the front gates came running toward us.

"Brone!" the tallest one said. "What happened?"

I couldn't see their faces with the lit sconces behind their heads, but it was obvious they were concerned.

"Take her to the Medical cabin, and wake Iskra and Zofia," I whispered. "She needs immediate help."

If there were two people I trusted most in the world to care for Coin, it was Iskra and Zofia. By working together, these two brilliant doctors had managed several successful minor surgeries and had even set up a station for blood transfusion which we'd used four times now, following severe animal attacks. I was confident they could save Coin and, with any luck, her leg.

The Night Watcher hesitated, no doubt taken

aback by the sound of my voice. "Just go," I said, waving a hand in the air. I wasn't in the mood to explain to them everything that had happened.

Together, the two Night Watchers scooped Coin off the ground, and behind them, the large wooden gates opened.

"Keep quiet about all of this," I said. "I want all the sconces out. All of them. As soon as—"

I stumbled forward and Biggie caught me.

"When morning comes, we'll deal with this," I continued with Biggie's arm around my shoulders. "No one leaves the Village. Are we clear?"

With Coin in their arms, the Night Watchers nodded.

"Go," I ordered, and they hurried across the Village and toward the Medical cabin.

The moment they disappeared from sight, Biggie squeezed my shoulder. "Girl, you need to rest."

"We all do," I breathed.

"Are we going to be safe overnight?" Rocket asked, walking through the gates.

"I highly doubt he kept up with us," I said. "That buys us time. And so long as we stay inside the gates, we're safe. Bullets might penetrate wood, but he'll be killed before anything happens. We couldn't do anything now even if we wanted to. It's the middle of the night and everyone's sleeping. Besides, none of us are in any condition—" I coughed and winced at the same time. "Go sleep. Recover. Tomorrow, we'll get ready for battle."

CHAPTER 9

The cabin door creaked as I opened it, and Ellie turned in her sleep. It was so dark that it was like I'd gone blind, but I knew every inch of this cabin, and every sound made by Ellie and Robin. Any second now, Ellie would wake up and ask me what had happened.

She was a light sleeper, and ever since Robin had come into the picture, she barely slept at all.

Still, hoping that I might allow her a few more restful hours of sleep, I snuck inside, shoulders slouched even though it made no difference whatsoever to the weight of my body on the wooden floorboards.

Another creak.

"Brone?" Ellie whispered.

"Hey," I said.

She shifted again, the bed groaning a little with her movement.

"Brone, what happened? Why do you sound like that?" she whispered.

"It's a lot to explain," I said, removing my clothes.

I snuck under the cotton sheet and inched my body against the warmth of Ellie's skin. Wrapping my arm around her soft waist, I let out a breath so long it felt like I'd been holding it all day.

"You're so warm," I breathed into her neck.

"Please tell me what happened," she said.

"A lot happened, Ellie. We found the plane. We also found a guy—"

"A guy?"

I nodded, my grimy forehead sliding against her chin. She'd likely bathed, smelling like coconut and pineapple, and there I was, smelling like three-week-old sweat, blood, and stomach acid.

"Yeah," I said, talking into her neck to prevent my rancid breath from climbing into her nostrils. "From one of the other penal islands."

She pulled away, but I held on. "Stay here," I said. "You'll wake Robin."

Resting a hand on my arm, she remained quiet, which I knew meant, *Go on.*

"He got to the island on a raft. I saved his life. Turns out the son of a bitch knew how to fly a plane. He manipulated us, and we led him straight to it. We almost left the island, Ellie." I paused, remembering how close I'd come to being forced to leave Ellie and Robin behind.

"Left? How?" she asked.

Although I couldn't see her face, I knew she was hurt. I hadn't yet explained the whole story to her, and she was probably thinking I'd considered leaving with the strange man.

What she didn't know was that I'd never leave her behind.

Kissing her neck, I pulled her in tighter. "I gave him shit. Told him to turn off the engines. Otherwise, he'd attract people to us. He wouldn't listen, and the next thing I knew, he was going full speed, preparing to take off."

"You should have gone," she said.

Taken aback, I pulled away. "Why would you say something like that?"

"It would have killed me," she said, "but you could have gotten your freedom, Brone. Why didn't you go?"

I scoffed, infuriated that she would even suggest such a thing. "First of all, there's no telling whether or not we'd have even survived the flight. And even if we had, what was I supposed to do? Stick my fucking thumb out at oncoming traffic and ask someone to drive me to my mom's? Then what? I'm a criminal, Ellie—"

"Brone, relax," she said. "I'm just saying I would have understood if you'd gone—"

"Well, stop it," I said. "I almost died fighting him off so I could come back to you and my people, and this is what I get? You telling me I should have left?"

"Brone, that's not what I meant."

Fuming inside, I held on to the fact that I was beyond exhausted and likely misinterpreting the intention of her words. The last person I wanted to fight with was Ellie, so instead of continuing the fight, I said, "Look, it doesn't matter. What matters is that there's another guy with a rifle."

When she didn't respond, I said, "Ellie?"

"I heard you," she said. "I—I don't know what to say or think. Was he from the plane?"

"I think so."

"He shot at you?"

"All of us, yeah," I said. "He got Coin."

"Oh my God. Is she okay?"

"She's with Iskra and Zofia. He got her leg, which is better than anywhere else. I don't get it. He was coming at us like he wanted us dead. It wasn't like we instigated it. We didn't even have our weapons on us. I was really careful *not* to look like a threat. It doesn't make any sense."

"Did he follow you?" she asked.

I hesitated, then said, "I don't think so."

Deep down, I knew it was a possibility, but I'd somehow convinced myself that this man didn't know the jungle, and there was little chance he'd managed to keep up with us through the denseness of the forest. It was easy to get lost in the trees, so how could a man from the outside possibly track down women who'd been living off the land for years?

"You're sure?" she asked.

"No," I admitted. I couldn't lie to Ellie. "That's why we're taking precautions. The fires are out, and first thing tomorrow, I'll assign guards to watch the towers. I want this son of a bitch dead before he steps anywhere near the Village."

"I can't believe this." She shook her head. "What are the chances—"

She kept talking, but her voice became distant and tunnel-like. I was so tired that within seconds, everything faded.

CHAPTER 10

I woke up to an empty cabin and a sound that made my stomach sink—women fighting.

Jolting upright, I grimaced. Every inch of my body was killing me, including my neck, which no doubt looked like wet cotton candy—deep blue, pink, and purple.

Throwing on my blood-stained clothes from the night before, I stormed out into the Village. At the very center, around the breakfast fire, were four women yelling at Rocket and Biggie, pointing fingers and throwing fists in the air.

Then, one of them stepped forward and grabbed Rocket by the hair. Biggie wasn't having it—with a swing of an arm, she slapped the woman upside the head, making her stumble backward and fall flat on her ass.

"What the fuck is going on?" I snapped, though it came out sounding more like a growl.

At once, everyone froze, and angry eyes rolled my way.

"Why aren't we allowed to leave?" one woman said. "We aren't prisoners!"

Feeling defensive, I almost said, "Technically, you are," but kept my mouth shut. Most of these women had suffered at the hands of the Northers—the last thing they wanted was to be confined within the walls of the Village.

"These two bitches ain't tellin' us what's going on," another woman said, pointing at Biggie and Rocket.

At the same time, both Biggie and Rocket raised their hands on either side of their faces and shrugged as if to say, *Hey, we're only doing our jobs.*

Poor Biggie and Rocket. I knew why they were being heckled—they didn't feel it was their place to tell everyone in the Village what had happened the day before. They were likely waiting for me to make that announcement, and all they *could* tell the people was that they couldn't leave the Village.

How were the women going to handle the news?

"What's going on?"

"Yeah, why are we stuck here? Are we in danger?"

One woman scoffed. "You aren't stuck. If you want out that bad, sneak out through the shit door at the back like everyone else did."

"What did you say?" I said.

The woman who'd delivered that last comment sealed her lips and looked away.

Was it true? Had women left through the back

door? Why the fuck had the guards not assigned someone to watch the door? I'd told them not to let anyone out. Why hadn't Ellie woken me? As the rage started to build inside, I reminded myself that exploding on these women wouldn't solve our problem. This was on me.

I hadn't ordered anyone to watch the back door. I'd been too tired to think about it.

These women needed a calm, level-headed leader. Not someone who was unable to maintain their cool in the face of danger or someone so easily capable of placing blame rather than finding solutions.

"What happened to you?" one woman asked, pointing at my throat.

I knew precisely what she was thinking—who could have done this? We'd defeated our enemy, so who could have possibly attacked us?

"The Village is on lockdown!" I tried to shout. It didn't come out loudly at all, but with how silent everyone was, my voice carried far enough. "Everyone in your tents until further notice!"

Voices exploded all around me—some angry, but most panicked.

What had I expected? They had no idea what was going on. Nobody moved as instructed. Instead, they stood around, rubbing their necks and bickering back and forth.

The idea had been to limit the amount of

information they had to avoid chaos, but ever since earning my position as leader, I'd made a point to be open and honest about everything.

Keeping things confidential wouldn't get me very far.

"All right, listen up!" I said, and the entire Village went so quiet children's feet could be heard stomping in the grass. "I'm going to tell everyone exactly what happened out there, but I need you all to remain calm."

Everyone shifted in their stances, no doubt fighting the urge to freak out.

"We're going to be okay as long as everyone stays calm, quiet, and follows my instructions. Can you all do that for me?"

The women nodded and remained quiet.

"We found the plane. It was a private jet. We weren't able to talk to anyone because we were attacked." I didn't bother going into the details of Number 73. The last thing I wanted was to spread additional panic by introducing the possibility of a new threat—male convicts from nearby penal islands. We had enough on our plate as it was, and we needed to deal with one issue at a time.

As women opened their mouths to begin protesting, I raised my hand, palm facing out. "We don't know who this man is—"

"Man?" shouted a woman. "How's that possible?"

One stern look was enough to have her retreat into the crowd.

"He had a rifle," I said.

Gasps filled the air, so I quickly added, "We have no idea what this person is after. All we know is that he wants us dead. Listen, guys, I wish we could talk this out, but if my suspicions are right, he's out there looking for the Village. I need everyone to remain silent until further notice. We don't want to draw him toward us. Anyone who's trained to use a weapon, follow me. And no one else leaves the Village, either. Get inside your tents and stay there." I turned sideways to find Rocket standing next to me, arms crossed over her chest and an expression so serious she didn't even look like herself. How was she still physically able to fight? It was a miracle we'd made it back to the Village in one day given how far we'd traveled to find the plane. "I'm going to head to the Working Grounds to gather the stray women there," I continued. "Once we're all inside the Village, no one leaves."

Women nodded all around me.

Eliot stepped out from within the crowd and women moved aside to let him through. With a puffed chest and clenched fists, he said, "How can I help?"

Although I was tempted to ask him to arm up, he was the only father these children knew, and it wasn't like we'd stumble across another one. We needed Eliot alive.

"Stay with the kids," I said.

Without a word, he bowed his head and turned away.

At once, everyone scattered, some rushing to their children, others straight into their tents. The women moved about so silently that it was a bit eerie.

Not once had the Village ever been this quiet.

"What can I do?" came Murk's voice.

Looking into her soft eyes, I sighed. "Spread the word. Let everyone know what's going on and make sure the women stay inside their tents. I don't want to see anyone standing in plain sight."

Murk nodded, gave me a look that said, *You got it, I'll handle this*, and stepped away.

Behind me, several dozen eager women stood confidently with heaved chests and angry scowls. They waited like trained soldiers, prepared to obey any command.

"Go see Hammer," I said. "Tell her I told you to grab any weapon you can. Throwable weapons are preferred."

"Um, Brone?" came one woman's voice. She stepped out in front of the crowd, her broad shoulders brushing against several others. "No disrespect, but Hammer's a bit, well, hardheaded. She won't believe us. She'll think we're rioting."

Sighing, I waved a hand toward the Tools tent. "Tell her I'm a monkey's ass."

A few women smirked, but their friends elbowed them until they stopped.

"It's our emergency code word," I said, walking away. "It'll work."

While it sounded idiotic, Hammer and I had chosen it together because we both knew no one in the Village would ever dare call me a monkey's ass.

Biggie, Rocket, and Elektra followed me outside of the Village and down the path toward the Working Grounds. Although beyond exhausted, I felt as if I'd been injected with a heavy dose of caffeine, and by the way my women carried themselves, it was obvious they weren't thinking about their pain or fatigue, either.

When this was all over, we'd likely collapse and sleep for three days straight. But until then, we needed to remain on high alert.

"The sooner we get those women out of the Working Grounds, the sooner we can seal the Village," I said, jogging down the muddy path.

In the distance, the waterfall's heavy flow became louder and louder, as did the voices inside the Working Grounds.

I turned around midjog, prepared to tell the others to spread out as soon as we entered the Working Grounds, when a nauseating sound filled the air around us—the sound of women screaming.

CHAPTER 11

The screaming was followed by a loud gunshot.

"Fuck!" I hissed, loading my bow.

Another shot was fired, and then another, and another.

All this did was amplify the sound of chaos—women shrieked and footsteps scattered. The moment we arrived at the Working Grounds, however, I couldn't see any of the chaos. A massive cloud of white smoke spilled out of the Working Grounds and around the jungle trees.

Throwing a hand over my mouth and nose, I took a step back.

"A goddamn smoke grenade?" Rocket said. "Fuck that."

She darted toward it, but I grabbed her by the back of her shirt, causing the seams to snap around her collar.

"Not so fast," I said. "Let's all go in at the same time. Whatever you do, don't breathe it in. There's no telling how toxic it is."

Sucking in a lungful of clean air, I bolted straight forward, entering the expanding cloud of white smoke.

The moment it touched my eyes, I squinted away tears. I ran until the smoke became less dense and I found myself standing inside the Working Grounds with light smoke slithering around my ankles.

At the same time, Biggie and Rocket came jogging behind me, slapping the air in front of their red, blotchy eyes.

Although I may have only stood there for a few seconds to take in the gruesome scene before me, it felt like an eternity. A man wearing a gas mask walked at a rapid pace in the distance, taking aim every time he saw movement in the Working Grounds' bay of water.

The white smoke—no doubt the result of smoke grenades—surrounded the entire area as if he'd strategically set them off to create a blinding wall. It had worked. Dead bodies lay in the sand across the Working Grounds, and by the way he kept pointing his gun toward the water, it was obvious that the surviving women had run away from the smoke and into the bay.

All of a sudden, a brown-haired head surfaced from the water and the man fired his shot as if playing Whack-A-Mole.

Blood and brain matter splattered into the air, and he reloaded his gun.

He was so preoccupied with hunting the

women in the water that he hadn't even heard us coming in through the smoke.

Aiming for his right thigh, I fired my arrow. It whistled through the air before piercing the middle of his leg. He let out a loud grunt and his rifle fell from his hands and remained dangling in one.

As much as I wanted to kill the worthless piece of shit, we needed him alive. I needed to know who he was, where he'd come from, and why he was hunting us like a bunch of wild game.

Almost falling over, he tore off his gas mask and his hateful eyes rolled up at me—the same eyes I'd seen earlier when he'd been hunting us.

Oh God.

This was my fault.

I had, in fact, led him straight here.

With a knot in my stomach, I stood there, trying to understand how I could have possibly allowed this to happen. He must have realized I was in my own head. Swinging half of his body for momentum, he regripped his gun and pointed it at me.

But he didn't have the time to shoot. In a moment, I shot an arrow into his right shoulder. It tore through, the colorful fletching now sitting at the front of his forest green shirt like a boutonniere on a tuxedo.

Dropping his gun, he collapsed to one knee,

barely able to hold himself up. He frowned and grabbed at his bloody thigh.

Got you, you bastard.

I took a step toward him, but at the same time, Rocket came bolting beside me with a sharp knife gripped in her fist.

Sand flew up into the air as she ran. "You're a fucking dead man!"

"Rocket!" I shouted.

She was so intent on killing him that she couldn't hear me.

"Stand down!" I ordered.

She couldn't hear me.

Behind me, Biggie shouted, "Girl, stop runnin'!" but Rocket kept on moving at lightning speed.

She raised her knife in the air, prepared to slaughter him, when I did the only thing I could think of; I shot an arrow in front of Rocket's feet.

The hit came so close that the arrow's shaft hit her shin and she lost her momentum. With narrow slits for eyes, she swung around and gave me a look that screamed, *Did you just fucking shoot at me?*

Had I been off by even an inch, I'd have caught her in the heel or the ankle. But what was I supposed to do? If she killed him, we had nothing—no information whatsoever.

Jogging toward her, I shook my head. "Don't kill him."

"Why the fuck not?"

The man smiled up at her, a look so detestable it made me want to pour battery acid on his face. He threw his head back and laughed. Why was he taunting her? How was any of this amusing to him?

Rocket ground her teeth and twirled her knife in her fist. It was obvious all she wanted to do was stab this man in the throat.

Bending down, I picked up the man's rifle and stared at him.

He sat in the sand with the weight of his body on his left elbow and bloodstains all over his clothes.

"You can come out!" I shouted, and one by one, heads started popping out of the water.

Women came walking out of the bay, some trembling, others crying.

One older woman with gray hair and smooth brown skin shook so hard her teeth clattered. "Wh-wh-who is that?"

I squeezed the grip of his gun, wanting nothing more than to break it with my bare hands. "That's what I'm gonna find out."

He parted his lips to say something—likely some smart-ass comment—when I turned the gun around and with its stock, smashed him square in the face.

CHAPTER 12

"You need to back off!" came Hammer's voice.

Then, Rocket's followed. "Brone gave you all an order! Back the fuck up!"

I didn't blame them for wanting inside the cabin. Had I been in their shoes, I'd have tackled my way through the crowd to get a punch in.

In front of me, tied to a wooden chair, was the man who'd taken the lives of sixteen of my women.

Any minute now, he'd wake up to find me standing in front of him, waiting for answers.

His nose, now a crooked, bloody mess, would be enough to make him talk. If it wasn't, I'd remind him of the break.

So I sat down across from him, closed my eyes, and waited.

Outside the cabin, women shouted and swore, while others cried. They wanted revenge, and that was understandable. Eventually, they'd tire themselves out, which may have been a heartless thought, but this situation needed to be managed without emotions.

I wanted him dead as much as the next woman,

but I needed my answers, first.

Finally, one eye cracked open, and then another.

He moaned and swallowed hard.

"Welcome back."

Our eyes locked, but he didn't say anything. It was difficult to even look at him when everything about him ignited a rage within me—his thick uncombed eyebrows, his dark soulless eyes, his square bearded jaw, and his slobbery pale lips that he kept licking repeatedly as if to feed a compulsion.

"Well, would you look at that," he said, his gaze searching the cabin. "You twits are capable of building things."

What the hell was his problem? What could we have ever done to him to deserve anything like this?

"Who are you?" I asked.

He scoffed as if answering me were a privilege I was unworthy of.

"You come here with your fancy plane," I said, clenching my teeth, "and you start shooting a bunch of innocent women."

"Innocent!" he shouted, his voice bouncing off the cabin walls. "So you're a murderer and you're an idiot."

Was that what this was about? The fact that we were convicted felons? Was he some sort of vigilante trying to prove something? Who the fuck flew this far out, on unauthorized land, to hunt down criminals?

"So you kill murderers," I said, "and you're doing the world a favor." Leaning forward, I rested my hands on my knees to stare him square in the face. "What does that make you?"

When he didn't answer, I grabbed the arrow's shaft sticking out of his shoulder and pushed it sideways. He cried out, slobber dripping from the corners of his mouth.

When I let go, he didn't speak.

Slowly, I stood up and turned away from him.

"You're going to start talking," I said, plucking my knife out of my belt. "Where are you from?"

Nothing.

I turned around again to catch him glaring at me with so much hatred I could almost see what he was picturing—holding me down and breaking every bone in my body. That's when I noticed the digital screen on his chest, right over his heart. I hadn't noticed it at first because the numbers weren't illuminated, but every few seconds, a green number flickered.

An electrical component had evidently been damaged when I shot him in the shoulder.

Moving closer, I squinted at it.

The number read: 16.

"What is that?" I asked.

This time, he offered a dignified smirk.

When he didn't answer, my nostrils flared and I rushed toward him, prepared to sever one of his fingers, or maybe even an ear. Although the idea may have caused projectile vomiting when I'd first landed on the island, it didn't phase me now, especially not when dealing with a piece of shit like this guy.

Without warning, I swung downward and stabbed my knife through his hand and into the wooden armrest.

He shouted, and outside, women cheered.

With clenched teeth, he scowled at me.

"Still don't want to talk?" I asked.

Nothing.

Bit by bit, I turned the blade, and he screamed.

"Fuck you!"

I tore the knife out and stared at the digital pad over his jacket. The number wasn't changing, and the format wasn't time. What the hell was that thing? It reminded me of a scoreboard. Could it be—

"Is that a counter?" I asked.

When the smile on his face returned, bile rose in my throat.

"You're keeping track of your fucking kills," I said.

It all made sense—although we hadn't removed the dead bodies from the Working Grounds just yet, I'd counted them, reaching precisely *sixteen*.

"What kind of sick fucking game is this?" I asked.

Something in his eyes lit up, almost as if he'd suddenly realized something.

"You're right," he said at last. "It's a game... A game thousands of people are watching."

"What are you talking about?" I asked.

He scoffed. "How do you think we got here? This island's protected by the feds. No one makes it to Kormace Island. And trust me, people have tried. Now and then, the news talks about how a plane was shot down for getting too close to the no-fly zone."

"What're you saying?" I asked. "The government's in on this?"

He shrugged his uninjured shoulder. "Depends on how you look at it. All they did was give us safe passage in exchange for half the profit."

I clenched my teeth so hard they squeaked. "What profit?"

He threw his head back and laughed maniacally, revealing large red tonsils at the back of his throat. "A shitload of money. I mean, the Organizer set the whole thing up and told us it was a lucrative market. Didn't actually believe the son of a bitch until he showed me the website."

"You're telling me this is online?" I said.

"Dark web," he said. "We can't be traced. People

are paying us to watch us clean up the island."

"*Watch* you?"

He glanced down at his jacket, where a small black dot hung at the end of a red and white wire. "Well, they can't see my shots anymore, thanks to you."

Pacing back and forth, I ran my fingers through my short hair. "What kind of profit are we talking about? Who's getting the money? What the fuck is this?"

"Well, before we landed, the pot was up to twenty-three million dollars. When we landed an hour later, it jumped up to forty-eight million. People can only watch if they pay the entry fee, which means more and more people are watching."

In an instant, I remembered the screen Rocket had shown me—it had indicated something close to fifty-two million dollars, and next to the amount was the word *Bid*. I wanted to vomit.

Was this truly happening? Why wasn't this page being tracked and shut down? Why wasn't anyone stopping this?

"The game ends in three days," he added. "After three days, whoever has the most kills wins a third of that pot. The rest of it is shared with the Organizer, the feds, and a small payout goes to whoever bid on the right player."

This couldn't be happening.

It couldn't be.

How the fuck would anyone allow something like this to happen? Hunting human beings for money?

I breathed in slowly, then exhaled through my nose.

"Listen, I can help you," he said.

Tempted to stab my knife into his temple, I tucked it back into my belt. "How the fuck can someone like you help me? You're here to kill us."

"Yeah, and so are another five people," he said.

I scoffed. "You think I'm going to believe anything you say? This whole thing's a fucking game. Why should I trust you? And why the hell would you *want* to help me?"

"Because I want to help *me*," he said.

When he didn't smile or make some other smart-ass comment, I bit my lip.

"I'm listening."

"Like I said," he continued, "there's another five players out there. There are six of us total, and the pilot, but he has nothing to do with the hunt. We saw your village when we flew overhead, so you can bet your ass the other players are on their way here. I hope you have weapons."

What was he doing? Why was he turning on his own people?

He must have noticed my confusion. Offering a pompous smile, he said, "Listen, lady, these people aren't my friends. We're all ex-military, highly trained, and we came here for one thing... Money. Whoever gets the most kills wins. Right now, I'm top player. That's why my number's green. Blue is second player, red third, and yellow means you're at the bottom of the list. So if you kill the other players before they raise their score, I win."

"Not if you're dead," I growled.

"Even if I'm dead," he said. "The contract states that in the event of a death, the funds will be distributed to immediate family. My wife knew the risks. All I want is for her and my kids to be taken care of."

How could such a horrible piece of shit even have a family or care about another human being?

His eyes widened, and he looked at the cabin's door as if to say, *Well, what's it gonna be?*

"What help are you offering?" I asked, even though the last thing I wanted was help from this guy.

"Information," he said. "First, I suggest you get to them before they reach your village. See my bag?" He threw his chin out at a large forest green bag. "There're grenades in there... Knives, and a shitload of ammo. Use my gun. Use whatever you want. Just wipe them out."

Walking toward his bag, I turned my head to look at him. "You're a sick son of a bitch, you know that?"

He smiled so big all his teeth became visible. "Maybe, but I'm about to win this motherfuckin' game."

PART THREE

PROLOGUE

Rocket marched through the Village with a raised chin and a crowd of armed women behind her. They'd been ordered to go out in search of the remaining players and commanded to kill without hesitation.

What I hated most about being the leader was ending up in positions like these—forced to request that my friends risk their lives to protect the Village. But what was I supposed to do? Ask those I care about to sit behind? I had to set aside my emotions and think with my mind, not with my heart. All our lives were at risk, and I needed the best of the best to defend our land.

The best happened to be my friends.

As Rocket came marching back inside, I could tell something was wrong. They'd left minutes ago, so why were they already returning? Slowly, I lowered Robin into the grass and stood up straight.

The women behind Rocket reminded me of our sworn enemies, the Northers. Most of them wore skull masks over their faces, fur on their shoulders, and boots up to their knees. While I hated the idea of using recycled Norther attire, it was to our advantage to do so. The more frightening we looked, the more intimidating we were to our attackers, and same as with wild animals, this was crucial to our survival.

"What's going on?" Ellie asked, leaning into me.

How could I answer that? I had no idea what was going on. The order that morning had been simple: exit the Village, spread out, and hunt down the remaining players before they could find the Village. Hammer had spent most of the night sharpening weapons to ensure they were ready for battle. Each Hunter was then assigned a team of women willing to fight with weapons, and it was their responsibility to lead their small group out into the forest.

As Biggie marched next to Rocket, she shook her head, and I couldn't help but feel like we'd been defeated before even starting.

The moment Rocket approached us, she threw an arm out in the air. "They fucking trapped us."

My eyes shot up toward the closing Village gates. "What do you mean, trapped?"

"These people are smart, Brone," she said. "They've got some sort of electric wire system all around the Village. We're trapped."

CHAPTER 1

"Explain it to me again," I said, my voice carrying throughout the crowd.

I hadn't meant to get snippy, but I didn't understand how anyone could have set up some electrical barrier around our entire Village overnight.

Frowning, I shot my Tower Guards a look. Did they fall asleep? How the hell did no one catch this? Rocket must have sensed my hatred toward the women assigned to protect us. She reached for my shoulder, and when I pulled away, said, "You asked them to keep the fire out. They couldn't see anything."

"They don't have fucking ears?" I snapped.

When everyone around me went silent, I realized I wasn't making the situation any better. They were likely freaking out as much as I was, and the last thing they needed was for their leader to lose her wits. I sucked in a long breath and stretched my neck to the side until something cracked.

"Okay," I breathed out. "It's okay. We can figure

this out."

Everyone stared at me as if I held the answer to the Egyptian pyramids. It was astonishing how much these women trusted my judgment, but I consistently got us out of trouble and saved lives, which meant I had to trust myself as much as they did.

"How many wires are there?" I asked, directing my gaze at Rocket. "Can't we walk over it?"

She shook her head and tightened her lips, which translated to, It isn't that simple.

"There's more than one wire," she said. With her hands, she drew lines through the air, trying to draw out a picture. "There's like, three or four of them, and they're all at different heights."

"So there's no getting through it," I said, more as a statement than a question.

Again, she shook her head.

"Where's the electricity coming from?" I asked.

"We haven't located the source of the power. To be honest, we didn't do much investigating at all. We came back inside the Village to inform you—"

"Then how do you know it's electric?" I cut her off.

Rocket cocked an eyebrow and raised her knife; its tip was as black as coal, as if she'd twirled the blade around in a pile of ashes.

"I tossed it at the wire and it almost came back

at me. This thing's fucking power—" She lowered her voice, no doubt trying to avoid causing a panic among the women. "It's basically an advanced electric fence."

"So you tested it," I said.

She nodded.

"Rocket, you could have gotten yourself—"

Playfully twirling the knife in front of my face, she said, "Girl, unlike some women here, I finished high school—"

"What the hell did she just say?" someone said.

Rocket laughed, her bright eyes turning into little moons. The woman who'd made the comment behind her—a half-toothed, middle-aged woman covered with sagging tattoos—craned her neck to look at us.

"All right," I said. "Rocket, Biggie, show me the way. The rest of you—stay here."

As we walked toward the Village gates, I twirled a finger in the air and the Tower Guards on either side opened them up. On the ground, two other guards helped pull the gates open, the weight of them making for a difficult task.

Behind us, women came in and out of their wooden tents, looking like curious hyenas around a dead carcass. They wanted to know what was going on, but they didn't want to leave the safety of their homes.

It wouldn't take long for word to spread, which

also meant women would panic. I needed to find out what had been installed around the Village and how to go about removing it. The fact that one of the players had taken the time and effort to trap us inside meant they had another plan lined up, and it was most likely a plan that involved mass murder.

"Ain't you worried we'll get shot at?" Biggie hissed, her back so slouched her lips almost touched my ear.

"If this player wanted a few kills, they would have shot at you when you all came out here this morning," I said. "It isn't a few kills they want. They want to win, which means they want all of us. So until they make their big move, we have nothing to worry about. Besides, they aren't the only ones with guns anymore."

Behind me, the sound of a gun being cocked echoed, and I turned around to find Quinn following us with a rifle in her hands and a strut in her walk. She stuck her chin out, smiled with her eyes, and said, "Let's get this son of a bitch."

Quinn knew her way around a gun, and if there was one person I trusted more than Coin with a rifle, it was Quinn. Although she hadn't gone into the specifics about her past, she'd made it clear that her knowledge of guns couldn't be matched by anyone on the island.

"Long guns, shotguns, rifles, pistols, revolvers,

semis, subs, automatics—" she'd rambled. "I've shot more guns than there are hookers in all of Toronto."

The other gun had been given to one of Quinn's friends—TunaHead. I'd asked her to repeat the woman's name three times until Quinn lost her patience and said, "Forget her name. It doesn't matter. The girl can shoot, and I promise you can trust her."

So I did. Now, TunaHead sat in the middle of the Village with the second rifle on her lap, responsible for the protection of our people.

"If anyone comes in here," I'd said, pointing a stiff finger in her face, "you kill them. Got it? And if that bastard inside the cabin somehow manages to get out—kill him too."

She'd nodded, her face expressionless, and stared intently toward the closed Village gates as if trying to anticipate an attacker on the other side.

The moment we stepped outside of the gates, I stopped walking. A few meters away from our Village's wooden blockade were silver wires intertwined to form a messy barrier. The first row ran at the height of my shins, the second row at the height of my waist, and the third at the height of my neck.

No way could we slip underneath without our backs getting caught, and with how high up it went, jumping it wasn't an option, either. Whoever set this up had a lot of experience, and it was clear they went above and beyond to ensure that none of us were getting out.

"See," Rocket said, standing stiff with her arms crossed over her chest. "We're fucked."

As I stared at the wiring that ran in both directions and around our Village, I realized something. "No, we aren't. Follow me."

CHAPTER 2

"Get the fuck out of there!"

"Get her out!"

"Mason, stop it! You heard Brone!"

With my stomach sinking, I sprinted toward the back cabins where a crowd of women had formed. The cabin's door—the one in which Player 1 was imprisoned—was wide open with women standing in the doorway.

What the hell was going on? I'd ordered everyone to remain away from our prisoner. I'd even assigned four armed women to guard the door. Why was it open? Why were women inside? Had they killed him?

As much as I wanted the man dead, we needed him.

Shoving women aside, I cried out, "Get the fuck out of my way!"

They'd disobeyed a direct order and weren't about to receive patience or kindness from me. My elbow caught a woman in the face and she stepped back, throwing her hands over her nose. But I didn't care. After everything I'd done for these women, how dare they disobey such a simple command? I was trying to protect all of them, and to do that, I needed this man alive. That's why no one was to go near him.

I understood the rage these women felt—the man had killed their friends. To compensate, I'd promised them that after the situation was resolved, I'd hand him over freely and allow them to do whatever they wanted with him. The one trade-off was that they had to remain patient and wait for me to hand him over.

"Mason, put the knife down!"

I stormed inside, the cabin's door slamming against the wooden wall.

On the floor was Player 1, still strapped to the chair with his legs sticking out in the air. Behind him was one of my women, Mason, on her knees with a grimace so pronounced it made her look hideous.

"He—he killed them!" she shouted, slobber spewing across his body.

That's when I noticed the knife she had pressed to his throat. For the first time, the man wasn't smiling. With his bulging eyes rolling pleadingly toward me, he seemed afraid for his life.

"Brone, we tried to stop—" said one of the guards behind me.

I raised a fist to tell her to shut up. If I opened my mouth, I was afraid I'd say something I'd regret.

"Mason." I tried to convey sweetness with my voice. "Let's put the knife down, okay?"

"Why?" she shouted, squeezing her knife until her knuckles went white.

The blade was now pressed so firmly into his neck it made a bloody gash.

"Because this isn't the way," I told her. "As much as everyone wants this guy dead, we need him alive for intel."

She hesitated, looking down at the slobbery mess beneath her, then regripped her blade as if she'd concluded that killing him was worth losing whatever intel we were after.

"Mason," I said again, my voice hardening this time. "Think about your daughter—"

"I don't have a daughter!" she shouted, her voice so loud that the women behind me stepped backward.

What was she talking about? Mason had a daughter. She'd named her Violet. Judging by how much her face had swollen and how deep purple it had become, I knew something was very wrong.

"I let her go with Schmitt to the Working Grounds this morning!" she shouted again. This time, she dug her knife so deep that Player 1 grimaced and tried to push his body off the ground with his head to alleviate some of the pressure. But with the restraints around his arms, wrists, legs, and shins, he couldn't move.

"I-I didn't shoot no little girl," he said. "I swear. I may be a killer, and you may think I'm a psychopath, but I'm not a monster. I'd never touch a little—"

"Shut up!" Mason cried. "Shut the fuck up!"

"I swear, I didn't shoot—"

Screaming at the top of her lungs, she raised her knife, and clenching it in her fist, smashed him in the face twice. His jaw shook violently, and something snapped.

Turning around, I leaned into the women behind me and whispered, "Has anyone seen Violet?"

The women shook their heads.

It didn't make any sense. If he hadn't shot her, what had happened? Why hadn't anyone located the child? I couldn't remember seeing Violet when we'd searched the Working Grounds for survivors.

"Mason," I said, fighting the urge to yell at her. "We haven't found a body, which means your daughter is probably still out there."

She breathed in and out through gritted teeth, bubbles forming at the corners of her mouth. If I hadn't known what was going on, I'd have thought she'd been bitten by a rabid animal.

"Put the knife down," I said, "and we'll go look for her together, okay?"

But she wasn't listening. It was as if she no longer possessed the ability to hear with her ears.

Instead, she watched us as if we were the enemy, probably creating nonexistent conversations in her head.

"Put the knife down," I said, my tone hardening.

When she didn't obey, I stiffened my stance. Slowly, I raised my hand until I felt the cold handle of my knife on my belt—a metal throwing knife I'd found in Rainer's lair. Mason was one of us, but she was still a convicted murderer. It was important not to forget how dangerous she, or any other woman in the Village, could be.

She would, without a doubt, kill this man if she was determined enough.

As the leader of the Village, it was my responsibility to do whatever was necessary to protect my people as a whole, even if it meant harming one of my own. She must have sensed my willingness to attack her; her wild eyes shot toward my hand and she growled something incomprehensible.

"Mason, I'm not going to tell you again," I said. "Put the goddamn knife—"

Suddenly, she screamed out—an unsettling shriek—and the veins in her forehead inflated. Her entire face darkened several shades of red, and the muscles in her arms bulged as she forced the edge of her knife into Player 1's throat. The entire event may have happened in all of two seconds, but the surge of adrenaline that burst through me at the sound of her cry slowed everything down.

Just as her blade punctured the side of Player 1's neck, I whipped out my knife and threw it as hard as I could, straight for the largest target on her body—her chest.

The impact didn't sound like impact all at—it was quiet, sliding right through her shirt and into her chest. The handle sat crookedly on an angle, which meant the blade had slipped through her ribcage. She sucked in hard, maybe the result of a lung being punctured, and dropped her weapon.

Falling back against the wooden wall of the cabin, she clawed at her bloody chest, the tips of her fingers hovering above the knife's handle. It was as if she wanted to tear it out but was too afraid to touch it.

She opened her mouth to say something, but a raspy breath took the place of her words. Dark red blood pooled in her mouth before spilling over her bottom lip. Based on the knife's position, it had likely punctured both her lung and nicked her heart, and with a blade that thick, there was no coming back from that.

As much as I'd wanted to catch her in the shoulder, or somewhere else without damaging vital organs, I wasn't a professional knife thrower. I'd practiced several times with Quinn and Rocket, but I'd been unable to hit the bullseye every single time. The only chance I had at stopping her from killing Player 1 was to act fast, and at that moment, my knife was all I had and her chest was the biggest target.

I felt awful watching her panic. Blood spilled out of her mouth and her eyes bulged as if being inflated with air. She couldn't breathe, and she had to be in tremendous pain. But what other choice did I have? She was about to kill the one person who possessed the knowledge to protect us from the other players.

"Mason!" one woman shouted.

Footsteps echoed behind me but soon came to an abrupt stop. Someone else undoubtedly stopped her from coming too close.

"Do something!" that same woman cried. "She's suffering!"

Fighting back the lump in my throat, I loaded my bow and aimed the arrow straight for her heart. She stared at me pleadingly, and I couldn't tell whether she was begging to be saved or begging for mercy. Knowing her wound couldn't be healed on this island, I stretched the elastic of my bow, my fingers grazing the side of my face.

Behind me, several women gasped and cried, but no one interfered.

Just as Mason gasped for another bubbly breath of air, I mouthed, "I'm sorry," and released the fatal shot.

CHAPTER 3

"You fucking bitch!" the woman shouted.

The next thing I knew, someone was on top of me, blasting solid hits to the side of my face. I swung back as hard as I could, feeling cartilage crack beneath my knuckles, but still, I had no idea who was on top of me or how to dodge the attack.

Biggie's silhouette appeared, and within seconds, the woman was dragged off me, fists pumping the air and feet kicking out as far as possible, trying to land a final blow.

"How could you do that?" she yelled, saliva landing all over Biggie's forearm. She appeared to be Mason's age—thirties or early forties—with dark skin and eyes to match. "She didn't do anything wrong! This man's a fuckin' terrorist!" She kicked again, but Biggie didn't let go. "You saved a fucking terrorist's life and killed one of our own!"

This woman, whose name I couldn't recall, was right—the man was a terrorist. He'd killed over a dozen of my women without so much as blinking and had done so for cash. What she didn't understand was that the intention wasn't to save him—the true intention was to save *us*.

Outside, women gathered and bickered with one another. News traveled fast on this island, and it wouldn't have surprised me to discover that the news of Mason's murder had already reached the other side of the Village.

"Brone wouldn't do that," one woman said in the distance.

"Are you sure? Let me see."

"Stop pushing!"

Women shoved their way into the cabin, squishing the rest of the audience against the cabin's interior like a bunch of sardines.

"Oh my God."

Within the dimness of the cabin, all I saw were the whites of women's eyes as they stared at me in disbelief.

Reaching for the swelling bump on my cheek, I said, "This man might be a terrorist, but he's the only one who has the information we need. Without him, we could all die."

No one said anything, which meant they were at least willing to hear me out.

"Do you think I wanted to save his life?" Suddenly, all I felt was loathing. I was disgusted that these women thought that killing Mason had been as simple as choosing between shorts or pants. Did they not know me by now? I didn't mean to get so upset, but it was difficult to stay calm when I felt I was being attacked for making an impossible decision. "You think I enjoyed killing one of my own? Like this is a fucking game to me?"

No one spoke, and some gazes quickly fell to the floor. Others, however, remained fixated on me with such abhorrence it was as if they were plotting my demise.

"All right. Everyone. Get out," Rocket said, assumedly realizing how angry I was.

"So she gets away with murder," said the woman who attacked me, jerking her body from side to side within Biggie's grasp. "You'll fucking get what's coming to you, you stupid bitch."

This was it.

This was the moment I knew would affect my reign over the Village. Although we'd lived in peace for the last few years, and although many of these women were good-hearted people who regretted the mistakes of their pasts, there was no denying that many others were still cold-blooded killers who, if given the opportunity, would attempt to climb their way up the hierarchal ladder.

But with the number of women who respected me and looked up to me, the bad ones found their places and kept to themselves. The few who'd tried to stand up to me in the past had been banished, and on one occasion, killed by Fisher when she'd tried to attack me from behind.

As I stared at the woman, grinding my teeth, a

thousand thoughts ran through my mind.

Was it better to offer her mercy? Or, should she be punished for using violence? She knew damn well that anyone living inside the Village was to abide by my zero-tolerance policy about violence.

But how could I punish someone after I'd killed another? Wasn't my job to be a mentor and an example to my people?

Even Biggie couldn't contain her shock. With bulging eyes, she chomped down on her bottom lip and waited quietly, her flabby arms still wrapped tightly around the woman.

I parted my lips, prepared to offer this woman a free pass given that I'd killed her friend, when I realized something: I had no one to answer to.

Not only was this woman showing utter disrespect to the leader of the Village, she was also blatantly threatening me. Not once had I been unfair to my women. If anything, I prided myself on being fair and practicing equality no matter the situation.

I was about to order Biggie to take her outside the Village gates and banish her from ever entering again when something overcame me.

Suddenly, all I knew was rage.

I felt betrayed, attacked, violated, and belittled all at the same time. I'd saved hundreds of women from a life of torture and enslavement. I didn't deserve this.

With gritted teeth, I charged straight toward the woman, grabbed her by the back of her hair, tore her out of Biggie's arms, and dragged her outside the cabin. She stumbled, tripping over her own feet, and reached for her hair in an attempt to free herself.

"What—what the hell—" she said, her strides long and awkward-looking.

The crowd that had accumulated around the cabin broke apart, forming a clear path for me.

I bit down on my teeth so hard they squeaked and walked straight toward the center of the Village, clutching her hair as tightly as possible next to my waist. Behind me, she kept tripping and catching herself and mumbling a bunch of broken sentences such as, "You think—," "The hell is—," and "Hey, let—stop it—"

Inside, it was as if a switch had been flicked. I couldn't stop the anger, nor did I want to. I'd done nothing but help this woman live a life she'd never dreamed of, and she'd turned on me—she'd hit me again and again and threatened my life.

I wouldn't tolerate it.

The moment we approached the breakfast fire, now a lonely pit full of ashes, I threw her into the grass. She rolled sideways until she stopped on her back to face me. "Yo, what the fuck are you doin'?"

Women had exited their tents now, and they

gathered around us like city dwellers after witnessing a horrible car accident. When I swung around to face my audience, most of them gasped, some pointed, and a few looked away.

"Who did that?" someone whispered, staring at what I assumed was a red swelling on my face.

"Was it Bridge?"

Their curious eyes rolled toward the woman, Bridge who'd hit me, and the bickering picked up again. How bad was the mark? Was there bleeding? Was that why they were pointing?

"As I'm sure you all can see," I said, "this woman attacked me, your leader."

Bridge glared up at me, pointing a finger my way. "The bitch killed Mason!"

No one spoke up. It was clear they already knew what had happened.

"What's wrong with you?" Bridge said. "Why aren't any of you pissed off about this?" Slowly, she stood and rubbed the back of her head. "How can you all stand there when this psychopath who calls herself our leader killed one of our own?"

Whispering broke out among the crowd, and it became obvious that no one knew what to do. Was Bridge in the wrong for having attacked me, or did they truly believe I was wrong for having killed one of our own?

Drawing my shoulders back, I made a conscious effort to look at as many women in the eyes as possible. "Not once have I ever done anything out of anger toward any of you. All I've ever cared about was your happiness and well-being."

The women nodded, mumbling words I couldn't understand.

"Yes, I did kill one of our own today, but not out of hatred or vengeance. I did what had to be done to protect all of you."

With a slouched posture, fists clenched so tightly they looked like triangles by her hips, and a bowed head, Bridge looked at me as if preparing to jump me again. "How is killing my friend to save a captured terrorist going to protect anyone here?"

"I don't have to explain my decision," I said coldly. "I'm here because you all trust me to guide you in the right direction. If you can't trust the decision I've made without demanding that I explain my thought process, then we have a problem."

At the back of the crowd, Ellie emerged, looking more worried than I'd ever seen her before. She knew what was going on, and if my plan backfired, things would take a turn for the worse within a matter of minutes. But this was the only way to go about it without causing a divide among my people. If I didn't involve everyone in this decision, women would do the one thing they knew how to do when angry or panicked—place blame.

Slapping both hands on my waist, I said, "The choice is yours. Her, or me."

It felt like we were standing on trial, waiting for the jury to deliver the verdict.

This time, the crowd exploded into loud chattering, and women turned from side to side, searching each other for guidance.

"If you think I'm unfit to be your leader, now's your chance to do something about it. I'm not a dictator—I'm not Rainer." Venomous scowls spread through the Village at the sound of her name. "If you're unhappy with how things are, I'll walk away."

"Stop playing your fuckin' mind games!" Bridge shouted.

Ignoring her, I kept going. "As your leader, I intend to banish this woman for treason. She's proved herself to be a threat, and if she refuses to go willingly or becomes violent in any way, I won't hesitate to do what needs to be done. So, what will it be? Do you vote that I step down as leader of the Village, or that Bridge—"

Yet before I could finish my sentence, rapid footsteps echoed behind me, and I turned in time to see Bridge charging at full speed. With her mouth wide open and her triangular fists held up in the air, she let out a hoarse cry as she ran.

Still filled with rage, I reached for my carving

knife on my belt and pulled it out, prepared to end this.

Before Bridge could even try to throw a blow at me, something hard hit her in the face, splitting her eyebrow in half. At once, she stopped running, reached for the blood over her eye, and blinked hard. At her feet lay a bone-made breakfast dish with speckles of blood on its edges.

"Brone!" one woman shouted.

"Brone!" said another.

And then, all of the women started chanting my name and pumping fists in the air.

Bridge glared at everyone like a caged dog, her teeth bared and her head turning from side to side so fast it looked like she was twitching. "You can't do this!"

Then, another bowl was thrown, this time, knocking her square in the mouth. Two of her front teeth disappeared, and blood spilled over her bottom teeth. Women in the crowd searched the grass and reached for any hard object they could find to use as a weapon.

As I watched Bridge on her hands and knees, scrambling to get back up, I remembered who I once was: someone who would have never allowed another person to get hurt even if they deserved it. But that was all it was—a memory. I didn't feel sorry for her. She was a threat to everyone in the Village.

Lydia would have felt sorry, but I didn't, and the truth was, Lydia didn't exist anymore.

Raising my chin, I stared at the crowd of furious women and nodded. With bowls, spoons, and forks clenched in their fists, everyone closed in on Bridge.

CHAPTER 4

Bending down to grab Player 1's chair, I turned to Biggie and Rock. "Help me out."

With a bloody gash on the side of his neck, Player 1 smirked up at me with a look that said, *I'm untouchable.*

It made me want to pull my throwing knife out of Mason's chest and stab him in the eye with it. Arrogant piece of shit. The sole reason he was still alive was that he knew things we didn't. Once this disgusting game was over, he wouldn't have anything to smile about.

In fact, he wouldn't be able to smile at all—he'd be torn to pieces by my women.

Biggie and Rocket each grabbed a part of the chair, and with a grunt, the three of us brought him back onto four legs. His chair landed with a thud, and behind him, Mason's limp hand fell to the floor, her knuckles hitting hard against the wood and her knife slipping out of her grip.

Once this was over, I'd allow the women to take her body to our burial site—a space we'd cleared near the Working Grounds. It was quaint and surprisingly good representation of a typical graveyard. Handpicked rocks with poorly drawn engravings lay above the bodies in the earth, and around the graves were figures constructed of wood and hay, like scarecrows. It prevented certain animals from approaching the holes and digging out the bodies. It wasn't a foolproof plan, but it was better than nothing.

Until Mason's body could be transported to our burial site and placed inside the earth, she would have to be wrapped in leaves and left outside. If we didn't end this war with the players, her body would start to decompose, attracting flies, insects, birds of prey, and even wildcats. The last thing I wanted was for a leopard to climb into our Village in search of food.

Crouching down beside her dead body, I closed her eyelids. Then, I made my way around Player 1's chair, crossed my arms, and stared him in the face.

"Thanks for that," he said, his smile returning.

Biggie stepped forward, her fist balled up by her face.

"It's okay," I said, touching her forearm. "He'll get what's coming to him."

Without responding, he elevated his chin, revealing the unsightly cut left by Mason.

I wiggled a finger at his neck. "Without treatment, that could get infected."

He shrugged so nonchalantly that I all I wanted

to do was kick him in the chest and send him flying on his back again. How was he so calm? So neutral? Was he not afraid of anything? He knew I had every intention of killing him after this was over. Was he delusional? Did he think he'd somehow survive? Had he planned for some sort of rescue mission?

"Do you *want* to die?" I asked him.

Again, he shrugged. "It's not about what I want. It's about providing for my family."

"What's he talking about?" Rocket asked.

His cold eyes slowly rolled from me to Rocket. "She hasn't told you?"

With arms crossed over her belly, Rocket rotated the upper half of her body to face me. "Told me what?"

I'd explained to everyone that we were being hunted by psychopaths, but I hadn't gone into the details about the money. The revelation of it all had already disturbed me beyond belief—why let my women suffer knowing that the lives of their friends had been lost for a game?

It wouldn't have helped the situation and might even have aggravated it.

But Biggie and Rocket were my friends, and I trusted them more than anyone. Closing my eyes, I sighed. "It's a game."

Biggie scoffed, but then her features hardened when no one else laughed. "A game? 'Dis some sort of horseshit? What're you talkin' about, a game?"

She punched her palm. "'Cause I ain't playin'."

"No," I said. "*He* is. And so are the other players out there."

"Playing what?" Rocket asked. "Some sort of killing game?"

"Basically," I said. "People are bidding on different players, and whoever wins gets half the bid money. The rest is split between the government and the bidders—"

"The government?" Biggie snapped. She threw both arms into the air and frowned, her bushy eyebrows almost touching each other above the bridge of her nose. "Are you tellin' me—"

"Why're you so surprised?" Rocket cut in. She had to tilt her head back to look up at Biggie. "We all know how corrupt the government is—"

"Listen, ladies," said Player 1, and both Rocket and Biggie turned toward him with flared nostrils, white-knuckled fists, and eyes so narrow it looked like they were trying to shoot him with invisible lasers.

"I hate to break up your little chitchat, but the more you stand around here talking like a bunch of idiots, the more danger—"

Crack.

Biggie shook her fist, wiggled her fingers, and smiled as Player 1 rolled his head back up and stretched his jaw muscles. I didn't even bother scolding her for the hit—it had satisfied me too much.

"Is that how you treat someone who's trying to help you?" he asked.

"Bullshit," Rocket said. "You aren't trying to help us. You're trying to help yourself. You've been caught, which means you can't play your fucked-up little game anymore." Her eyes shot toward me. "Am I right? Is that what this is about? He's willing to help us out so that his competitors can't beat him." She stopped talking and forced a choppy laugh when she noticed the green digital counter on his chest. "Let me guess... This is your kill counter. You sick motherfucking piece of—"

Crack.

Even though Rocket had been the one to clock him on the other side of the face this time, Biggie grinned from ear to ear. "That's my girl."

With his hands tied behind his back, all he could do was open his mouth wide to stretch out the tension. "Hit me again, and you won't be getting my help—"

Clenching my fist as hard as I could, I swung a punch right into his ear. It must have hurt him enough; he let out a pathetic pained cry and shook his head, looking dazed.

"Listen here, you little shit," I said. "You don't tell us what to do. You're the one strapped to the chair, and your counter is still green, which means you're still winning the game. So unless you want to lose millions of dollars, I suggest you drop the arrogant act, pull your head out of your ass, and answer our questions without being a smartass dick about it. Got it?"

He stared at me a bit longer than I would have liked and then nodded without saying anything. "What information do you need?"

"Someone trapped us inside the Village," I said.

When he arched a brow, I added, "There are electrical wires all around us."

"Of course," he said, the corner of his lip pulling upward. By the way he stared intently at the wooden floor panels of the cabin, it was obvious he knew what I was talking about.

"That's BlueVolt's fine work," he said.

"BlueVolt?" I asked, feeling stupid even voicing the name aloud.

"We all have online names," he said. "I don't know his real name. All I know is that he's a mastermind when it comes to electricity. I checked out his profile before entering the game, and he brags a lot about his own handmade weapons. On the plane, he didn't say a word—no one did. We didn't want to get into one another's heads or give anyone an upper hand. But I do remember that damn profile, and you can bet your ass that guy has weapons you've never even dreamed of." Biting his bottom lip, he searched the ceiling. "The guy has some weird weapons on him.

I can't say what they are for sure, but I'm willing to bet he's planning on using them. He had this one bag full of ornament-sized balls, and one of them fell—"

"What's your point?" I snapped. "We're trapped. How does that give him the advantage? It's not like we're going to be stupid enough to try to pass the fence."

"Good," he said, "because whatever that fence is, you can bet your ass it's military-grade. These guys, and women," he corrected, "are professionals. There's a reason we're being paid the big bucks. So if he trapped you, it's because he plans on killing all of you without you being able to escape."

"How?" I asked. "He can't even come in himself."

"Well, he could if he wanted to, but that's not what he's planning." Then, he smiled so big he looked like a kid who'd been handed their first A-graded assignment. "Fucking genius... I can't believe it."

"Can't believe what?" I asked.

"How does the sky look?" he asked.

My eyes involuntarily rolled toward the ceiling. Was this some sort of joke?

He laughed again. "When you were out there. How'd the sky look?"

"What the hell—" Biggie started.

I raised a fist and she went quiet. Player 1 wasn't an idiot, and he wasn't playing mind games. If there was one thing I remembered most from science class, water and electricity were each other's worst enemies.

"Cloudy," I admitted.

"Those balls I saw him carrying around," he continued, "well, he dropped one and it rolled out onto his seat. He didn't think anyone saw, but I did. The thing looked like something out of a video game. It was silver, had a blue light on one end, and red stripes running on the sides. I didn't realize what it was until now. It must be some sort of electrical grenade."

"Electrical grenade?" Rocket asked. "What, it explodes with energy?"

"Not exactly," he said. "It probably fires out a powerful, high-voltage electrical current, electrocuting anyone within a certain radius."

But he didn't have to explain anything further for me to figure it out.

"He's waiting for it to rain," I said. "And then he'll start throwing them inside."

CHAPTER 5

Player 1 pointed his chin at the wooden floorboards as if trying to draw out an image with his face.

"I'm guessing the fence is what, six feet high?" he said.

Rocket nodded. "Something like that."

"Most people would try the whole short-circuiting method to fry the fence, but as I said before, this thing's the real deal. Unless you have professional tools to get the job done, there's no short-circuiting that fence or cutting through it. The only way to beat this guy is to get around the fence, find the source of the power, and shut it down."

"How're we supposed to get around a fence like that?" Rocket asked.

She'd lost the attitude, perhaps realizing that regardless of the sick reasoning behind this man trying to help us, he was giving us valuable information.

"You're a bunch of barbaric island dwellers... almost animals," he said, glancing up at her. "Figure it out."

When she took a step toward him, I threw my arm across her chest. "He's right. We're resourceful and we can figure something out." Shifting my attention to him, I asked, "What does the power source look like? And won't BlueVolt, or whatever his name is, have some sort of system in place to protect the source?"

Player 1 smirked, and it seemed almost condescending as if he hadn't expected an *island dweller* like me to think this far ahead.

"I'm sure he does," he said. "I can't tell you what the power source looks like, other than that it'll be attached to a wire leading to the fence. Could be a box. Could be a huge panel. And as stupid as this might sound, when you do find it, shutting it down is probably as simple as hitting the off switch. Question is, can you make it to the source without getting killed?"

"Let us worry about that," I said.

"I'm on the line here too, sweetheart," he said.

I grimaced at the word and contemplated telling him to go fuck himself, but I knew he was only trying to get a rise out of me. It was better to ignore his belittling comments and get on with saving our Village.

"All right, then let's get moving," I said, moving toward the door.

"Um, sweetheart?" said Player 1.

I cringed and pulled my shoulders back, filling them with tension.

"Why haven't you asked me about the other players?"

Seriously? Was he enjoying our little chats? What did the other players have to do with the life-threatening situation I was trying to handle? I'd deal with the other players after BlueVolt was dead. Besides, for all I knew, they were far out at the other end of Kormace Island.

He must have sensed my irritation. Sighing, he said, "Get annoyed all you want, but at the end of the day, if you kill my competition, I win, which means all I'm trying to do is make sure you don't get yourself killed."

"Okay. What about the other players?" I asked begrudgingly.

"Well," he said, "I told you I'm the tracker."

He paused as if we were somehow supposed to understand where he was going with this.

"We all had profiles," he continued. "I know everyone's specialty, which means they also know mine."

Pinching the bridge of my nose, I growled out, "Are you telling me they followed you to us?"

He shrugged, though it was barely a shrug with his hands tied behind his back. "Anyone who's smart, which they all are, would've taken advantage of my specialty, for sure."

"This doesn't make any sense!" Rocket snapped as if she'd been holding her breath for the last three minutes. "If you guys are so eager to outkill each other, why not kill off the competition yourself?"

"This is a sport," he said as if he were talking about something as mainstream as basketball. "There are rules in place. For one, if you kill another player, not only are you disqualified, but you have a ransom on your head when you get back to the US."

"So then set some traps—" Rocket tried.

Player 1 clicked his tongue. "Same rule applies. Disqualification. You can't set kill traps unless you're standing there monitoring them. Those traps I set up near the landing site? All they did was alert me. Besides, traps wouldn't do anything for your score. The camera has to see—"

"Camera?" I asked, stomping toward him.

"Relax," he said. "You killed mine when you shot me in the shoulder."

He glanced down at his injured shoulder at a small black lens that appeared to be shattered. As his head rolled back up toward us, I noticed the excessive sweat shining on his forehead. His eyes, too, were puffy and sitting over deep blue bags.

Was he in pain? Not once had he given any indication he was suffering. I'd been so busy trying to pry information out of him that I'd forgotten I shot him with an arrow.

"I'll have someone come in and disinfect that," I said, pointing my chin at his shoulder.

Forcing a laugh, he said, "Don't bother. I'll be dead soon anyway."

How was I supposed to respond to that? It was true—he would be. Helping us didn't diminish the fact that he had killed dozens of my women or that he'd agreed to sign up for this twisted game in the first place.

No way was he coming out of this alive.

"So that's why you aren't even trying to escape," I said, staring at his broken camera. "Even if you got out of your restraints and managed to kill a few more of us, it wouldn't count."

"You got it," he said.

"All right." I nodded. "So about these players, I'm listening."

"There are six of us in total, but five players. The sixth is the pilot, who shacked up somewhere a few miles away from the plane until this is over. You know about me and about BlueVolt. Then there's Detox, SkullCrusher, and BlackPanther."

Biggie scoffed. "Black Panther, like the superhero?"

Player 1 shook his head. "No, not really. He's a night freak. He's got all sorts of gear for seeing in the dark, silent weapons, some weird suit, and too many martial arts black belts to list."

"That's great," I said. "Not only do we have to shut down this fence and kill some electrical maniac, but now, we can't even go to sleep."

"Basically," he said.

Breathing hard through flared nostrils, I said, "And what's your name? I keep calling you Player 1."

Beaming, he said, "My online name is Grizzly, because, well, bears have one of the best senses of smell, which makes them amazing trackers, but I think I prefer Player 1. I am, after all, in first place."

Rolling my eyes, I said, "Who's Detox? And who's SkullCrusher?"

"Detox is one hell of a smart cookie," he said, "and I'm thinking she's extremely underestimated. That woman has degrees falling out of her ass. Apparently, she worked in a top-secret facility as a chemist. It doesn't take a genius to figure out what she was doing there... Creating chemical weapons. Her profile was clean, straightforward, and a bit modest if you ask me. But she's a bit of a weirdo. Didn't talk to anyone on the plane. Instead, she kept writing mathematical equations in her diary and mumbling a bunch of shit that didn't make sense to any of us." He burst out laughing. "Bitch knows how to use a gun, though, which came as a surprise to all of us when she loaded her rifle.

"Is Detox the only female player?" I asked.

"Yeah, she is—"

"Well, she's dead," I said.

His eyes popped out and he sat up straight. "What? How? I mean, she didn't look like the outdoorsy type, but I thought she'd surprise all of us with some crazy chemical attack—"

"We found her hanging in an Ogre trap," I said.

"Ogres? What the f—"

"They're wild women," I said, not wanting to be bothered by having to overexplain all the different types of *island dwellers*.

"Jesus," he said, looking genuinely surprised. "I didn't think she'd win this because, well, I knew I would, but I was still kind of rooting for her, you know? Female power and all."

"Female power?" Biggie said. "How the fuck is signing up to some human huntin' game got anythin' to do with female power?"

"Hey, I'm not being sexist here. I'm pointing out science, and science says men are more physically aggressive—"

"This isn't about the aggression," Biggie said. "You can be aggressive as fuck and not sign up to murder a bunch of people. I don't give a shit—"

"All right, enough," I cut in. "We don't have time for this. We have three players left to take out, and the longer we sit here bitching about stuff that doesn't matter, the more time we're wasting." Letting out a sharp breath, I looked at Player 1. "Okay, SkullCrusher, go."

Player 1 let out a long whistle. "The guy's a beast. Ever heard of the Stone Man? You know, the famous wrestler?"

When none of us responded, he continued. "Well, that wrestler's six feet seven and two hundred and forty pounds of pure muscle mass."

"Let me guess," Rocket said, looking bored. "SkullCrusher looks exactly like him."

"Nope," said Player 1. "He's bigger."

"Okay, seriously?" Biggie said. Pacing back and forth in the cabin, she searched the ceiling. "Come on, tell us the truth, man. You're from some show, ain't you? This is some reality TV shit and this whole thing's some messed-up prank. Where're the cameras? You got another one on you?"

Player 1 stared at Biggie with a wry expression as she ranted.

Biggie shook her hand in the air, snapped her fingers, and a massive grin stretched her face. "Man, are we all gonna get paid for this?"

"Biggie," I said.

Slapping a hand over her wide smile, she said, "First thing I'ma buy is a goddamn cheeseburger."

"Biggie!" I snapped.

This time, her smile disappeared and she straightened her posture.

"This isn't a joke," I said, "and we aren't on some fucking reality show, okay? Put your big girl pants on and get ready to fight for your life, do you hear me?"

Biggie was one of my best friends, and the last thing I wanted to do was be harsh with her, but this wasn't the time for her to slip into a delusional state. We needed all hands on deck, and I especially needed to know that Biggie was in this with a clear mind, prepared to survive.

"So, he's big and strong," I said plainly. "So what? Size doesn't stop bullets or arrows. What's his specialty?"

Looking taken aback by my response, Player 1 said, "That is his specialty. He works with that. The guy almost got disqualified from the game because his gear was too heavy for the plane. He had to leave a few things behind."

"Gear?" I asked.

"He's got some crazy metal suit that protects him from head to toe. When we got off the plane, he started putting it on, looking like some Roman gladiator."

Instead of reacting, I held my breath. How were we supposed to fight against these players? They were trained professionals. Rainer had been tough to beat, and she didn't have any military background.

"An electrical freak, a monster, and some ninja of the night," I said.

Player 1 pursed his lips, which I knew translated to *You got it.*

CHAPTER 6

Biggie and Rocket followed me outside of the cabin, where two guards stood with their backs facing us.

Like the Queen's Guards in England, they didn't move a muscle at the sound of us stepping out. Instead, they stared straight ahead with spears jabbed into the grass, the sharp stone heads pointed at the sky. They were probably too embarrassed by what had happened earlier—how they'd allowed Mason and other women to push their way into the cabin—to even look at me. But, it also meant they wouldn't allow something like that to happen again.

The moment I stepped out into the Village, a cold droplet of water landed on the tip of my nose. Crossing my eyes, I stared at it as if it were somehow responsible for all of my problems. Another droplet fell, landing on my wrist this time. Craning my neck back, I stared up at the thickening clouds overhead. They moved swiftly, blending into each other like chocolate and vanilla soft serve ice cream.

"We need to shut that fence down, and we need to do it now." Turning to the two guards assigned to Player 1's cabin, I said, "Can you please have someone take care of the body?"

They both nodded at the same time, looking like a pair of twin robots.

"Brone?" came Ellie's voice.

Behind me, Ellie stood looking as beautiful as always; yet this time, she wasn't holding Robin.

"Ellie," I said, a bit sharper than I'd intended. "What're you doing here? Go back inside."

"What's going on?" she asked.

Rushing next to her, I whispered, "Listen, it's complicated and dangerous."

"Brone—"

"No, Ellie, you have to trust me. If I don't do this properly, we're all dead."

She touched her lips and glanced back toward our cabin.

Following her gaze, I wrapped an arm around her shoulder and kissed her clammy forehead. "Take care of Robin, okay? I'll figure this out and put an end to it. Whatever you do, don't get out of your cabin, especially if it's raining."

"If it's rain—"

"Go," I said, planting a kiss on her cheek this time.

Ellie wasn't afraid to put up an argument when it came to my safety. Today, however, she could probably sense how serious I was. This wasn't some Ogre lurking nearby, or a long-lost Norther who'd come back for revenge. We were talking about highly trained professionals with a specific goal in mind—to kill as many of us as possible.

"What's the plan?" Rocket asked.

At once, Quinn appeared beside her, as did Hammer and Proxy. I was surprised Proxy wanted to take part in any of this—she avoided violence at all costs.

"Proxy," I said the moment she looked at me.

"I heard you have a puzzle," she said simply.

"A puzzle?" I asked.

"Yes," she said. "I hear there's some sort of electrical fencing outside of our Village. I'd like to help."

Of course. Why hadn't I thought of this? Proxy lived for science and anything to do with hard, solid facts.

Smirking, Quinn threw her thumb out at Proxy, who, although the same height as Quinn, looked like a skeleton in comparison.

"Figured we could use that big brain of hers," Quinn said.

Proxy didn't smile at the compliment. Instead, she kept nodding like one of those old bobblehead toys. I couldn't tell if it was some sort of tic, or if the wheels in her head were turning. "What is the voltage?"

"We don't know," I said.

"Is the energy spread through electrical pulsing?" she asked.

Cocking an eyebrow, I stared at the others. "We have no idea, Proxy—"

"Doesn't matter," she said. "Quinn tells me these people are highly trained, so it's doubtful they would be using farming equipment. The voltage must be very high—enough to kill someone."

"Well there were a few dead birds—" Rocket said.

Proxy kept nodding. "I'm certain you're already aware that you can't do anything about it unless you get to the source."

"Yes," I said. "Player—" but I stopped myself, realizing that no one other than Biggie, Rocket, and I knew about what was really going on. In an instant, I turned to Biggie, who I knew wouldn't be of much help in this specific situation as she wasn't adept at climbing. "Can you fill everyone in? Proxy and I will keep talking. I didn't want everyone knowing what this was about, but anyone carrying a weapon needs to know what they're up against, and the women who aren't fighting need to know how serious this is."

Biggie nodded and extended her arms so far away from her body it was as if she was preparing to pull us all in for a group hug. Instead, she waved her outstretched hands as a way of saying, *Come on, let's move,* and guided Hammer, Quinn, and a few other women who'd assembled.

"We don't have much time," I said. "It's already starting to rain, which will make it even harder to climb—"

Proxy's eyes lit up, and she shot a finger toward the sky. "Climb? Are you planning on climbing over the fence? I assume your goal is to shut down or destroy the power box."

"That's our one option," I said. "Let's get some rope. All we have to do is scale our own fence and climb up a tree."

Rocket rubbed her chin, looking worried. "Um, Brone, we don't have many trees left around here."

Although she was right—most of them had been burned down during the massacre—there were still a few standing strong despite their lack of leaves. All we needed was a sturdy branch that reached over the electric fence. Once on the other side, finding BlueVolt wouldn't be too difficult given the lack of density in the forest.

Where was he hiding, anyway? Sure, thick bushes and countless plants had emerged from the ashes, but the Dead Zone was rather empty in comparison to the close-knit trees that had once surrounded us.

"Well—" Proxy said.

"We'll find a good branch," I said. Then, I turned

my attention to Rocket. "Rocket, can you go to Hammer's tent? She should have some solid rope in there."

"Who's climbing?" Rocket asked.

"Theoretically—" Proxy said.

"I'll do it," I cut in. "I may not be the best climber, but I'm a good shot. And that's all we need... one good shot to take out BlueVolt. Once he's out of the picture, I can locate the box and shut it down."

"Okay," Rocket said. "I'll be right back."

"Do you two ever stop talking long enough to listen to someone else?" Proxy said.

Both Rocket and I froze with our mouths open. Not once had Proxy ever shown attitude before, so to hear even an ounce of snarkiness in her voice took me by surprise.

"I apologize," she said quickly. "But you're both going on and on about climbing this fence, and about relying on one person to complete the task. What happens if Brone is killed?"

Pulling my face back, I stared at her. I wasn't certain whether I was more shocked by her bluntness or by her lack of confidence in me.

"I mean no offense, Brone," she said, perhaps sensing my confusion. "I'm thinking logically, here. For all we know, this opponent has other tricks up his sleeve. The fence may not be the only trap, and sending one person to do the job is equivalent to buying a lottery ticket." She scratched her chin with her index finger. "Well, perhaps equivalent to a scratch card. I suppose the odds aren't as high as a nationwide lottery game."

"What's your point, Proxy?" I said. "Do you have a better idea? Because we're running out of time. This fence needs to be shut down before the sun sets."

Flicking her finger up into the air again, she smirked. She had such a know-it-all look on her face that all I could picture were her beady eyes squinting at us from behind fogging, rectangular-shaped glasses. "As a matter of fact, I do."

CHAPTER 7

Reaching for one of Hammer's metal-headed shovels, I turned to Rocket. "It doesn't have to be all that deep—but deep enough so that we can roll underneath the first wire."

"May I suggest something else?" Proxy asked.

This time, I listened to her. Anything Proxy had to say was worth listening to.

"I would have women dig a hole in two different areas. You want two different access points for several reasons: in case of panic, for simplified access, and to increase the speed at which your soldiers can cross over."

Although not a fan of the word "soldiers," Proxy was right. I pulled the shovel off the wall's bracket, the weight of it causing my biceps to bulge, and inspected its head. It was astonishing how much work had gone into handcrafting the tools in this tent. Had I been anyone else, Hammer would have come storming toward us with a puffy red face and arms flailing in the air. But, given the situation and the fact that I was the one scavenging through her tent, all was forgiven.

Handing the shovel to Rocket, I said, "Find us some diggers, five or six other women." I reached for the second shovel, which was the only other one, and pulled it off the wall. "Once you have them, meet us at the back gate. We have two shovels, so we'll have to rotate to conserve our energy."

Proxy parted her lips, which I knew meant, *May I say something else?*

Raising both eyebrows at her, I waited.

"You shouldn't be doing any digging, Brone."

What did she mean by that? I was perfectly capable of digging out a bit of dirt.

"Unless you dig on a daily basis, you'll be utilizing muscles such as your quadriceps, hamstrings, abs, lower back—"

"So what?" I said.

"You're our number one Archer," Proxy said, matter-of-factly.

I was a bit taken aback by the sound of my old title, *Archer*. Not a single person had referred to me as an Archer since the war. But I'd never stopped shooting—every day, I made my way to the Working Grounds to practice with other women, and every time, I surprised everyone with my unbeatable accuracy.

"Did you not say you'll be the one to take out BlueVolt?" she asked.

"Yeah—"

"Then I strongly suggest you preserve your energy for that. If you weaken your muscles through an activity your body is unaccustomed to, you may end up with shaking muscles, causing your aim to be off."

Not once had I ever thought to *conserve* energy. My mentality had always been to give it all I had, but Proxy was right—why dispense energy digging when other women could do it for me? Wasn't that my role as leader of the Village? To assign tasks and delegate responsibilities?

Planting a hand on Proxy's bony shoulder, I said, "Thank you," and she flinched.

It was obvious that Proxy didn't like being touched, but it was important she knew how valuable she was to our society.

"Why don't you join the others?" I asked. "Let them fill you in on what's going on. I'm sure you'll have some ideas on how to beat the other bastards."

"There are others?" she asked.

I nodded and my eyes rolled toward Rocket, who, like me, knew how much danger we were in. "Yeah, and if we plan on eliminating them, we need to strategize."

Nodding hard, Proxy twirled on her heels and marched out of the Tools tent.

The moment she stepped out, Rocket shook her head and smirked. "I know she's a bit weird, but that girl's got one hell of a brain." She grabbed the other shovel out of my hands and said, "I'll get us some diggers and meet you at the gate."

* * *

"I want everyone to keep their eyes open," I said, taking the time to look every woman in the eye. We all know what it's like out there without the trees. We'll be moving targets. Let's dig as fast as possible so we can get to the other side."

Rocket handed her shovel to the strongest-looking woman of the bunch—Baldwin if I recalled correctly. She grabbed the shovel, gave me a firm nod, and waited for further instruction.

"Rocket, take them around the back, right over there." I pointed behind the Village, where half a burned tree stump lay across the jungle floor. "Dig beside that log so we remember where the hole is. When you're done, come get me. No one crosses over until I say so."

The women followed Rocket around the curved wooden barrier and to the back of the Village.

"Baldwin, right?" I said.

Baldwin nodded again, lips sealed tightly. I'd only ever seen Baldwin smile once, and when it had happened, she'd thrown her hand over her mouth to cover the rotten mess. I couldn't even begin to imagine how much pain she was in daily with all of that decay.

"As soon are your arms or your back starts to

burn, rotate with—" I hesitated, staring at the two other women standing behind Baldwin.

"Lex," the taller of the two said, and the other one cleared her throat and said, "Penny."

"Okay," I said. "Lex, Penny, you got this?"

Lex stared at me, her eyes cold and empty. Penny, on the other hand, stretched her neck and wiggled her fingers as if preparing to play the piano.

"You okay?" I asked Lex.

She gave me a phony a smile, and said, "Of course. You're the boss."

Who was this woman, and why had Rocket picked her to dig with us? Was it because of her size and broad shoulders? She looked like she could handle herself, but the way she was staring at me made it seem as though she wanted to handle *me*.

Was this about Mason? Hadn't I already dealt with this? Even if the whole Mason situation hadn't happened, this wasn't the first time a woman gave me attitude for being the leader. For the most part, women respected me and appreciated that I was in power. But every once in a while, I received backlash or attitude, mostly from newer drops who didn't believe in my methods or who wanted to take my place. Maybe the whole Mason situation had sparked something.

I'd spoken to Murk about this, and she'd told

me that no matter what I did, I'd never please everyone—especially not a crowd full of convicted murderers. She'd explained to me that newer drops were even more difficult to manage since they knew nothing about our ways or our history. It was easy to maintain the respect of women who wouldn't be alive had it not been for me. But new drops... they had a mind of their own, and while most of them shut their traps to survive the island, there were always a few odd ones who spoke out or acted out.

Since the war, I'd banished six women in total, and four of them were new drops. The other two, having once been slaves to the Northers, had uncontrolled rage problems that almost led to the death of several of my people. If there was one person I'd have expected to banish, it was Snow Face. But, since we'd defeated our enemies, she'd changed entirely. Most days, she sat in the Working Grounds, building toys and dolls for the children to play with.

When Baldwin handed Lex the shovel, I took a step back, my hand hovering over my knife. Was I being paranoid? Something was off about her, and I wasn't going to waste my energy worrying about being attacked when I had the entire Village to worry about.

"Lex," I said, "hand Penny the shovel."

She turned around, sweat dripping off the tip

of her nose. "What? Why?"

"Because I said so," I said.

With nostrils flared, she jabbed the shovel's head into the dirt and used the handle to stand up straight.

"Not satisfied with my work?" she asked.

This was the kind of attitude that made me want to punch a woman in the face. But being the leader of the Village, it was my duty to remain fair and professional with everyone.

"You seem bothered," I said. "Why don't you go take it easy for a bit. Thank you for your help."

She wiped her nose with the back of her hand—another gesture full of attitude. "I'm not bothered."

Without saying anything, I arched both eyebrows at the shovel as a way of saying, *I'm not asking.*

"Just give Penny the damn shovel," Baldwin said, two veiny hands on her waist. "You're wasting our time."

Lex scoffed, pulled the shovel out of the dirt, and walked toward Penny. But as she extended the shove with her right hand, a sour scowl replaced the cocky smile on her face. Without warning, she gripped the handle of the shovel with both hands and swung her body full circle, the metallic end coming straight for my face.

Everything happened so fast that I didn't even realize what was happening. All I knew was that

Lex was shouting something and I was about to get pummeled in the face with hard steel. I tried to step back, but I was too slow to pull away. Suddenly, a swift breeze tickled my face as the shovel's head grazed the tip of my nose.

I blinked, trying to understand what had happened, when I caught Lex stumbling backward with Baldwin pulling her by the shirt. The shovel came crashing into the dirt as Lex fought to catch her fall, but what she didn't realize was that she wasn't falling—Baldwin was pushing her. With muscles bulging, Baldwin growled, and with the weight of her body, she pushed Lex straight into the electrical fence.

A blinding blue light exploded behind Lex, and flames burst out all around her. On instinct, I covered my face with my arm and turned away as sparks flew toward me. Heart pounding, I lowered my arm and found that neither Lex nor Baldwin were anywhere to be seen.

"Where are they?" I shouted.

Penny stood still, her mouth wide open and her eyes bulging. She was likely too traumatized by what she'd seen to react. Behind me, footsteps approached and I swung around to find Rocket and one of her diggers jogging toward me.

"What the fuck happened?" Rocket said, her eyes twice their usual size.

I opened my mouth to explain the altercation

when something caught my attention. Against the Village's wooden barrier smoke drifted into the air.

Curious, I stepped toward it.

Where was it coming from?

Then, I saw them—Lex's and Baldwin's bodies, both of which were stuck together and scorched beyond recognition.

CHAPTER 8

"Oh my God," said one of Rocket's diggers.

She covered her mouth and turned away as I swept a hand through the air, trying to clear the smoke coming off their bodies.

"Lex tried to attack me," I said, "and Baldwin saved me."

No one said anything. How could they? We were staring at two electrocuted bodies so charred they smelled like fried meat. Their clothing was burned, and in some areas, missing entirely. The back of Lex's neck, where the wire had clearly touched, had melted through skin and muscle, revealing her spinal cord.

"Are they—" Rocket tried.

Pushing a finger up underneath my nostrils to block the smell, I nodded.

As the other diggers approached, Rocket yelled at them to turn around.

"No, it's okay," I said. "We need help finishing our hole. Penny, go back inside, and everyone else, split up evenly and keep digging."

Two of Rocket's diggers brushed past her and

made their way over to my trench. As they walked, they couldn't keep their eyes off the bodies.

"Let this be a lesson," I said. "Our enemies are extremely dangerous. If we don't shut this thing down, everyone in the Village is going to end up looking like this."

As I said that, three thick droplets of water landed on my head. Both Rocket and I looked at each other, and before I could say anything, she said, "I'm gonna go to get more help, and I'll get our fighters ready. As soon as those holes are dug out, we need to move."

Nodding, I turned away and watched as my two new diggers started pulling dirt out, their bodies tilted as far away as possible from the lowest wire. The stance was so awkward it was a wonder how they managed to do any digging at all, but every time one of them pulled back on their shovel, the hole got deeper.

* * *

The women stood silently, weapons in their hands and eyes darting toward the burned bodies.

"It's simple," I whispered, pointing at the dug-up hole. "You crawl underneath, careful not to touch the wire above it. If you have weapons on your belts, I suggest you take them off. You don't want any added bulk as you cross over. I'll lead the way. All I need is for you all to watch my back. I'm hoping to take BlueVolt out with one shot, but the other two could be out there, waiting. Keep your eyes peeled and get ready to fight. And if anything happens out there, I don't want you all running here in a panic. You saw what happens if you touch the metal." I shot a glance toward Baldwin and Lex, or at least, what remained of them. "The last thing we need is for you guys to start shoving each other to try to get back into the Village. Does everyone understand?"

With grimy faces, they nodded, and I pulled my bow off my back. Bending forward in front of the trench, I threw it on the other side, along with my quiver full of arrows. Empty-handed, I dropped to my stomach and crawled underneath.

When I reached the other side, I picked up my weapons, pressed a firm finger over my lips, and signaled the rest of the women to follow. Both Rocket and I had already warned everyone that once we crossed over, no one was to speak a word. Being that we were moving around in the Dead Zone, we weren't protected by full trees or curtains of vines. Any noise we made would travel quickly, alerting the enemy.

I hoped to God that BlueVolt, or the source panel, wasn't anywhere near the back wall of the Village. Rocket and I had inspected the space before digging the trenches and there had been no sign of him.

"Hey," Rocket mouthed, walking toward me

from the other trench. Behind her, women followed with axes, spears, and even a few bows. Hopefully, they knew how to use the weapons. I'd seen several women practice archery in the Working Grounds, but how well would they do in battle? Practice shooting and firing at a moving enemy full of adrenaline were two very different things.

Jerking my head sideways, I moved forward, leading my people around the Village's perimeter. We moved so quietly I had to turn around every few seconds to ensure they were all still following. As instructed, everyone searched the forest around us, their eyes darting from side to side.

It was a relief to know I had several dozen eyes looking out for me. Had I done this alone, I could have easily been blindsided. With two fingers, I pointed at my eyes and then at the fence's metal wiring. As I'd explained to the women before—and as Player 1 had explained to me—the source of the power was coming from somewhere, which meant we had to keep our eyes open for a wire running from the fence and out into the jungle.

How far had BlueVolt positioned the source panel? Had he taken every precaution necessary and remained as far away from the Village as possible? I searched the ground, sliding dirt out of the way with the tip of my boot. It had to be here somewhere.

Behind me, half of the women stared at the ground as they moved, their heads bowed and their backs rounded. The other half kept their attention aimed at the Dead Zone around us.

The ground was moist but not wet—at least, not yet. Every few seconds, several droplets of water landed on my head, and every time I looked up, I expected to be blinded with pouring rain, but instead, the quickly forming clouds taunted me.

How long did we have?

As I walked, I kept tapping the earth with my foot. Sooner or later, I'd find something that didn't feel quite right—a bulge, soft earth, or something hard. BlueVolt was obviously a professional, as Player 1 had indicated, which meant his setup wouldn't be amateur. Without a doubt, he had covered his source wire quite well.

Where was this son of a bitch? How far out had he gone? We continued our way around the Village's perimeter, passing the front gates and crossing the path that led to the Working Grounds. I kept my bow up in front of me, my metal arrowhead swaying from side to side as I searched the trees.

Suddenly, a sound caught my attention and I instinctively pulled on the elastic of my bow.

But the second I found the source of the sound, I realized we weren't in any danger. Next to one of the dead tree's roots was a white-striped squirrel, its fluffy tail whipping the air behind its body. It leaned forward, it's little round butt aimed at the sky, and dug into the dirt as if trying to find a long-lost acorn.

I stopped moving and raised a clenched fist—a signal that meant, *Don't move.*

The squirrel kept digging as hard as it could, coming up for air every few seconds. Jerking my head sideways, I moved toward it. Its ears twitched at the sound of my footsteps and it darted straight up into the nearest tree.

When we got to its digging spot, I saw it. Underneath the dirt, where the squirrel had dug a small hole, was a black, rubberlike tube. I bent down, and with my finger pushed aside a bit more dirt. The tube was long and seemed to lead from the fence and out into the forest.

"Got you, you son of a bitch," I mouthed.

CHAPTER 9

BlueVolt had covered up his wire with leaves, dirt, and branches, making it almost impossible to keep track of it. Every few feet, we were forced to scratch away a patch of dirt to ensure we were going the right way.

Rocket pointed at the ground, ordering some of her Hunters to track the wire. As we continued, the wire led us across the Working Grounds' path and around the Village's wooden barrier.

He couldn't be too far, could he? With my bow still held up in front of me, I led the way, searching the trees. Where could he be hiding? It wasn't like there was much to hide behind in the Dead Zone.

As we passed by the Working Grounds, I cringed at the thought of all the dead bodies we had yet to recover. There was a good chance that prey animals had gotten to them first, and as much as it made me sick to my stomach to imagine one of my women being crunched by some wildcat, I couldn't focus on that. After Player 1's massacre, we'd been forced to retreat within the safety of our Village walls. Burials were something we would have to consider once all of this was over... if there was anything left to bury.

Suddenly, a crack of a branch pulled my attention away from the Working Grounds. It had come from up ahead, and although I didn't see anyone, I was certain something was there.

An animal?

Or, was it BlueVolt?

I swung around to find Rocket nodding fiercely, her wide-open eyes aimed ahead of us.

She'd heard it too, and by the way my women were tightening their fists around their weapons, it was obvious they'd also heard it.

Bright blue light flashed overhead, followed by cracking thunder—it hit so hard that I felt the vibrations in my bow. A cold droplet of water exploded on the tip of my nose, and then another, and another. I glanced up into the leafless trees, squinting in time to avoid rainwater from landing in my eyes. The few droplets that had fallen had been nothing more than a warning. Rain exploded from the clouds overhead, drenching me in an instant.

We'd run out of time.

Jerking my head sideways as a way of saying, *Let's hurry*, I darted forward, launching myself into a silent jog. Sneaking around was no longer an option. If BlueVolt was anywhere nearby, we needed to get to him before he attacked any women inside the walls.

What was he going to do? Throw grenades over the wall? Player 1 had made it quite clear that BlueVolt had all sorts of high-voltage electrical weapons. There was no doubt in my mind that he could take us all out without even stepping foot inside our Village.

If we didn't reach him in time, we risked losing everything.

I hurried through the dirt as it turned to mud, careful not to slip.

Why couldn't I see him? The noise had come from up ahead, yet no one was there. As I turned to look at Rocket to express my confusion, something shiny came swirling through the trees beside us. At first, it looked like a trick of the eye—a light being reflected off of something.

But within a split second, I realized it wasn't a trick of the eye at all. It was a ball of metal, about the size of a baseball, with a silver casing and cracks filled with bright neon blue light. In haste, I turned my bow and fired an arrow, hoping to stop it midway, but the ball was moving so fast my arrow missed.

It came landing hard against the woman standing next to Rocket, and the moment it made contact, fiery blue light exploded all around her, and her entire body convulsed as if she were having a seizure on her feet. The woman standing next to her stiffened just the same, her terrified eyes aimed straight ahead as her body rocked uncontrollably.

Everyone jumped back as far away as possible as both women shook violently, the sound of electrical current buzzing around us. The air filled with the same scent I'd smelled earlier—burning flesh, and at the same time, both women collapsed to the floor, convulsing with foam at their mouths. The whole thing may have lasted all of ten seconds, though it felt much longer. At last, the shaking stopped and both women lay still, their hollow eyes wide open.

The women standing around them stared at me, looking petrified with fear.

As much as I was worried too, we couldn't stop now. If we didn't stop this son of a bitch, he was going to do this to every woman inside the Village.

"Now we know where he is," I said. "We charge, and we go for the kill. Stay behind trees as much as you can—"

Suddenly, another woman standing several feet away from the two bodies clenched her jaw, tightened her back, and started convulsing. She gripped her knife so hard that her knuckles looked like canine teeth. Within seconds, she was down on the ground.

"Get back!" Rocket shouted, throwing protective arms across several chests. "The current is spreading through the water on the ground!"

Everyone split apart, running far away from the electrical grenade.

"Charge!" I shouted, pointing toward our attacker.

As the rain began to pour, we charged straight ahead, our feet stomping through wet mud and our weapons held high.

CHAPTER 10

It was like looking at something out of a science fiction movie.

He wore a full-body suit that resembled something worn by medical professionals inside a quarantine unit. Unlike medical professionals, however, his suit wasn't white. Oddly, it matched his surroundings perfectly—gray, white, and black. No wonder it had been impossible to see him; he was perfectly camouflaged.

How had he known to wear those colors? Or, had he brought several different outfits to choose from? Obviously, he was prepared.

His head was covered with a dark, square-shaped hood, and at the front of his face was a plastic screen. What was the purpose of this outfit? Was it to protect him from his own electricity? It had to be.

He reached down into an oversized cargo bag and pulled out several grenades. They rolled in his arms as he struggled to turn them on. The first one lit up, and he threw it as hard as he could. It cracked against the bark of a dead tree and rolled into the leaves on the ground.

As he turned on the next ball, he dropped one.

Was he panicking? Had we taken him by surprise? It almost looked like he hadn't expected to be confronted by an army of angry women. He'd been the coward in all of this—he'd trapped us inside to kill us without ever having to do any dirty work.

How would that work on his score, anyways? Player 1 had explained that all kills had to be caught on camera.

It didn't matter, at least not now. All that mattered was that we take this bastard out once and for all.

Another bright silver grenade came spinning through the air.

This time, we weren't so lucky. Although it didn't hit anyone, it landed right next to a woman's foot as she ran, and the combination of her speed and the shock sent her flying through the air.

The woman who'd been running next to her contorted her face, spun her spear in her right hand, and threw it as hard as she could at BlueVolt. He dodged awkwardly, several grenades bouncing out of his arms, and bent down and reached deep inside his bag.

What he pulled out next, however, wasn't something I had anticipated.

In both hands, he held what looked like a gun,

but it was the size of a rocket launcher. He loaded it up onto his shoulder and pressed a button. Suddenly, the tip lit up to create a bright green ring, and a high-pitched sound filled the air around us.

Shit.

I ran sideways, searching for a clear shot through the countless trees, until at last, I found one. As the high-pitched sound became so intense that my ears hurt, I fired an arrow straight for his chest. It made impact—a loud cracking noise—and he stumbled backward, clutching at his heart.

He removed his hand and looked down to see what had hit him, and that's when I realized the arrowhead hadn't penetrated.

How come? Was he wearing some sort of protective armor under there? Was there anything this asshole hadn't thought of?

I fired another shot, this time, aiming for his face.

The arrow hit hard enough for his head to rock back, but it didn't kill him. The one benefit it provided was to throw him off his game—with arrows being shot at him, he couldn't fire his massive gun.

Every time he raised his gun, I fired an arrow.

Rocket shot a glance my way, perhaps realizing that all I was doing was distracting him. It was up to them to take him out, and that meant they had to act fast because I didn't have an unlimited supply of arrows.

Rocket shouted as loud as she could—a war cry that reminded me of our war against the Northers—and ran forward with her hunting spear pointed at BlueVolt. Although the others weren't as fast, it was obvious they were trying as hard as they could; leg muscles bulged, bellies jiggled, and features became so hard it was as if they were trying to murder him with their looks.

BlueVolt must have realized that with my arrows coming at him, he'd never get to shoot his gun. Evidently, there was a technique to it that required careful attention, and I was making it impossible for him to properly control his weapon. So instead, he dropped it to the ground, reached for two grenades, and lit them up. I fired an arrow at one of his wrists, sending the blue and silver ball flying into the air, but with one ball still in his grip, he threw it straight at Rocket.

My stomach sank, but the next thing I knew, Rocket lunged sideways and kept on running.

The closer they got to him, the more dangerous the situation would become. BlueVolt would simply turn on his grenades and throw them at anyone who dared touch him.

There had to be another way.

As I pulled back on the elastic of my bow, prepared to fire another distractive shot, I realized something: my new arrowheads were made of metal. The idea I had in mind was a huge gamble, but it was worth a shot.

As he lit up another grenade, I aimed for the ball itself and released my arrow, my bow's elastic snapping against my leather arm guard. It wouldn't kill him, that much I knew, but killing him wasn't my intention.

The second the arrowhead made contact with the ball, the whole thing lit up like a Christmas light and started zapping, little blue bolts firing out around the arrow's shaft. BlueVolt, taken aback by his grenade's malfunction, stumbled backward and dropped the zapping ball to the ground.

It stopped rolling when it hit his cargo bag full of inactive grenades. Whipping out another arrow, I aimed it for the bottom of his bag and fired the shot. The metal arrowhead slipped right past the sporadic, damaged grenade, potentially grabbing some of its charge, and tore through the bottom of his bag. A wide tear split horizontally, and one by one, silver balls rolled out.

With another arrow loaded, I waited.

Suddenly, one of the balls made contact with the damaged ball, crackled loudly, and mini bolts of electricity flickered in every direction.

"No!" BlueVolt shouted, running toward his precious weapons.

But he didn't have the time to stop it. After the

second ball went off, it created a domino effect and every other ball inside his bag started exploding. The bag bounced up and down as the balls went off, burning holes through his bag and sending smoke up into the air.

"No, no, no!" he cried out.

I fired my last arrow at the bag and it exploded. BlueVolt threw his hands over his masked face and stepped back.

This was my chance—he was off guard.

Reaching down, I picked up a log the length of my body and charged straight for him. There was no telling how far the electrical current was spreading, so it was important that I not get too close. BlueVolt bent forward, inspecting the ground for what I assumed were undamaged grenades. But before he even had time to reach for one, I threw the log as hard as I could and it crashed right into his chest.

The impact threw him flat on his back, a loud thump on the ground. In a panic, he flailed his arms wildly at his sides as if trying to create a mud angel.

I ran in a circular trajectory, far away from the burning bag, and made my way to him from behind.

"Brone!" Rocket shouted.

She, along with every other woman, had stopped running and were slowly stepping backward. With how wet everything was, walking anywhere near BlueVolt and his bag of high-voltage grenades was a huge risk.

What if I stepped on the wrong spot? One wrong move and I'd be gone forever.

"You're too close!" Rocket said.

Quickly, BlueVolt flopped over onto his stomach and by sticking his butt into the air, managed to get back up onto his feet. His head snapped sideways, his fogged plastic face screen aimed at the gun he'd tried to fire earlier.

Shit.

If I stepped any closer, there was a good chance I'd die. But if I didn't, there was a good chance he'd fry all of us. Something on the sleeve of his wrist caught my attention—a small hole. Had my arrow done this? I'd shot at his wrist to make him drop the grenade. If his suit had torn, it meant his sleeves and pant legs didn't have the same impenetrable protection as his chest, back, and head.

I shot Rocket a look but didn't have to say anything for her to know what I was thinking. At once, she threw me her spear and I caught it by the shaft. Right when BlueVolt picked up his gun, I launched the spear as hard as I could into his left thigh.

Although an excellent archer, I wasn't as adept at throwing spears. It didn't stab him the way I'd hoped, but the throw had been aimed well enough to tear another hole in his suit. He swung around, his gun aimed at me, and pressed a button.

It charged up within a matter of seconds, and he placed his finger over the trigger. Although I couldn't see his face behind the scratched, foggy screen, I had a feeling he was smiling at me.

Before he had the time to press the trigger, though, another spear came twirling through the air, catching him in the calf. And then, several arrows followed, one of them catching his arm, and the other, his left thigh.

In an instant, he cried out and dropped his gun, but it was obvious he was doing everything he could to stay upright.

In one swift motion, I reached down and grabbed the closest and longest branch I could find, held it firmly in both hands, and swung it like a baseball bat.

The other end hit him square in the throat and he stumbled backward. As he did so, the heel of his heavy boot landed on one of his grenades and he slipped as if having caught a patch of black ice. His entire body went up into the air, his limbs flapping in a desperate attempt to save himself.

But it was no use.

He came down hard, right into a shallow puddle of muddy water, and his suited body shook violently as sparks of blue light zapped all around him.

CHAPTER 11

The walk back was nearly as difficult as the search for BlueVolt—not because of pain or fear, but rather, heartache. Several women cried for their lost friends, while others held onto each other, their eyes red and glossy.

"Any of you wishing to return home can do so," I said, throwing my chin out at the Village's wooden walls. "Be careful going under the fence—"

"No," Rocket cut me off. "We'll all come with you in case." She turned around to look at the remaining survivors, who wiped their eyes and nodded.

"It shouldn't be too far," I said, following the same rubberized wire we'd tracked earlier.

Without the fear of BlueVolt attacking us from behind, the search didn't take long at all.

"Right there," Rocket said, pointing ahead.

Attached around the base of a tree was a black box with a metal door. BlueVolt had taken the time to push dirt up against its sides to make it more difficult to spot.

We approached it cautiously, inspecting the space around it. There didn't appear to be any traps. BlueVolt had been guarding it himself from a distance. It was obvious he had anticipated an intervention, but he hadn't expected our number to be so great.

I walked up to it and crouched down. On the front door was a small rubber handle that seemed responsible for opening and closing the door. So I pulled on it, and sure enough, the panel opened up to reveal a red switch on the inside.

Could it be so simple? Was it only a switch that turned the power on or off? It must have been one hell of an advanced piece of equipment to hold so much power in such a little box. As I thought about this, another wire caught my eye. I followed it up the tree, where odd-looking panels stuck out of the tree's trunk.

What were those things? Some sort of advanced solar panels?

"Think it's a trap?" Rocket asked.

I turned my head to look at her. "Not sure. It could be."

A woman standing next to Rocket—Carolina—leaned forward with a scowl on her face. "That thing's what's powering the fence?"

Carolina was one of our cleaners and often went around the Village picking up pieces of bone, fruit seeds, and even cleaning out dirty dishes left by a few lazy women. She had short curly hair, cheeks as red as blood, and an open mouth as she breathed in and out faster than anyone else. I couldn't tell whether she was exhausted, angry, or frightened.

"Yeah," Rocket said, pulling away from what I could only assume was the woman's raunchy breath.

Carolina tightened her grip around the wooden club in her hands and flared her nostrils so hard they went as red as her face. She raised her weapon above her head and growled.

"Whoa!" I said, stepping in front of her.

I must have taken her by surprise. She awkwardly lowered her club, then tilted sideways to look at the box again.

"What the hell are you doing?" I asked.

"Doing what needs to be done," she said. "I'ma break that piece of shit." She breathed in loudly, no doubt fighting back tears. "That fence... That fucking fence killed—"

"Easy," I said. Turning my attention to Brook, a tall woman with a gun tattoo on her neck, I said, "Can you please bring her back inside the Village to cool off? Smashing the box probably isn't safe. If she hits that thing, it could kill us all."

The truth was, I had no idea how the box was going to react. Not only did I know nothing about electricity other than that it was both useful and dangerous, but I also knew nothing about military-grade technology.

Brook nodded, wrapped a comforting arm around Carolina's shoulder, and walked her away from the crowd. I reached for the nearest spear I could find—a finely-carved wooden shaft with a dark stone blade—and spun it around in my hands. Although I'd heard that most rocks didn't act as conductors, I'd once been told that others, depending on the type, had higher electrical conductivity.

Not wanting to take the risk of blowing anything up, I used the wooden end of the shaft and aimed it at the red lever. Although this would have been far easier had I been using my hand, the last thing I wanted was to be electrocuted to death after falling victim to some well-designed trap.

Wincing, I aimed the end of the spear under the lever and pulled. It slipped a few times, both because it was difficult to latch onto something using a dull end, but also because the switch had a weird shape. The rain was also still pouring down, making me blink hard every few seconds.

Finally, something caught, and I pulled the lever down. It clicked as it switched into the off position, and a loud humming filled the air before disappearing entirely. I turned to Rocket, who appeared as confused as I was, and stared out toward the fence.

Had it worked?

"Who has a sword?" I asked.

One woman stepped forward, handing me an old Norther sword.

I gripped it by its handle and marched toward the electrical fence. Had we truly done it? Could we now cross over safely to the Village?

"What're you gonna do?" Rocket asked, jogging to catch up with me. "This isn't like earlier, Brone. It's raining. The whole thing's wet. You can't go touching the tip of it on one of those wires. What if it's still active?"

"Relax," I said, staring straight ahead.

Everyone else followed me up to the fence, excited whispers firing back and forth.

"Stay back," I ordered, extending an arm out at my side.

Everyone took several steps back, and I aimed the sword's blade at the middle wire. One touch was all it took—if there was still electricity coursing through the wire, the sword would either be thrown off or would create a blinding spark.

Right?

With that in mind, I threw the sword forward and prepared myself for a reaction. When the blade's metal hit the wire, it bounced off and fell into the dirt.

"It's off!" one woman shouted, running forward.

"Don't be a fuckin' moron," said another one.

"You can't be sure of that. What if it has pulsating current?"

"Doubt it," said the excited woman. "You saw how fast it killed—"

But then, everyone went quiet. Player 1 had already admitted that this wasn't like a fence you'd find to keep farm animals within a certain confined area. It was unlikely that the current swept through from time to time. This thing was designed to kill people on a regular basis.

"Throw something else, to be safe," Rocket said.

Someone else handed me one of their swords and I grabbed it by the handle. Eyes glued to the fence, I swung my arm back and forth for momentum.

"If you can hit the blade on two wires at once," Rocket said, "that's even better."

Right as I prepared myself to let go of the sword, something caught my eye. At the base of the fence was a small squirrel similar to the one we'd seen earlier. Its tail flicked in the air, and its ears moved back and forth. It pranced in circles several times, then made its way to the lowest wire. It sniffed it, rested one of its hands on it, and chewed at the metal.

Smirking, I turned my head sideways. "Looks like we're in the clear."

The women behind me cheered, some hugging

and others high-fiving each other. Rocket grinned, dropped two fists on her waist, and shook her head. "You did it again, Brone."

Although I wanted to smile, I couldn't. The truth was, we had two more players to worry about.

"We should head back," Rocket said.

Several women started walking toward the Village's gates, but I didn't follow.

"What're you doing?" Rocket asked.

Bending down next to the electrical box, I tore through the rope holding it in place. "We have a human-killing fence around our entire Village"—I glanced up into the tree—"and an electrical box connected to what I assume are solar panels."

I didn't have to say anything for Rocket to know where I was going with this. Her eyes lit up, and she smiled like a kid receiving her first bike.

"We have fucking power," she said. "Like, real power... Unlimited power. And metal. Holy shit, Brone." She put both hands on her head and paced back and forth.

When the women saw her reaction, they crowded around me and the power box.

"What's going on?" one of them asked.

With my knife, I cut off the last rope and the box loosened in the dirt. Standing, I smirked at everyone. "First, we kill these sons of bitches. Then, we create light."

PART FOUR

PROLOGUE

No one knocked on my door in the middle of the night unless it was an emergency.

Had Black Panther infiltrated the Village? How could he? We'd turned the electric fence back on, and with the power box now inside the Village, we controlled it.

Blinking hard, I sat up in my bed, careful not to wake Ellie. But she was already awake and sat upright at the same time I did, a tired moan slipping out of her mouth.

"What's going on?" she asked.

"Not sure," I whispered.

Whatever it was, it wasn't good.

My heart raced. All I could imagine was that we were under attack. I should have listened to my gut—I should have stayed up to watch over the Village despite my exhaustion from the fight earlier that day.

I threw the hemp sheet off my body and rushed to the cabin door, wincing as my blistered feet met the floor. Before I could open the door all the way, Fisher's face appeared, her hardened features illuminated by the lit torch in her hand.

Although it wasn't raining anymore, the clouds had remained overhead, concealing the stars and the moon.

In the darkness behind Fisher, the Village appeared to be still—women weren't running about in a frenzy, weapons weren't clashing against each other, and no one was screaming.

That was a good sign.

I'd stationed twice the number of guards at the towers to ensure we had eyes everywhere. Although I'd ordered all fires to remain unlit, I'd made it clear that if anyone was seen trying to get inside the Village, I wanted all fires lit up for visibility.

If this Black Panther guy was nearby, we had to spot him before he found a way inside.

I didn't have to say anything for Fisher to know I wanted details and I wanted them now. What could warrant her waking me up in the middle of the night if we weren't under attack?

"There's crying," she said.

"What? What're you talking about?"

With how exhausted I was, it took everything in me not to yell.

"Outside the Village walls," she said. "It sounds like a kid crying."

Staring at her, I ran several scenarios in my head.

Was it really a child? Or, was this some trap? If it wasn't a trap, would this child survive the night if we didn't go out there? Was it worth opening the Village gates and shutting down the electric fence? We'd have no visibility out there, so we'd be forced to walk out with fire. And it wasn't like we could cross the fence through the holes we'd dug out earlier that day. I'd ordered women to fill them back up.

"What do we do?" she asked.

I bit my bottom lip. What the hell was I supposed to do? "You think it's real?"

Fisher planted two hands on her waist as if the answer were obvious. "Unless one of those gamer guys has some sort of audio recording and an amazing speaker system, there's no question that it's real."

CHAPTER 1

I stomped through the grass to keep up with Fisher. "Where's it coming from?"

She led me to the north side of the Village and pointed at a small group of women gathered next to our wooden wall.

"Sweetheart!" one of them shouted. She tilted her head back and cupped her mouth as if her words were tangible and capable of being strategically thrown over the wall. "We're right here, okay?"

Clenching my teeth, I ran toward her. "Shut up!"

She cowered at the sight of me running and raised two hands as if to say, *I mean no harm.*

"You have to stay quiet," I whispered, my glare traveling through the crowd. There were five women in total and several more walking toward us. "We don't know who's out there, and if you keep shouting like that, you'll attract them to us."

"I-I'm sorry," the woman said. "She's just a kid... And it sounds like she's all alone. She's crying, and—"

I raised a fist to get her to stop talking.

On the other side of the wall came a little girl's voice.

"H-h-hello? M-m-mommy?"

She sucked in a quivering breath and sniffled what I could only imagine were snot bubbles.

Who was that? How the hell had a kid managed to get out? I'd been very clear when I'd ordered everyone to remain inside the Village. With countless mothers and Eliot watching in earnest, how had one slipped through the cracks?

"Maybe it isn't real," said one of the women in the dark.

It was comforting to know I wasn't alone in thinking this. While I didn't like the idea of a child being left alone in the jungle at night, I couldn't risk the lives of all my people. The moment we turned off the electricity, we became vulnerable. Wooden walls would only protect us for so long.

If this Black Panther guy was as agile as Player 1 had described him to be, he likely had the tools necessary to climb over a wall without any difficulty at all.

"Does that sound fake to you?" hissed the first woman I'd told to shut up.

"All right, everyone, back to your tents," I ordered. "Fisher and I will take care of this."

"You aren't gonna—" the frantic woman tried.

"Please," I said. "Let us take care of this, okay? I

promise I'll do everything in my power to make sure that little girl is safe."

Although seemingly unconvinced, she nodded as the rest of the women wrapped their arms around her and guided her toward the wooden tents. If I hadn't known any better, I'd have assumed this woman was the child's aunt or godmother.

"What's your plan?" Fisher asked.

"I don't have one," I said. "What am I supposed to do? It's pitch black out there."

"Mommy!" came the little girl's voice again.

"You think that's fake?" Fisher asked.

"Honestly, I don't know what to think anymore," I said. "These bastards have weapons I've never seen before, so yeah, it's crossed my mind. What if this is some ploy to get us to turn off the fence?"

Fisher shrugged, her dancing orange flame following her movement. "It could be, but what if it isn't? What if that is a little girl out there. She's alone, Brone, and it's the middle of the night."

"Yeah, I get that," I said, folding my arms. "I'm trying to think."

We both went quiet, listening to the little girl's sniffling and whimpering. Then, a branch cracked and leaves crunched.

Was she moving? Was she trying to find her way inside?

And then, it hit me.

The fence.

What if she tried to climb it? What if she grabbed onto one of the wires? Isn't that what kids did? Touch things they shouldn't be touching?

My thoughts must have surfaced onto my face. Fisher's mouth hung open and her owl-like eyes shifted between me and the wall.

"The fence," she said. "It might be protecting us, but the second she touches it—"

"She's dead," I said.

The longer we stood around trying to figure out a game plan, the more at risk this kid's life became.

"Get some women armed and ready," I ordered. "We're going out there."

Fisher nodded. "You got—"

And just then, the little girl shrieked at the top of her lungs.

CHAPTER 2

"Turn it off!" I ordered.

The guard to the right of the gates flipped the power box's switch.

A low humming sound filled the air, and at the same time, two other guards opened the gates. I hadn't had the time to arm anyone—Fisher and I were going at this alone.

Rushing through the open gates, Fisher held her torch with a stiff arm in front of her, its glow casting an oval light across the jungle floor.

"P-p-please!" the little girl cried.

By the shrill sound of her voice, the one thing I could imagine was a wildcat pawing at her or a monkey trying to pull her up into the trees.

What if it wasn't an animal? What if it was a person? One of the players? Even though I could barely see anything ahead of me, I held my bow straight up, my metal arrowhead aimed into the darkness. As we moved closer, two little blue shoes appeared inside of Fisher's light.

Above these shoes were two light brown ankles, scabbed legs, and a fluffy blue dress. With the fire's glow lighting it up, the dress looked green.

When the light enveloped her entirely, she turned around with wet brown eyes and wiped a glob of snot from her nose. Her bottom lip trembled like a caterpillar stuck on a branch during a windstorm.

"Hey, sweetheart," I said, my voice as soft as possible.

Before I landed on this island, I would have never called anyone *sweetheart*. I wasn't nurturing or motherly in any way whatsoever, and being nice to kids wasn't my forte. To me, they'd always been annoying little brats. But ever since Robin had come into my life, things had changed—that, along with the other kids who, when they weren't throwing fits, made my heart smile.

She tried to say something but instead sucked in a broken breath.

Lowering my bow, I leaned forward and rested my hands on my knees as if preparing to tell her a bedtime story. "We heard you screaming over here. Are you all right? Are you hurt?"

Without warning, she squealed again and hopped sideways, her feet landing in a pile of wet leaves. It made a sloppy squishing sound and she winced so hard her brows almost touched her cheeks.

It was obvious she wasn't hurt—she was scared,

and I knew why. Beside her, a small frog had bounced out from the leaves before disappearing again.

"Are you afraid of frogs?" I asked.

Without opening her eyes, she nodded fast.

"Did someone tell you they're dangerous?" I asked.

She nodded again.

"What's your name?" I asked.

She popped one eye open. "V-Violet."

Violet. It all made sense now. Her mother, Mason, was the one who'd tried to kill Player 1—the woman I'd been forced to kill. I felt sick to my stomach.

How had little Violet managed to escape the Working Grounds when Player 1 started shooting everyone? She must have found a hiding spot and sat there for hours.

Oh God. Had she witnessed the shooting? Had she seen her guardian, Schmitt, get murdered? No one had seen her after the shooting, which led me to believe she hadn't made it out alive. No wonder Violet was terrified—she was traumatized.

"Hey," I said softly, and she opened her other eye. "We're here now, okay? You're safe. And I can promise you that the frog bouncing around is a friend. You probably couldn't see its color because it was too dark for you, but I saw him. He's green with cute red eyes—" I needed to add the word *cute* because in any other context, red eyes were anything but cute. "That frog's called a red-eyed tree frog. It has sticky feet and likes to climb things, even wet surfaces."

"S-s-urf—" Violet tried.

Could she even understand what I was saying? Violet had been born a few weeks after the last battle, which meant she was about two years old.

"Come here," I said, extending my arms. "I'll get you back home safe, okay?"

She hesitated, scanned the leaves around her feet, and then hopped as far as she could as if jumping over a deep puddle. At the same time, I swung my bow around my back and scooped her up.

Bouncing Violet in my arms, I followed Fisher as she led the way back. When we approached the front gates, they creaked open, and we were welcomed inside.

"Turn it back on," I ordered."

That same humming sound filled the air, and we were safe again.

As I stepped inside the Village, two women came running toward us, choppy breaths coming from their mouths with every stomp.

"Oh my God, Violet!"

The other woman didn't say anything, but when she heard Violet's name, she ran even faster. I didn't even have to hand the child over—the woman, a plump, sweet-looking lady, plucked Violet right out of my arms and kissed her hard on the cheek, the forehead, and then on the cheek again.

"Oh, honey, you're okay... you're okay," she said, bouncing her up and down.

Her big wet eyes met mine, and she nodded as a way of saying, *I can't thank you enough.*

I wasn't certain what her relationship was with Violet, but there was no denying that Violet meant the world to her. That didn't come as a surprise. Most women in the Village had developed family-like relationships with each other and the children after the war.

In a sense, I owed the Village's stability to the birth of these children. While I may have been responsible for ending our suffering, most of the violence, hatred, and resentment dissipated after the mothers gave birth.

How could women focus on fighting each other when innocent lives were around them every day? People—at least most level-headed people—didn't want to fight in front of a child. Plus, the children had brought out many soft sides within our society, and for the most part, people stopped being destructive and instead became nurturing.

How could they not? I'd gone to sleep to the sound of women crying countless nights—not because they were prisoners on this island, but because the possibility of ever being a mother had been stripped away from them.

Now, everything was different.

While I was grateful for our new dynamic, it saddened me in a sense because it confirmed that most of the violence and hatred among my women had been the result of their poor emotional states. Many of these women, all convicted criminals, were here because they'd done awful things in the past. What about before their crimes? Had they been miserable? Had they been living hectic lives? Were they destitute? No one's misery excused killing another human—*ever*. Some nights, however, my mind was all I had to keep me company as Ellie lay sleeping next to me. I'd lie there, staring into nothingness and wondering how many women's lives could have gone in totally different directions had life offered them a different hand of cards.

"Brone?"

Fisher's voice pulled me back to reality. She pointed her chin toward the gates. "Why aren't we closing them up?"

Loading my bow, I said, "We're going back out there to do a sweep."

CHAPTER 3

"Keep the gates closed until we come back," I ordered the guards.

Before we stepped out, I reached for an unlit torch and swept it across Fisher's. With my newly lit torch in hand, I led us out beyond the Village wall but remained within the electric fence.

A loud creaking sound filled the space around us, and within seconds, the gates were closed.

"How're we doing this?" Fisher whispered. "Shouldn't we be getting backup?"

"No," I said. "We don't have time to go waking everyone up. Besides, this Black Panther guy's all about stealth, which means we aren't going to find him standing in the dark, prepared to fight. He's all about surprising his victims. If he can avoid a face-to-face altercation, I'm sure he will. All we have to do is make sure he didn't come in."

"What about FaceCrusher?" Fisher asked.

"SkullCrusher?" I said.

She rolled her eyes. "Whatever. Maybe he got in."

Although it was improbable that a man geared

up from head to toe would sneak inside, we couldn't rule it out. For all we knew, both he and Black Panther had rushed past the electric fence after we'd turned it off. I hoped to God that wasn't the case and that no one had infiltrated. Regardless, I needed to sweep the Village's perimeter over and over again until I felt certain my people were safe.

"You go that way, and I'll meet you on the other side," I said, twirling a finger in the air.

Fisher's brows came together over the bridge of her nose. "You want us to split up? That's the dumbest—"

With flat eyelids, I stared at her—a look meant to convey, *Do you seriously want to argue right now?*

"If we don't split up," I said, "we could be walking circles all night. If someone's stuck between the fence and our wall, we need to trap them."

"And if one of us gets attacked?"

"Then you scream," I said. "That's what the tower guards are for."

Fisher didn't seem convinced of my approach, and I didn't blame her. Going at this alone was a risk, but the longer we stood here bickering about the endless possibilities, the more time we were wasting. What if one of them was trying to dig a hole under our wall or setting up some sort of climbing mechanism? Every minute was crucial.

"Keep your knife on you and get ready to fight," I said.

Going forward with this plan was a bit reckless, but what option did we have? I held onto the idea that it was doubtful one of the players had rushed past the electric fence. For all I knew, the two remaining players were far away from here and had yet to find us.

On the other hand, if Player 1 was right, every other player had taken advantage of his tracking skills and had followed him to the Village.

Clenching both my sword and torch, I lifted them in front of me and nodded at Fisher. When she turned around, I did the same, making my way along the left side of the Village.

As I moved, my eyes darted toward the blackness of the jungle. If there was one thing I despised more than venturing through the jungle at night, it was doing so with fire on me. It reminded me of the real world and how my mom used to leave her blinds open at night. I hated that. Anyone bold (or creepy) enough to stare into our window could see everything inside as if my mother and I were on display. Across the street from us was another apartment, and several tenants there did the same thing as my mom. Had I had binoculars—not that I had any interest in other people's day-to-day lives—I could have easily watched their every move.

As I followed the dirt path along the Village wall, I tensed, anticipating an attack from out of the dark. If either of the remaining players were skilled with guns or throwing weapons, I didn't stand a chance. I might as well have been walking with a huge neon sign above my head.

The only control I had was speed. Quickening my pace, I hurried toward the back of the Village, searching for Fisher's orange glow. While I wanted to inspect the ground for footprints, it was no use—there were already far too may footprints and the ground looked like disturbed earth.

At the far end of the back wall, an orange glow came into view. Same as me, Fisher jogged my way, the fire of her torch dragging with the wind.

"Anything?" she hissed.

"All clear," I said. "Nothing suspicious on your side?"

She shook her head.

I gazed into the darkness of the jungle as if last minute, I might catch a glimpse of a figure. "Let's head back."

She nodded, her shadowed brows and cheekbones making her look angry, and followed me when I turned around. But before I took a step, something appeared in the corner of my eye.

"You okay?" she asked.

Slack-jawed, I turned the upper half of my body

and raised my torch, its warm glow illuminating the Village wall's wooden planks.

"Holy f—" I breathed.

"Are those—" Fisher said, her mouth agape.

Up along the entire height of the wall was something I hadn't expected to find—muddy footprints. They were laid out so perfectly as if their wearer possessed antigravity technology.

"That can't be—"

I didn't give her the time to finish. Swinging around with a tight grip on my sword, I charged toward the front gates. "He's inside!"

CHAPTER 4

It was almost as if these women had forgotten the meaning of danger. The assigned Village guards, who had been specifically trained to handle high-stress situations, stared at me with big bug eyes and wrinkled noses.

Had they forgotten how to speak English? What the fuck was wrong with them?

"Now!" I shouted, pointing at the Village sconces.

Nodding, they scattered in different directions in pairs of two, ordering the tower guards to light the Village sconces. One by one, balls of fire lit up the Village perimeter, casting an orange blanket across the wooden tents and cabins.

"Close the gates," I growled.

If this son of a bitch was still in here, he wasn't getting out.

Turning to Fisher, I said, "Get me the horn."

She hesitated, which was understandable. We'd never once used the emergency blowing horn. When the Hunters brought back their first water buffalo after the war, I'd asked Hammer to carve off one of the horns and turn it into something capable of producing a sound loud enough to reach the entire Village and the Working Grounds.

* * *

"You sure it works?" I asked. Before she could respond, I pressed my lips against the small hole at the end of the horn and blew out a mouthful of air.

Hammer rolled her eyes and yanked it out of my grip. "You have to blow hard." The corner of her lip twitched upward, and she squinted playfully. "So, if I can do it—" she mumbled, placing the horn against her mouth.

With ballooned cheeks, she blew air through the horn and a deep musical sound filled up her entire tent. It was so loud that I instinctively cupped my ears and she stopped.

"See?" she said, handing it back to me.

Brushing my fingers along its rough grooves, I smiled up at her. "This is perfect, Hammer. Thank you." She'd done an immaculate job. The horn was massive—easily the length of my entire forearm—and curved upward with a wide opening at one end. She'd even wrapped a decorative rope around it and fastened a suede string from one end to the other to create a handle.

While I didn't want to worry the women by explaining to them that a new emergency protocol was to be implemented, we needed to remain vigilant even if our enemies had been defeated. There was no telling what else was out there; having an alarm system was crucial.

The blowing horn signified one thing: imminent danger to every life inside the Village.

I'd already decided on the different tonalities and their meanings. One blow would signify a predatory threat, ordering every single woman inside the Village to prepare for battle—with the exception of mothers. Two blows would signify a natural disaster, ordering women to seek immediate shelter.

* * *

Fisher rushed back with the blowing horn in her hands.

Without saying anything, I took it from her, raised it to my lips, and did as Hammer had taught me. I filled my stomach and lungs with as much air as possible, sealed the tip with my lips, and blew out hard.

Vibrations tickled my hands as the powerful sound exploded from the instrument and spread across the entire Village. At once, doors flung open and women rushed out with clenched fists and startled looks. While I didn't allow women to carry any form of a weapon inside their sleeping tents, I'd clearly explained to them that if the horn were to ever be used, they were permitted to rush to Hammer's tent and grab any weapon they wanted.

As women came running out, more and more sconces lit up, lighting up the entire Village.

No one spoke. It was almost as if we'd trained for this daily since we'd won the war against the Northers when in fact, we'd only practiced the blowhorn twice—once by creating a fictitious scenario in which an entire clan had infiltrated the Village, and the other in preparation for a natural disaster.

But these women were prepared. They ran in silence, created a line outside of Hammer's shop, and passed weapons to each other.

When I caught a glimpse of someone in my peripheral, I turned sideways to catch Ellie poking her head out of our cabin. With a tight grip on my bow, I ran toward her, my feet slapping the cool grass.

She stepped back as I rushed inside. Behind her, Robin moaned in her sleep, but she hadn't completely awakened, which was shocking given how loud the blowing horn had been. Ellie stared at me, her plush lips parted and her brows high on her face.

She didn't have to say anything for me to know she was freaking out.

"It's okay," I whispered. "I'll take care of this, okay?"

"What the hell's going on, Brone? You've never used that thing. I didn't think you'd actually ever have—"

Grabbing her fingers, I stepped closer and planted a kiss on her cheek. This seemed to soothe her.

"I think one of the bad guys made their way inside the Village," I said. Realizing I was sugarcoating the truth, which was something Ellie hated, I cleared my throat. I didn't *think*—I *knew*. "Black Panther made his way inside."

"H-how do you know?" she said. "I mean, how's this even possible? We have the electric fence and everything—"

Sighing, I bowed my head. Was this my fault? Had he snuck in the moment I'd shut off the fence? Or, had he been in here for quite some time, and the reason we'd found out about it was *because* I'd turned off the fence?

"I know, I know," I said, gently brushing the back of her hand with my thumb. "But we had to turn the fence off, there was a kid—"

"You did *what*?" she said.

While part of me understood why she was so upset, another part of me couldn't help but feel resentful that she was questioning what I'd done. I already had the weight of the entire Village on my shoulders—the last thing I needed was to be made to feel guilty about a difficult decision I'd made in a split second.

That's what being a leader was all about—

making impossible decisions. I wouldn't always make the right choices, but it was better to choose than to choose nothing at all.

Swallowing my frustration, I said, "It was a risk, Ellie, but there was a kid stuck outside the electrical fence. What did you want me to do? Leave her there? Risk her getting mauled by an animal? Burned to a crisp if she grabbed the fence?"

Ellie averted her gaze. "N-no."

She must have sensed my anger. Although levelheaded and calm in almost every situation, Ellie wasn't the type to back down when she felt passionate about something. And while my people were more important to me than anything, so was the life of an innocent child.

Surely, she understood that.

"You would've done the same thing," I said.

With a blank expression, she stared ahead and nodded. "Y-yeah. You're right. I would have. So what now? What's the plan? What do you need from me?"

"I need you to stay inside with Robin," I said. "Lock the door and don't let anyone in."

Before I turned around, she pulled me in tight. "Be careful."

"I will," I said, pressing my lips against the warm skin of her neck.

Regripping my bow, I opened the cabin door

and stepped out into the firelit Village, where countless women stood carrying weapons and waiting for my command.

CHAPTER 5

The women stared at me with bloodshot eyes. Despite how fatigued they must have been, the adrenaline coursing through them was enough to prepare them for battle.

"We're after one man, but he's extremely dangerous," I said. "He's somehow managed to get over the wall. Everyone, split up, stay vigilant, and search everywhere. Remember to keep your eyes on the walls at all times. if he's still in here, I don't want him getting out. When you find him, kill the son of a bitch."

Everyone pumped their weapons into the air and let out deep growls before running in opposite directions. They scattered across the Village, their footsteps causing the ground to tremble, and searched everywhere.

He had to be in here somewhere, right? Was it possible that he'd snuck out as fast as he'd come in?

"You think he's still in here?" came Fisher's voice, as if she'd somehow read my mind.

I wanted to say, "Yes, and we'll find him," but I

wasn't convinced.

This guy was supposed to be an expert—a professional in his field. If that was true, it meant he wasn't an amateur and he wouldn't be so easily caught. It wasn't like we'd find him standing at the back wall surrendering with two hands in the air.

For all we knew, he had advanced camouflaging equipment.

Sighing, I turned to Fisher. "I have no idea. If he is, maybe we can trap him before he escapes. But for all we know, he's already gone."

"What would've been the point of that?" Fisher said. "Why infiltrate a village simply to run away a few minutes later?"

"It's obvious he's cautious," I said. "And we have no idea when he came in. Maybe he's preparing something the way BlueVolt did. Some sort of trap..."

Then, Rocket appeared, along with Elektra, Biggie, and Quinn. Seeing my friends reminded me of my other friend—Coin. I'd gone to check up on her before going to bed that evening, and Iskra had assured me that she was recovering nicely. She'd managed to kill the infection in Coin's leg and dose her with some heavy-duty pain killers—some concoction Tegan had made using coca leaves.

With any luck, she'd be back up on her feet soon.

"Listen," Rocket said, "we'll find him, okay?" She

stared at me a bit longer than necessary, no doubt trying to ease my guilt. It was as if she understood that being the leader of the Village took a huge toll on me by making me feel responsible for everything, including any death.

While I hated that feeling, I appreciated that Rocket understood it. In a sense, it made me feel a bit less alone.

"Let's get out there," I said, preparing my bow.

Fisher followed me, and together, we walked along the Village's perimeter, searching the wall for more prints.

"Where the fuck is this guy?" Fisher hissed. "People don't just disappear into thin air."

"Player 1 warned us," I said. "This guy isn't your average killer. He's trained for this. God knows how many years he spent in the military. We have to be prepared for anything."

Around us, women crouched, stretched, and even contorted their bodies to search every inch of the Village. Some women even protested as their tent doors were kicked in, but it was crucial to search everything—not merely the land outside.

Black Panther might have snuck inside one of the tents to use it as a hideout. It would have been the perfect plan. Women didn't alternate between sleeping tents. Everyone had an assigned space, and out of respect, no one stepped foot inside someone else's tent. So if he was hiding out in a tent, the only way to find out was to search every single one.

"What the hell do you think you're doing?" one woman snapped. She slapped the woman who'd entered her tent and slammed the door shut.

The one who'd been slapped charged for the door again, blasting her fists against it. I didn't blame her—all she was doing was precisely what I'd ordered her to do.

"Fucking bitch!" she shouted, still pounding away.

I let out a sharp whistle and her eyes shot my way. This wasn't the time to pick a fight, and my stare must have translated that. Straightening her posture, she moved on to the next tent and opened it up.

"What the hell?" came a shrill voice.

The women inside the tents being searched were likely terrified and doing their best to protect their children. So when an armed woman came barging in, it was no wonder the mothers reacted with so much aggression.

"We have to inspect everywhere!" said the woman who'd entered the tent.

"See anything?" Fisher asked, pulling my attention toward the Village wall.

I shook my head. Why weren't there any prints? If he was still inside, why couldn't we find him? This didn't make any sense. Was he *that* good?

Good enough to conceal himself from several hundred women?

Walking faster, I made my way around the Village—the sooner I ruled out Black Panther's escape, the sooner I could start helping with the real search. When I reached the halfway point, however, a high-pitched scream sent shivers down my arms.

I swung around to find women charging toward a single cabin, their weapons held up in front of their chests. Had they found him? My heart thudded hard against my ribs—a rhythmic beat reminding me I was still alive. Without saying a word, I charged toward the cabin, shoving women out of the way to get by.

Why wasn't anyone fighting? Why were they all standing around like a bunch of sheep? Had Black Panther been killed? Were they staring at his dead body?

"Move," I ordered, elbowing my way through.

When I entered the tent, however, my stomach clenched. Black Panther wasn't there—at least, not anymore. Instead, beneath the dim glow of a poorly lit torch was a pale woman lying in her bed, eyes wide open and a bloody gash across her throat.

CHAPTER 6

"Would someone shut that thing up?"

"Thing? It's a fucking baby!"

"I don't care! Shut it up!"

The dead mother's baby cried so hard her plump little face darkened three shades of red. It was a bubbly cry so heart-wrenching that one woman rushed toward the crib, reached inside, and scooped her up. "Shhh, it's okay, sweetheart."

One woman carrying a battle-ax scoffed. "It's okay? How the fuck is any of this okay? We aren't even safe in our goddamn homes!"

A few more women joined in on the outrage, so I quickly raised a hand to silence them.

"You're right. This isn't okay. What's happening here is beyond disgusting. These people are playing with our lives for money. You should be outraged. I know I am." Saliva sprinkled out of my mouth and into the air, but I didn't care. I was fuming. And to think that the corrupt government took part in this game made me sick to my stomach. "So whatever anger you're feeling, bottle it up and get ready to use it on the son of a bitch who did this." I pointed at the dead woman without looking at her.

Women nodded with determination, their jaws clenched and nostrils flared.

Stepping toward the body, I bent forward and rested the back of my hand against her forehead. It wasn't cold, at least not yet, which meant this killing was recent.

"Check the other cabins—all of them," I ordered, and the women scattered throughout the Village.

Before I could step out of the tent, Fisher appeared, leaning against the slanted doorway. She brushed her slick black hair back, scratched her forehead, and sighed. "You should get some sleep."

I stared at her as if she'd told me one plus one equaled ten. Was she insane? How could I sleep knowing some trained killer was inside our Village?

"All right, all right," she said and threw her hands in the air. "After we catch him, you should get some rest. You're a mess, Brone."

What did she mean by that? A mess? Did I look as awful as I felt? Probably. My muscles ached so much I wanted to vomit. Over the last three days, I'd gotten little, if any, sleep. I was still functioning solely because of my adrenaline and will to survive.

"Let's just finish looking for prints," I said, brushing past her.

She followed me as I headed toward the back wall, and we continued our path from earlier with our weapons in front of us. The problem with searching for prints on the interior wall was that if he had run up with some sort of cable or climbing mechanism, he would have jumped from grass onto wood, which meant there was a good chance prints would not be visible.

We'd seen them on the exterior wall because the prints were muddy. There was a good chance that the wet grass inside the Village had cleaned the soles of his shoes. We weren't looking for muddy prints—we were looking for wet prints, which gave us a narrow window to work with.

If we didn't find them in time, they'd dry out. Or, they'd already dried, and there was no way of telling whether or not he'd left.

I was about to share my thoughts with Fisher when she let out a soft whistle. Turning sideways to look at her, I threw my chin out to say, *What is it?*

Without a word, she aimed her gaze toward the wall beside her. What was she trying to show me? I didn't see anything. So I moved closer, squinting to try to figure out what I was looking at.

When I still didn't see it, she said, "Don't you have perfect vision, Archer?"

Ignoring her comment, I took another step forward. At last, I saw it. It was barely visible, and I couldn't even understand how Fisher had managed to see it, but there it was. Right against the Village's wooden wall was a faint outline of a boot's print. It was so faint that it looked like nothing more than the texture of wood grain.

"How the hell did you see that?" I asked.

Shrugging, she said, "Honestly, I'm not sure. It's almost dried up. Look, there's another one." She pointed a bit higher this time, and sure enough, the faint outline of a boot's heel was several feet higher. "Guess he's gone."

Our eyes locked. Was he? How did we know for certain? Prints on a wall didn't prove anything, as much as I wanted them to. This guy wasn't an idiot. What if this was a setup? What if he'd intentionally left prints without leaving the Village?

"What's up?" Fisher asked, no doubt realizing my mind was racing. "What're you thinking? Talk to me."

"What if this is a trick?" I said. "What if he isn't gone?"

Fisher's eyelids flattened. "When's the last time you ate?"

I scowled at her. "What does my diet have to do with—"

"Brone, you're exhausted. It's all over your face. I think you're overthinking this one a bit. The dude's gone."

"How do you know?" I said. "If he left, how the

hell did he get past the electric fence?"

"Maybe he left when we shut it off," she pointed out.

I scoffed. "So, what? He's been camping outside the wall ever since we reactivated BlueVolt's fence?"

Fisher stared at me but didn't say anything.

Goddamn it. This was getting too complicated. There were too many possibilities without any certainty. I hated that. And I hated to think that maybe she was right—maybe he'd been playing us far longer than we knew.

"No," I blurted. "It doesn't make sense. There's no way he crossed back over into the jungle. The whole point of this game is to get as many kills as possible, right?"

Fisher nodded.

"So why try to run away when you have a bunch of live bodies right at your fingertips? He's playing the long game, but there's no way he gave up and fled the Village."

"Well—" Fisher said, rubbing her chin.

"What?" I asked.

"What if he has the winning score? That'd be reason enough for him to back off and try to survive."

Impossible. As far as I knew, he'd killed one of us, while Player 1's green counter displayed 16 kills. No way had he caught up to Player 1. At least, not unless he'd found other clans or stray women in the jungle.

"I doubt he does," I said, but the truth was, I couldn't be certain. Holding my breath, I tapped my cheek as if it would somehow help me think better. "Let's go see Player 1. If his score isn't green anymore, it means someone else is beating him. If that's the case, then Black Panther's winning, which means that maybe... just maybe, he *did* back off."

Without hesitating, I twirled on my heels and darted toward Player 1's cabin.

CHAPTER 7

"Are you fucking kidding me?" I said.

Fisher didn't speak. Instead, she stood there with two hands gripping her waist and tight lips that translated to, *Well, he's useless now.*

With his wrists still tied behind his chair, Player 1 lay flat on his side, eyes open and skin as white as the moonlight shining through the cabin's door.

"That didn't take long," Fisher said.

"He refused medical help," I said. "It was only a matter of time before the infection spread or before he bled out."

Fisher cocked an eyebrow at me. "Why do you sound so pissed off about it? The *cabrón's* dead. Ain't that a good thing? He killed a bunch of our—"

"Yeah, no..." I said, shaking my head. "I mean. I'm glad the son of a bitch is dead, but I still wanted him alive for intel. Besides, I promised my women they could tear him to shreds after all this was over. Now they won't get to."

A sly smirk pulled at the corner of her lip, revealing a short canine tooth. "Geez, Brone, you've changed. You're upset because women won't get to literally tear a man apart."

Although nothing about this situation was funny, I couldn't help but smile at how ridiculous I sounded—Fisher was right. Who the hell had I become?

"Come on," I said, "help me out."

Bending forward, I grabbed Player 1 by his uniform vest and arm and pulled back as hard as I could. Fisher did the same until we managed to place him flat on his back, revealing the death counter on his chest.

In bright green digits, it read, 16.

"So he's still winning," Fisher said.

Inhaling deep to catch my breath, I nodded. The simple act of shifting his body over had drained me. Fisher was right. I needed to sleep as soon as possible. Yet I wasn't certain I'd ever fall asleep—not while we were in danger like this.

"You okay?" Fisher asked.

"Yeah," I said, still breathing hard.

In the distance, I heard my name being called out.

"Where is she?"

"Brone!"

"I saw her go in there."

Footsteps approached the cabin, so I stepped out to find a woman running toward me. Her mouth hung open and her chest puffed out as she breathed heavily.

"B-B-Brone," she said, sucking in a lungful of air. "Th-there you are."

Why did she look so distraught? Then, I realized she wasn't alone. Behind her, next to our main gates, a small crowd had formed, and women closed in with bowed heads and curious gazes.

"What's going on?" I asked.

"There's been another attack," she said.

Clenching an arrow in my hand, I glared toward the crowd. "When did it happen? Did anyone see the attack?"

She shook her matted hair and looked back. "N-no. I found the body. It's one of your guards, Brone. I have no idea when this happened. The other guards beside her didn't see anything, either."

"How the fuck is that even possible?" I stomped forward, wanting to punch the woman in the throat although I knew she wasn't responsible for the attack.

I hated feeling this enraged, but I couldn't help it.

"I-I don't know, Brone. No one knows."

"Are any other guards hurt?" I growled.

"N-no. B-b-but—"

"But what?" I snapped.

"There's something else, Brone."

I glared at her intently without saying anything. If I opened my mouth, I might say something I regretted. Exhaustion was no excuse to treat my women like shit.

"It's... it's the electrical box."

I clenched my fist so hard my knuckles cracked. "What about it?"

"W-well... Someone... It's broken."

CHAPTER 8

For a moment, I forgot about SkullCrusher and
Black Panther. All that mattered was that the
electrical box was damaged. At one end, wires had
been cut, and on top, the wire connecting the solar
panel to the power box itself had been severed.

How had this happened? My heart pounded so
hard the thudding radiated into my head. While
not having our electrical fence up and running was
beyond dangerous, my one thought was that our
hope of ever being able to advance technologically
with electricity was now nothing more than a
shattered dream.

Was the box beyond repair? Had we truly lost
our chance at getting light? Heat? Cooking
technology?

"Brone?"

I must have stood there for several minutes,
imagining a dark future stuck in our archaic ways.
That box had changed our society's entire outlook.
And now, that outlook was nothing more than
wasted hope.

"Brone."

This time, it was Fisher's voice that pulled me out of my daze. She had a way of doing this; every time she spoke, I was inclined to listen. Maybe it was the close and trusting relationship I'd developed with her, or maybe it was that every time she spoke, there was a sense of purpose in her tone. Anything she said was worth listening to.

"I get this is shitty, but we need to act fast if we plan on catching this asshole," she said, staring intently at me.

As always, Fisher was right. I'd simply have to set my emotions aside and deal with the facts.

"Where's Zelda?" I asked.

Fisher glanced back toward the Village. "I'm not sure, I saw her a few minutes ago. I'll find her."

Zelda was a burly German woman with years of experience working with electrical equipment. She'd worked alongside her father—a skilled electrician—in the small town of Bacharach, Germany, when she was a young girl.

Though she hadn't obtained her license, she knew everything about electricity—circuits, amperage, voltage, watts, wiring... which were all things I knew nothing about. Zelda was the woman responsible for helping us set up the electrical box inside our Village walls. If there was anyone who could fix the damage Black Panther had done, it was her.

Fisher came back with Zelda walking by her

side. She walked in long strides, her thick arms swaying back and forth. Her massive size, serious demeanor, and rough-sounding accent made her seem intimidating, but Zelda was a kind woman at heart. Even when she wasn't frustrated, the way she carried herself and the way she spoke made everyone think she was pissed off.

Despite her constant scowls and permanent frown, there was a soft look in her eyes that spoke to me. Deep down, she was more sensitive than anyone knew.

I was also fond of Zelda for her name alone, which always brought me back to my early childhood when I'd spent hours every day playing my favorite game—the 2077 edition of Nintendo's *The Legend of Zelda*.

"Vat is it?" Zelda said, her tone coming out as harsh as usual.

Pointing at the damaged box, I raised both eyebrows. "I don't know how this happened, but Black Panther managed to get ahold of it."

She stepped forward, sighed heavily, and leaned the weight of her body onto her knees. "*Dummkopf,*" she said, hovering her finger over the damaged wires. Although I didn't speak German, the way it came out of her mouth made me assume it meant something like *moron* or *idiot*. "He knows nossing about electricity. He cut vatever he could, probably as fast as possible. I'm surprised he didn't kill himself."

With arms crossed, I stared at her furrowed eyebrows, her rounded back, and her fast-moving eyes. "Can it be fixed?"

She let out another long breath through her big nostrils and without looking away from the box, nodded slowly. "Yes, I should be able to fix zis for you."

"How long will it take?" I asked.

Without warning, she grabbed the entire box with one arm and stood up straight. The thing easily weighed over fifty pounds—I knew because I'd asked Fisher to help me carry it.

"Not sure," she admitted. "I vill tell you vonce I'm done."

It wasn't like I could order her to work faster. Zelda was the only woman I trusted to work on this thing. A few other women had stepped forward, proclaiming that they'd once been contractors and hired to do anything and everything from home renovations to pool installations to electrical wiring. While I didn't think they were being dishonest, I wanted the best there was in the field of electricity—not a Jacky-of-all-trades.

As Zelda pulled the box up to the Village's wooden wall, I turned to Fisher, squinting as the morning sun blinded me.

"We need to keep looking."

"We are," she said. "Women are everywhere,

Brone. They're climbing the towers, moving bushes around... They've gone into every single cabin."

"What about the rooftops?" I asked.

"They've already checked those."

I felt like my lungs were going to explode. I hated this feeling of uncontrollable rage, and I hadn't felt it in so long that it scared me. What if I blacked out again as I'd done several years ago?

And why was I even feeling this way? Two years had passed without any incidents. I'd healed, hadn't I? Or, was this what Proxy had talked about during one of her educational sessions? She'd gone in-depth about PTSD, which seemed to shake up the women. It was almost as if some of them hadn't realized how much they were suffering, and to hear Proxy's explanation of their feelings somehow validated them.

She'd given everyone assignments—tips to deal with symptoms and methods to cope with the pain it brought. The plan was to lead women on a healing path, especially after everything they'd gone through.

Although I'd denied it for so long, it eventually made sense to me. I may not have served in the military, but the gruesome and horrific things I'd seen were traumatic. No human being should ever witness the things I'd seen. Some nights, I'd wake up in a cold sweat with a graphic image in my mind and wonder if it was a memory or some twisted fabrication pieced together by my damaged brain.

The pain, the suffering, the torture... All of it still haunted me, as much as I wanted to believe it was too far in the past to matter. As Proxy had explained it, PTSD didn't just go away—at least, not in most cases. She'd gone on and on about how even years later, a single trigger was enough to bring someone to their knees.

I remembered the word *trigger*; the crowd of women had blown up into an immature conversation about guns, probably to mask their discomfort and pain.

I'd been standing at the back of the crowd, arms crossed over my belly and eyes focused on Proxy as if she were the only woman standing at the center of the Village.

* * *

"Maybe you're mixin' up your words," one woman said. With a partially toothless grin on her face, she turned to her friend, elbowed her in the ribs, and let out a choppy laugh. "My doc told me that those soldier folk are the ones who get PTSE—"

"PTSD," her friend corrected, leaning into her.

"I understand," Proxy said, "but your doctor was mistaken." She paced back and forth with a hand behind her back as if she'd practiced teaching her entire life in preparation for this very moment. Either that, or she'd been a teacher in the real world. While I didn't want to pry, I'd always wanted to know how Proxy got herself on the island. She appeared so level-headed—so calm by nature.

With her free hand, she pointed at the clouds. "Post-Traumatic Stress Disorder is often believed to be a mental illness that is limited to veterans. This is not true." She paused, her glance grazing the tops of everyone's heads before landing on me.

Several years ago, Proxy had attempted to explain this to me, but I'd been too defensive about it to let it sink in.

"Anyone can suffer from PTSD," she went on. "Seeing a pet get hit by a car could be considered a traumatic event. Anything that causes severe distress—"

"What about your husband throwin' your kid off a bridge?" one woman shouted.

Everyone's eyes doubled in size, and the woman standing next to her wrapped an arm around her shoulders.

Without showing any emotion, Proxy nodded. "Absolutely."

"What about seeing a suicide bomber blow up in pieces?"

"That too," Proxy said.

"Or your friend getting stabbed in the throat by a fuckin' Norther."

"Getting raped by a group of guys."

"Watchin' your mom be beat up by your piece

o' shit dad every night."

"Finding your dead boyfriend in the kitchen with a needle in his arm."

This time, Proxy didn't say anything. Instead, she clasped her hands together and nodded at the crowd.

"These things may haunt you forever," she said. "Even if you think you are doing well, one day, a single trigger may send you spiraling down a dangerous path you cannot seem to divert from." She paused again, this time, her eyes aimed at the ground. Was she talking about herself?

Proxy wasn't the type to talk about herself— ever. I'd never know what she'd been through, but it was obvious that whatever it was, it still tormented her.

"Trigger?" one woman shouted. "Like a gun?" She stuck her hands together to form a pistol and made shooting sounds with her mouth.

Another woman played along, slapping a hand over her chest and stumbling backward.

"Would you two idiots grow up?" shouted a tall, dark-skinned woman with a thick accent. "You are being children! Have you not heard a single thing? This is not a joke."

The woman with the fake pistol lowered her hands inch by inch and cleared her throat.

"A trigger," Proxy said, "is a psychological stimulus that brings your memory of the traumatic event back to life." Then, she pointed an open palm at the woman who'd spoken of her child and the bridge. "Seeing a man hold a child high up into the air may be a trigger for you."

The woman parted her lips but didn't say anything. Instead, she turned her head from side to side, and the ladies standing next to her patted her on the back. Finally, she turned back toward Proxy, her lower lip trembling. "It... it makes sense now. Y-you're right... I can't stand watching Eliot play with the kids."

As I stood there watching one of the most powerful educational sessions I'd ever seen, I felt a strange sense of belonging. At the end of the day, we were all the same—severely damaged yet wanting nothing more than to live a normal life.

* * *

"Brone?"

I blinked several times until the evening purple sky came into view.

"Jesus," Fisher said. "Are you okay?"

"Y-yeah," I mumbled. How long had I been standing here? My feet felt like they were bruised on the inside, and my legs trembled.

"You've been here for hours, staring at the ground," Fisher said. When I didn't respond, she parted her legs at shoulder's width and planted two firm hands on her waist. "Listen, we've been searching all day. He isn't in here, so those footprints we saw earlier, they're real."

"It doesn't make any sense," I said. "Player 1's dead, but he's still winning. This Black Panther guy isn't done doing whatever it is he's doing."

"Maybe he'll be back tonight," Fisher said. "We can prepare for it. We'll catch him this time."

I scoffed—not because Fisher wasn't making sense, but because for the first time, *everything* made sense.

"He might come back," I said, "but he might not."

"What're you saying?" Fisher asked.

"This is his fucking plan," I said. "He's playing with us. He's causing sleep deprivation to weaken us."

CHAPTER 9

As the evening sconces were lit, I approached Zelda. She was crouched over the electrical box, muttering to herself in German.

"Any luck?" I asked.

Turning her head a bit to the side, she said, "*Nein.*"

Fighting the urge to sigh, I turned around to find Rocket, Biggie, and Hammer standing behind me with arms crossed over their chests.

"Go sleep," Rocket said.

I parted my lips to tell her to watch her tone, when Biggie cut in, "That's an order."

Was this some sort of joke? Even Hammer stared at me with hardened brows and a pout no doubt meant to signify that this was anything but a joke.

"You don't give orders—"

"As your friends, we do," Rocket said. "Brone, you're beyond exhausted. You probably aren't even thinking straight."

Rocket wasn't wrong. I kept hallucinating moving objects in my peripheral and my body felt like it had been flattened under a steamroller. But how was I supposed to go to sleep while all of this was happening? These women needed me.

"You've done everything you can do," Hammer said.

I rubbed my hand over my face. "No, I—"

Biggie pinched the air in front of her, a gesture that I knew meant, *Zip it.*

It was a strange feeling to be bossed around after I'd spent the last two years giving orders, but their commands were coming from a place of love. The truth was, I couldn't believe I hadn't yet collapsed, and if I continued trying to lead my women like this, I'd end up making an unforgivable mistake.

"Okay," I breathed. "Then let's do rotational—"

"Already got that covered," Hammer said.

At times, it was almost as if my friends were able to read my mind. I was so thankful to have them by my side.

Although too tired to smile, I managed to say, "Thank you."

Biggie wrapped an arm around me. "Come on, girl. Let's get you to your cabin."

As we walked toward the back of the Village, Ellie stepped toward me with little Robin in her arms, but she was stopped by Fisher. They exchanged a few words, their eyes darting my way every few seconds, and although they were too far for me to hear anything, I knew exactly what Fisher was telling her—let me rest.

Biggie led me inside my cabin and I dropped myself into bed. It was both painful and satisfying at the same time.

"Don't you be stressin' about a thing, okay?" she said. "We got eyes everywhere, and that sneaky fucker ain't gettin' inside o' here unless he has a death wish."

I managed a smirk.

"So you sleep, and if we need you for anythin', I promise I'll be the first one at your door."

She may have said something else, but I couldn't be sure. Within seconds, I was out.

* * *

Rainer stood tall, her metal-plated shoulders drawn back and a hefty sword held in her right hand. At her feet, women cried out, begging for mercy. At first, the screaming was pleading—long, desperate whimpers. But then, Rainer raised her sword above her head. Behind me, the entire city roared.

One elephant even stood on its hind legs before dropping down, deep vibrations causing bits of earth to jump like popcorn.

"Don't beg," Rainer said. "It's unbecoming." And with that, she sliced her sword through the air and several heads rolled across the dirt.

"Brone!"

I jolted upright and wiped a line of drool from

my face. My back, cold and damp, sent shivers down my arms. Where was I? What was happening? Excruciating pain radiated throughout my entire body, almost as if I'd been tensing so hard that my blood had stopped flowing through me.

"Time to get up," Biggie said, trying to catch her breath. She dropped my sword at my feet and jerked her head sideways as if to say, *We don't have any time to waste.*

Grabbing the cold handle of my sword, I jumped to my aching feet. "What's going on? What happened? Are we under attack?"

"There was an explosion," she said, fighting to catch her breath. "Someone's tryin' to blast the gates open." Her big belly expanded as she breathed, and she wiped a streak of sweat from her forehead. "This ain't good, Brone. I ain't tellin' you what to do, 'cause you're the boss, but I *really* think you need to order an evacuation."

An evacuation? We'd already run once. No way was I fucking running away from my home.

Clenching my teeth, I threw my bow and quiver over my shoulder, pushed my way past her, and kicked my cabin door open.

The second I stepped out into the Village, another explosion shook the earth beneath my feet. At the Village gates, a bright orange and yellow flash forced me to turn and cover my face.

The few women who stood closest to the gates—those trying to fire arrows from the towers—were sent hurling through the air, their bodies crashing against the ground.

Out of nowhere, our large protective gates blasted open as bits and pieces of wood flew in every direction.

Who had set off the bombs? Was it Black Panther? Had he decided to change his approach to throw us off our game? The smoke was heavy and dark, expanding inside the Village as it doubled in size. Women screamed, running toward the back of the Village, while others stood strong with weapons in their hands, prepared to fight whatever was making its way inside our home.

But as our attacker entered, my stomach sank.

CHAPTER 10

At first, it was difficult to make out what this thing was, but as the smoke slowly dissipated, the body's shape came into view, barely looking human at all. He stepped into the Village, his massive metal-plated body moving almost robotically.

His head, which was at least six times the size of mine, was protected underneath a gladiator-like helmet with slits for eyes. It wasn't even the metal covering him from head to toe that made my stomach feel like it was caught in a vise; across every inch of his metallic armor were razor-sharp spikes sticking out like a porcupine's quills, making it impossible for anyone to get near him. In his gloved hands, he held a giant war hammer with a sharp point at one end.

How was anyone supposed to fight him? We couldn't use any throwable weapons—they would bounce off his armor. If anyone got too close, he'd swing his war hammer. And, if by some miracle someone managed to slip past his hammer, a simple swing of his spiked arm would be enough to tear someone's face off.

This guy was unbeatable.

"Holy mother of—" Hammer said, staring blankly ahead.

Rocket stood beside me, her jaw hanging as low as Hammer's. From the crowd came Fisher with an unusual limp in her strut. Over the last few years, her leg had healed pretty well since the crocodile's attack. But now and then, it seemed to flare up when she exerted herself. She'd been on her feet for more than twenty-four hours—it was only natural for her to be aching.

"Guys?" she said, but it came out as more of a question.

Was Biggie right? Was evacuation our sole option?

Turning to look at the back emergency gate, I realized that several women were already using it. Part of me resented them for running away without being given the order to do so, but the human part of me knew that these women were scared beyond belief.

How could anyone stand up against someone like this?

Suddenly, he let out a cry so deep its effect mimicked the vibrations of his steps. Several women fired arrows at him, but all it did was aggravate him. He lunged forward, moving far faster than I'd have expected for someone his size, and swung his war hammer over his head and spun in a circle, reaching it as far as his arms would allow.

Three women found themselves standing too close, unable to dodge in time. The hammer literally picked them up off the ground and threw them several meters back. As blood splattered into the air, the sound of bones shattering spread throughout the Village.

"Brone?" Fisher hissed. "Give a fucking order!"

Hundreds of eyes shot my way as women waited for my command.

I considered telling Fisher to grab the guns—the one that had belonged to the woman in the trap, and Player 1's rifle. But even I knew that shooting at a metal target was a terrible idea. There was no telling what kind of metal he was wearing, but I was willing to bet he'd made certain it was impenetrable, even by bullets. It also meant that a fired shot might ricochet and kill some of my women.

The grenade.

Would it work? Maybe. But too many of my women were around him. If I threw a grenade, the explosion would take several lives, not only his.

What was I supposed to do? This was a goddamn suicide mission. As much as I didn't want to back down, I couldn't let women run to their deaths. For what? By the end of it, there wouldn't be enough of us to even sustain a society.

We needed to evacuate. If we could find a way to isolate him inside the Village, maybe then the grenade might prove itself useful.

This thought process might have lasted all of five seconds, but my five-second delay was too long. At the same time, several women pumped their weapons in the air and screamed at the tops of their lungs, no doubt enraged by the murder of their friends.

"Stand back!" I shouted, but I was too late.

Women were charging at full speed, their mouths wide open as wordless shouts came out, filling the entire Village with so much hateful energy that more and more women followed them.

I grimaced as SkullCrusher did what his name signified—as women came at him, he swung his weapon, splitting heads open and disfiguring women. One woman even tried to jump at him but impaled herself against his body armor instead.

My heart pounded so hard I thought I might faint. Everything felt so surreal, like at any moment, I'd wake up inside the darkness of my cabin with Ellie by my side.

Shit.

Where was Ellie?

Swinging around, I narrowed my eyes toward my cabin. The door was closed, so I hoped to God she'd gone back inside.

"We can't just fucking stand here!" Rocket

shouted, little veins bulging out from her grimy red forehead.

What was I doing? I was the leader of these people, yet I couldn't move. I'd faced difficult situations before—very difficult—but this, by far, seemed like the most difficult of all.

I blinked hard and swallowed several times, hoping to regain my grip on reality. At long last, my surroundings came into focus and I felt grounded.

This was life or death, and although I couldn't save everyone, my job was to make sure I saved as many as possible.

"Get everyone you can to evacuate, now!" I shouted.

Without hesitating, my friends ran toward the crowd, grabbing shoulders and pointing at the back door. Some women pulled away with twisted features and charged straight toward SkullCrusher.

As inappropriate as it might have been, I suddenly thought of his kill counter, which was likely sitting beneath his armor. Had it turned green? As much as I despised Player 1, right now, I hated SkullCrusher far more than the sick son of a bitch who had at least helped me. In a sense, he was the better of two evils.

"How good's your aim?" Fisher asked, leaning into me.

I turned to her but didn't respond. Without

saying anything, she raised a flat seashell-tipped arrow in front of my face.

Was she insane? I almost laughed at her, even though nothing about this situation was funny, but when I caught her frowning, I knew she was being serious.

"If you can get the perfect shot, it'll fit," she said.

The idea was so insane that I found myself considering it. What other option did I have?

Grabbing the arrow from her fingers, I prepared my bow. "Do you have any more of these? In case I miss."

She stared at me without blinking. "Don't miss."

CHAPTER 11

The empty space around SkullCrusher widened. Women were no doubt realizing they didn't stand a chance. To make up for this, he stomped forward, swinging his war hammer as far as his massive arms would allow.

Unfortunately, he caught a few more women—one square in the jaw, and the other in the neck. I turned away before seeing any of the damage, but the crunching and oozing sounds made my stomach sink.

With no time to waste, I raised my loaded bow and stared down the arrow's shaft. The pointed, pearl-colored shell hovered in the air for a few seconds as I concentrated on SkullCrusher's right eye. I chose his right eye seeing as it was the one closest to me, and every few seconds, he swung his body to the right, his metallic helmet following his movements.

You can do this.

From where I was standing, the slits over his eyes appeared to be about half an inch in height, and two inches wide. All I had to do was ensure my arrow slid right through the crack. For this to happen, it was important that my arrow not spin. Most arrows I practiced with had either metal or stone heads. There was no telling how well this arrow would handle, and at that moment, I wished I'd practiced with shell arrows when Elektra had asked me to shoot one.

I'd told her that we didn't craft shell arrows anymore, so there was no use practicing with them.

SkullCrusher took a step to his right as one woman ran past him with a spear pumping over her head.

Pulling the bow's elastic back, I let out a long breath to empty my lungs. For some reason, I always found this to help me concentrate and stabilize my hands.

One shot.

And then, with all of my focus directed at the slit over his eye, I released my arrow. It flew through the air so fast I didn't see it—what I did see, however, was SkullCrusher's head jerk backward. He raised his metal-gloved hand over his eye.

Had I hit him?

But when he lowered his hand, looking confused, I knew I'd missed my target. All I'd done was disorient him, perhaps from the sound of impact against his metal helmet.

"Fuck," I muttered.

Fisher breathed out hard through her nostrils. "It's okay, Brone. You did the best you could."

Without looking at her, I whipped another arrow out from my quiver. I'd been so taken aback by SkullCrusher's size and the spikes coming out of his bodysuit that I'd forgotten we'd faced a similar threat several years ago.

"We took out Isaac and Rainer," I said. "There's no reason we can't kill this son of a bitch too."

And with that, I fired another arrow straight for his head. It dinged off his helmet, and his foot stopped midair as he searched the Village to locate the source of the attack.

Loading another arrow, I glared at him—I wanted him to know it was me. If he charged at me, he'd stop swinging his war hammer at my people.

"Over here, motherfucker!" I shouted.

"Brone!" Fisher hissed, but I didn't give her the time to dissuade me from continuing my plan.

"Go help Rocket and the others," I said. "Anyone who isn't holding a weapon needs to get out of the Village. Get Ellie out, too."

"But—" Fisher tried.

"That's an order!" I shouted, saliva sprinkling onto her face.

With slanted brows, she nodded, though it was obvious that leaving my side was as difficult for her as it was for me.

The second she swung around, however, Rocket came running toward us with huge eyes taking up a good portion of her face.

"What's going on?" I asked.

She leaned forward, resting her hands onto her knees, her cheeks rosy and her chest glistening with sweat.

"This... This is really bad," she said.

"What is?" I said.

With SkullCrusher heading my way, the last thing I had was time, so whatever was going on, I needed to know now.

"The... the back gate," she said. "The other guy's there."

My eyes shot up toward the back gate, where women now ran inside the Village, rather than out.

"He was hiding outside, waiting for us," she said.

"So fucking kill him!" I snapped.

"I tried," Rocket said. "My arrow bounced right off the guy."

Clenching my jaw, I stared at the man—Black Panther—as he entered the Village with what appeared to be two bloody Samurai swords held in his hands. His body, similar to SkullCrusher, was covered from head to toe in some strange fabric that seemed to change colors as he moved. Whatever it was, it was impenetrable. These sick bastards had thought everything through. Over his face were strange-looking goggles. At first, I'd have assumed they were night vision goggles, but it was broad daylight, which led me to believe they were an advanced piece of equipment—sensors maybe—to warn of potential attacks.

His suit flickered several times, and the next thing I knew, I couldn't see him anymore, or his swords. It was almost as if he'd gone invisible. Had he blended so well with his surroundings that it was impossible to see him? Were his swords also able to camouflage?

"Yeah, and there's that," Rocket said.

"You have got to be fucking kidding me," I said.

I parted my lips, prepared to tell Rocket to go search Player 1's bag for any other weapon we might be able to use, but I didn't have the time.

The next thing I knew, the earth under my feet rumbled, and I glanced up to find SkullCrusher charging straight for me.

CHAPTER 12

At first, I thought maybe I was hallucinating.

Were there two SkullCrushers? With my arrow aimed straight in front of me, I blinked once, then twice, trying to understand what was going on.

Behind SkullCrusher, charging at twice the speed, was another figure covered from head to toe in medieval-looking armor. The armor looked familiar, too, but I couldn't put my finger on it.

He raised what appeared to be a metal battle-ax with a wooden handle and ran even faster, his slits for eyes aimed at the back of SkullCrusher.

When I saw Hammer pumping her fists behind the second armored man, I realized what was going on—this man was no stranger; it was Eliot wearing his dead brother's armor. Hammer must have collected it and stored it after the war.

Eliot was gaining speed over SkullCrusher, but SkullCrusher was getting too close. Realizing Eliot might not make it in time, I stumbled backward, tugged my arrow back, and shot my attacker in the shoulder, hoping to slow him down.

But it accomplished nothing. If anything, it

aggravated him more.

SkullCrusher, who was now yelling at the top of his lungs, must not have heard his attacker coming from behind.

Eliot might have been half SkullCrusher's size, but he moved with such force and stamina that for a second, I imagined this battle ending in our favor.

Would he make it to our enemy in time? Did he have the strength to slice his weapon through SkullCrusher's armor?

I was running out of time.

I stepped backward and shot another arrow, hoping to slow him down, but my foot landed on a piece of wood and my shot missed.

Eliot wouldn't make it in time.

I clenched my fists, preparing myself to be sliced in half, when a spear came twirling through the air, followed by another, and another.

Several meters away, to the side of my opponent, were Hammer, Quinn, and Bushtail, a woman who spent most of her days sewing clothing for the children. Not once would I have ever imagined her a fighter, yet there she was, her features twisted and muscles popping from her frail arms.

At their feet were piles of spears, and behind them, a fast-growing crowd. One by one, women picked up anything they could and threw it into the wind. While only a few of the weapons managed to hit SkullCrusher, their effort to defend me gave me hope.

Dropping my bow, I tore my sword out from its sheath.

Maybe I was out of time, but I wasn't going out without a fight.

Gripping my sword's handle as tight as I could, I bent my knees and held my breath as SkullCrusher's raised his hammer over his head. He was so heavy that his stomping caused my legs to tremble. With another loud shout, he swung his heavy weapon sideways, its massive head slicing through the air horizontally.

It came at me so fast all I could do was drop to my knees. A gust of wind swept my hair atop my head as his hammer tore through the cabin behind me. Wood cracked and snapped, and broken pieces landed on my neck and shoulders. I raised my arm in time to block a heavy plank from crashing onto my head.

Why wasn't SkullCrusher swinging at me again?

I glanced toward him yet realized his hammer was stuck in the cabin's wood. He yanked backward, trying to free it, and more wood snapped—so much so that the cabin's entire right side started to collapse.

This was it. I had to make a move.

The handle of his hammer caught my attention.

Was it made of wood? If I managed to slice my sword through it, he'd be at a disadvantage. Gripping my sword's handle with two hands, I stood up, but as I did, the handle of his hammer glistened in the sun like the hood of a car on a hot summer day.

It wasn't made of wood at all. If I tried to cut through it, I'd damage my sword or injure myself.

SkullCrusher let out a throaty growl and tugged hard one last time. This time, his hammer came out, as did two solid beams of wood. I snatched my bow from the ground and rolled away as the cabin collapsed into pieces.

But the moment I landed on my back, SkullCrusher appeared at my feet, his weapon held in both hands. He stared down at me, his helmet blindingly bright, and with another loud grunt, raised the hammer up over his head.

I wanted to roll sideways the way actors did in the movies—one quick roll to dodge the lethal blow—but everything happened so fast. As his hammer came down toward my chest, I closed my eyes as hard as I could.

I felt my stomach crush flat as a loud crashing sound exploded all around me. The pain was so intense that I stopped breathing.

But then, I sucked in a gasp.

Wasn't I dead? Why was I still breathing? Cracking open one eye, I glanced down at my belly, afraid to see my intestines surrounded by rib fragments.

How was this even possible?

I was uninjured. I touched my belly, my arms, my face. I wasn't a ghost; I was very much alive.

Had my brain been so convinced of my death that it had made up the pain?

I flinched when wood came hurling my way, almost knocking me out cold. That's when I noticed that Eliot and SkullCrusher were in the pile of wood and debris kicking and punching each other. Eliot had somehow landed on top of his opponent, his metal armor deforming against SkullCrusher's pointed spikes.

How solid was Eliot's armor? Would his enemy's spikes puncture him?

Grunting, Eliot grabbed SkullCrusher's helmet by two large spikes and pulled upward. The helmet came flying off, revealing a man with dark skin, a short unkempt beard, glossy black eyes, and so many bright pink scars across his face that I found myself thinking of Zsasz. He grimaced up at Eliot, his teeth covered in blood, and swung a metal fist so hard against the side of Eliot's head that he threw Eliot right off him.

He landed hard on his back, his helmet halfway up his face. On his chest and thigh plates were small puncture holes with droplets of blood coating its edges.

Shit.

SkullCrusher's armor had, in fact, hurt Eliot.

As SkullCrusher climbed back to his feet, Eliot repositioned his helmet and quickly crawled backward in a desperate attempt to get away.

This was it.

A clear shot.

I ran on my hands and knees through the grass to find my bow, but the second I swung around with a loaded arrow, SkullCrusher was standing in front of Eliot with his helmet back on and his war hammer in his hands.

He raised it over his head, and although I couldn't see his face anymore, all I could picture was a sadistic smile on his lips.

"No!" I shouted.

CHAPTER 13

Her shouting was enough to make SkullCrusher turn his head sideways.

Out from in between two tents came Zelda with the heavy electrical box held in one hand, and two unevenly cut wires in the other. She ran hard and in an awkward fashion, her bare feet stomping through the Village. Her mouth, a wide-open black hole, let out a cry so loud it masked the sound of women screaming at the other end of the Village.

What the hell was she doing?

She was running straight for SkullCrusher.

At once, he swung around, prepared to pummel her with his hammer, but he didn't even have the time to swing it. So instead, he jabbed its head toward her chest—a blow powerful enough to break her bones. But as the hammer's head came straight for her, she smiled, refusing to back down or attempt to dodge his attack.

With a scowl on her face, she held both wires up, their tips pointed at the head of SkullCrusher's oncoming hammer. It all happened so fast that I had almost no time to understand what was going on. In seconds, bright blue light exploded between the two of them, and both bodies were propelled into the air in opposite directions.

Zelda landed with a thump on the grass, her body scorched and the damaged wires gripped in her fist. When it was SkullCrusher's turn to hit the ground, it sounded like loose change being dumped into a bucket. The pieces of his armor clanged against each other—not only upon impact, but also for a few seconds after his fall as his body convulsed.

"Holy shit—" someone said beside me.

I couldn't believe what I was looking at. He wasn't moving, and out from in between the cracks of his armor came light gray smoke, licking every edge.

Eliot got up with a grumble, picked up his fallen ax, and charged toward SkullCrusher, no doubt wanting to ensure the job was done.

"Eliot!" I shouted.

The sound of my voice was enough to stop him midrun. He turned around, his plated shoulders bouncing up and down with every heavy breath.

"Don't touch him," I said. "It could kill you."

He looked confused. Eliot didn't understand electricity despite Proxy's attempt to explain it to him. How could he? He'd been raised on the island. Electricity was difficult enough to understand as someone who used to use it daily. I couldn't expect

Eliot to grasp the concept.

Although he didn't know *why* touching SkullCrusher might kill him, he trusted me enough to lower his weapon and take a step back. His gaze, however, didn't leave SkullCrusher. He hovered near him, prepared to strike if necessary.

"Trust me," I said, "that killed him."

Eliot nodded but didn't budge.

A few other women gathered, their curious eyes darting between SkullCrusher's motionless body and Zelda, who lay dead in the grass, her hollow gaze fixated onto nothingness.

How had she gotten the power back up and running? It didn't matter. She'd sacrificed herself to save us all. I bowed my head as a way of showing respect, and everyone followed, some even lowering themselves onto their knees for her.

But our moment of silence didn't last long. A scream spread across the Village, followed by the sound of rapid footsteps and weapons clanging.

Black Panther.

Had Rocket not taken care of him? How was *he* still alive, while SkullCrusher was dead?

With my bow still in hand, I charged toward the back of the Village. Women ran in random directions, looking more confused than anything. Was this because of his camouflaging technology?

Out of nowhere, one woman's throat split open and she reached for it, blood spitting out over her knuckles. She fell to her knees as several other women shrieked, weapons held up by their faces.

The guy was almost invisible. How the fuck were we supposed to defeat him? Every few seconds, I saw a blur—something that looked off— but I couldn't pinpoint his location. Some women even dropped their weapons and ran away, maybe realizing they didn't stand a chance against someone like him.

Now that SkullCrusher was out of the way, we had one threat remaining. If I could eliminate him, there was no need to run away.

I aimed my arrow's point in his general direction. Maybe he'd reappear, even if only for a second. At the same time, the sound of a gun being cocked came from beside me.

Flinching, I turned toward it.

"Let's kill this son of a bitch," Coin said, a crooked smirk pulling at the corner of her lip.

"Coin!" I said.

Her leg was wrapped up in a bloody bandage, but she was standing on it. It was obvious the weight of her body was causing her pain, but I knew Coin, and pain wouldn't be enough to stop her from putting up a fight.

"I'm fine," she said. "I think if we both start firing at the same time, we'll have more odds of hitting him."

"You better be one hell of a good shot," I said,

staring toward the few women still trying to swing their clubs and swords at their camouflaged enemy.

"I am," she said.

Then, on my other side came Quinn's voice. "Me too."

I swung around to find her standing tall with our second rifle in her grasp.

"And if shit goes south," came Rocket's voice, "we always have plan B."

"And plan C," Hammer said.

Behind us, Biggie, Hammer, and Elektra stood with arms crossed over their chests. In front of them was Rocket with shoulders drawn back, speckles of blood across her cheeks, and two grenades in her fists. "Don't forget plan D."

"I thought—" I started.

"Don't you know me by now?" she asked. "I'm fast. I got in the cabin and grabbed Player 1's bag before the cabin came down."

Throwing my chin out at the others, I said, "I'm assuming you guys are plan C?"

Hammer punched her palm. "Fuckin' right."

Smirking, I nodded. "All right, let's do this."

CHAPTER 14

Every time Quinn and Coin fired a shot, I flinched.

The sound was deafening. For the first time, I understood why people in movies wore earmuffs when target shooting.

Beside me, Elektra and Rocket held bows, loading them every time I loaded mine.

The approach was simple—two simultaneous gunshots followed by three arrows.

Surely, we'd hit him this way, right? Who could dodge five different simultaneous shots?

Bits and pieces of our wall's wood shot up in fragments as bullets tore through it. While I hated the idea of damaging our wall, it was only material—it could be reconstructed. Right now, all that mattered was eliminating the enemy and securing my people.

The small crowd that had been swinging clubs and swords at their opponent dropped their weapons, covered their ears, and ran away from the fight.

As bullets flew, debris and dust created a translucent cloud.

Why weren't we hitting him? And why couldn't I see any strange movement anymore?

"Stop," I said, and everyone paused, weapons held up by their faces.

"I don't think he's there anymore," I said.

Rocket glared down her arrow's shaft. "Then where the hell is he?"

A shrill cry masked the sound of women panicking and made me swing my entire body in the opposite direction. Near the blasted Village gates was a woman with a huge puncture hole in her chest. She stared at me, almost pleadingly, and reached for the hole. She looked puzzled, as if trying to figure out what was going on. Her lips parted, but nothing came out. Instead, she dropped to her knees and life disappeared from her eyes.

No one even dared run toward her—instead, women ran wildly, reminding me of confused cattle in the midst of a coyote attack. They didn't know where to go. How could they? They couldn't even see our attacker.

Was this it? Was Black Panther going to be the one to massacre us all one by one?

I turned to my friends, not knowing what to do when the strangest sound caught my attention. At first, it sounded like a faint fluttering, but it grew louder and louder until at last, everyone stopped running as if forgetting we were under attack and aimed their eyes toward the sky.

My jaw hung loose as I stared up.

What the hell was that thing?

It was unlike anything I'd ever seen before.

Mighty gusts of winds blew downward as the flying vehicle's multiple helicopter-like propellers spun over its body. The wind was so powerful that grass blades danced around our toes, and tree branches swayed.

I wasn't certain who to fear anymore—Black Panther, or this giant aircraft.

It descended slowly, casting a looming shadow over us.

Too stunned and confused about what was going on, I couldn't say anything. I flinched when two warm hands gripped my waist.

"Brone!"

The sound of Ellie's voice calmed me. She squeezed my midsection and I placed a hand over hers.

"What is that?" she asked.

I shook my head to say, I *have no idea.*

This was it. I had to make a decision.

Was it better to run, or to stay? I'd lost hope too many times in the past to even consider the possibility of this being a rescue mission. It was likely Black Panther's ride home, which meant whoever was in there wouldn't hesitate to kill us all.

And judging by the look of the aircraft—a phantom black, military-grade machine—there was no doubt that whoever was in there was as dangerous as Black Panther, if not more.

I wanted them dead—all of them. Whoever had orchestrated this disgusting, inhumane game deserved to die. But the reality of the situation wasn't so simple. Around me, dozens of dead bodies lay across the Village and the surviving women looked terrified beyond belief. They stared up with bulging eyes, their bodies trembling so badly their heads shook from side to side.

I wanted to order everyone to arm up, but this wasn't about winning the war—this was about survival.

"We have to run," I shouted, my voice barely carrying over the sound of the propellers.

Everyone looked at me.

"I don't want to start over," I said, "but we have to. We have no idea who's in there, and the longer we stand here waiting for them to touch down, the more lives are at risk."

My friends went silent, no doubt thinking the same thing—after all the work we'd put into rebuilding the Village, the thought of having to flee our home again was devastating.

"Brone's right," Rocket said.

The others nodded solemnly, and when I turned to face my people, I realized their petrified gazes were fixed on me, waiting for my command.

Clearing my throat, I drew my shoulders back and grasped Ellie's hand in mine. But as I opened my mouth, a loud, unfamiliar male voice filled the air around us.

"Liam T. Saunders," the voice exploded through some megaphone-like device. "You're under arrest for twenty-one counts of first-degree murder. Surrender yourself now."

CHAPTER 15

No one moved.

Who was this man? This voice? And who was Liam T. Saunders? Was that Black Panther's real name? Was this aircraft on our side? My head spun, and I searched the Village, hoping to see Black Panther without his camouflaging abilities.

If this was him, would he surrender? Doubtful.

When nothing happened, a metallic device came hurtling through the air. It landed in the grass, right beneath the aircraft. Atop the device was a red flickering light that flashed intermittently, making my stomach sink.

Without thinking anything through, I pointed toward the Village gates. "Run!"

As we stampeded away from the flashing box, a figure appeared in front of the Village gates, stopping us in our tracks.

The figure, which was awkwardly hunched forward, held its face as if suffering from some intense migraine. "Make... make it stop!"

Slowly, the glitching stopped and Black Panther came into full view: his suit, a deep blue skintight fabric covered him from head to toe, and at his feet were two Samurai swords. While clawing at his head, he reached for his goggles and tore them off. "S-s-stop it!"

This time, his voice cracked.

He was squeezing his masked face so hard it was a wonder he didn't crush his head.

Was this the device's doing? Was it hurting him?

I spun around to look at the gadget again when a dozen armed men and women who looked like they were members of a SWAT team came falling from the aircraft on what appeared to be rappel ropes. A loud hissing sound was emitted as they slid down, and the moment their feet touched the grass, they pressed something on their belts, sending the loose ropes swaying in the air.

At once, the entire group of armed soldiers, or whatever they were, raised advanced-looking rifles to their faces. At the same time, all of my people raised their weapons. Some shouted, jabbing their spears in the air as if prepared to die to defend our Village.

But their guns weren't pointed at us. Instead, they were aimed at Black Panther. Collectively, they ran toward him, their black leather boots stomping through the grass and over dead bodies.

"On your knees!" one man shouted, jabbing his gun in the air at Black Panther.

Black Panther fell to the ground, his hands shaking over his head.

Whatever piece of equipment they'd set off was causing him tremendous pain. Was it his suit? Was the electric device interfering with it? It must have been.

The first soldier to reach Black Panther removed the player's mask and forced him onto his stomach. Dropping to one knee, he extracted a set of handcuffs that appeared to be made out of energy—blue rings that looked hot to the touch.

"You—you can't do this!" Black Panther shouted.

The man who'd arrested him didn't say anything. Instead, he pulled him up so aggressively that Black Panther let out a pained cry.

With my bow held in my hands, I rubbed my thumb against the elastic. That son of a bitch wasn't getting off that easy. I stared at him as he walked forward, the large soldier guiding him from behind and holding him by his cuffed wrists.

I was an excellent shot—I wouldn't miss.

When Black Panther's eyes shot my way, a sly smirk spread across the lower half of his face. I clenched my bow so hard the wood made a cracking noise. I knew why he was smiling—dead or alive, he'd won the game.

Across his chest was a green digital font that read: 21.

He'd killed twenty-one of my women.

Without wasting any time, I drew my arrow back.

"Brone!" Ellie hissed.

Suddenly, a female soldier eyed my loaded bow and raised her rifle at me. At the same time, another handful of soldiers did the same.

He deserves to die. Even if it kills me.

"Lower your weapon!" shouted the blond woman with the rifle.

I didn't.

Instead, I pulled back on my elastic, teeth grinding and my hateful stare fixated on Black Panther. That smug smile on his face disappeared in an instant. What had he expected? Did he honestly think he was safe behind a bunch of armed soldiers? After everything he'd done, he didn't deserve to live. And he didn't deserve the satisfaction of knowing his family had inherited his blood money.

All around me, countless women prepared their weapons—spears, clubs, and even rocks.

This wasn't going to end well.

"Excuse me," came a soft voice...so soft it caught my attention.

Without lowering my bow, I glanced sideways to find a woman walking toward me. She wore a white button-up blouse, high-rise pants, and tall brown leather boots. Her hair, groomed and shiny-looking, sat in a bun at the back of her head with a few strands dangling along her dark cheekbones.

"My name is Ingrid Swanson," she said.

Was this supposed to mean something to me? And why the fuck was she looking at me like that? With kindness? Like she knew me? Or, like she wanted to help me?

I must have been scowling ferociously at her; she held two hands in front of her as if to calm me. "I was sent here by Eliza Petrie, President of the United States."

At this, I scoffed.

Did she think that because I'd spent several years on the island I'd lost my intelligence? What kind of sick game was this?

"I may be wrong," she said, "but by the way these women look at you, I believe you are in charge."

"What's your point?" I growled.

"May I show you something?" she asked.

I was losing my patience. It was almost as if she were trying to distract me.

"It'll only take a moment," she said.

With one hand still floating in front of her face, she reached to the side of her belt, and dozens of spears turned toward her.

"It's okay, it's okay," she said, pulling up a small blue gadget. It was flat, circular, and no larger than the bottom of a mug. She pressed the top of it and a holograph appeared in front of her.

Several women gasped—probably the ones who'd spent too many years on the island to have seen technology's speedy progression.

"What's your name?" she asked.

I didn't answer.

"Anyone?" she said.

One woman cleared her throat. "Bree... Bree Chetzsky."

Ingrid smiled warmly at her and slid her finger across the projection. At once, an image of Bree's face appeared, along with small text beside it. Ingrid's eyes scanned the screen. "Convicted of murder approximately seven years ago, sentenced to serve three years on Kormace Island."

"Been more than three fuckin' years!" one woman shouted.

Then, another woman chimed in. "Who the fuck are you?"

Ingrid raised her trembling hand even higher. It was obvious she was uncomfortable but doing her best to stay calm. "I'm President Petrie's Executive Assistant—"

"Right," came someone else's voice. "'Cause we're supposed to—"

"Enough!" I shouted, and everyone went quiet.

This woman wasn't a fake. She had Bree's information, which meant she likely had all our information, too. But what for? What did she want?

Who was she, really? I needed to know more.

"What do you want?" I asked her.

Looking confused, she shook her head. "*Want?* I don't want anything. I was sent here to bring you all back home."

CHAPTER 16

The Village became so loud that I had to order everyone to shut up several times. At one point, I even turned my loaded bow onto several of my own to get them to back off.

"Is it true?" one woman shouted.

"Are we going home?"

"You can't believe this bitch."

"A female president, my ass."

"Quiet!" I shouted again. "If this woman is telling the truth, you'd better listen up if you want to go home. Do I make myself clear?"

It seemed to work. Women nodded, while others looked away from my piercing gaze.

Lowering her voice, she stepped toward me. "Maybe this would be easier if we spoke in private."

Staring coldly at her, I said, "Whatever you have to say to me, you can say to everyone here."

She cleared her throat and nodded quickly. "There's a lot of information to go over," she shouted, her voice reaching across the Village. "A lot has changed within the United States federal government. For one, President Seth is no longer in power. It's a long story, and one you'll be hearing about for years to come, but that's a discussion for another time. Right now, my priority is getting you back home. Now, due to the gruesome conditions you've been exposed to, many of you will be returning to America as free women. The only condition to your freedom is your cooperation in taking part in a rehabilitation program. For those of you who received lifelong sentences for your crime, a reputable lawyer will be assigned to your case free of charge. If you are to be relocated to a high-security penitentiary to serve out the remainder of your life sentence, I assure you that you will be relocated to one of the best facilities in the country."

"Rehabilitation program?" someone asked.

Ingrid nodded. "It's a twelve-month program located in one of America's finest centers. We want to ensure that you're properly reintegrated into society and that you don't pose any danger to yourself or anyone else. Those who cannot integrate or fail to pass the psychiatric evaluation will be given a different treatment or transferred elsewhere. Of course, everyone will be dealt with on a case-by-case basis."

"'Cause we're criminals," one woman said.

"Precisely," Ingrid said. She didn't sugarcoat anything, which I appreciated. "Technically, you were all sentenced to Kormace Island for murder, so I'm certain you can appreciate the fact that the government needs to approach this delicately."

"And what about those of us who spent even longer than our sentences?" I asked. What I wanted to ask was, *Are we going to be compensated for all this bullshit?* But the truth was, being rescued and brought back home was already enough on its own.

She glanced sideways at me but didn't answer my question. Instead, she smirked and turned her attention back onto the crowd. "The reason things took a turn so fast is actually because of Kormace Island."

"What do you mean?" I asked.

"This Death Game," she said. "The information became public after a team of hackers broke into the organizer's secret page. Let's just say the public couldn't swallow the idea of the government handing over a bunch of money to take part in human hunting. People were already upset with President Seth's dictatorship and feared speaking out. This game, however, was the final straw. It led hundreds of private investigators to dig up a lot of dirt on President Seth. President Petrie is still cleaning up the corruption left by her predecessor, and it's a slow process. The situation was far worse than we thought. Our search-and-rescue teams have already extracted several thousand bodies from around the islands."

"Islands?" I said. "Why are there so many bodies in the ocean? I heard there were four islands. You can't tell me that many people weren't able to swim—"

She cocked an eyebrow at me, confusion clouding her face. "Four islands? We've located twenty-seven different islands with survivors, and the bodies found in the ocean were nowhere near the islands, which means they were intentionally dropped into the water to be killed."

No one said anything, without a doubt too shocked to speak.

Ingrid sighed and rubbed at her temples. "What happened to all of you was unacceptable, and while we cannot go back and fix the past, I can assure you that President Petrie is going to do everything in her power to ensure America becomes once again the country everyone deserves it to be—the land of the free."

"And what 'bout us who've been livin' 'ere for years? Or people who ain't even from America?" came one woman's voice. She stepped forward, and it was obvious by her missing teeth and sun-damaged skin that she'd spent countless years on the island. "Ain't like we got anybody waitin' for us back home. I'll tell ya what's gonna happen. I'm gonna end up livin' on the streets. No thank you. I'm stayin' here."

Without any reaction at all, Ingrid asked,

"What's your name?"

The woman, looking taken aback, searched her friends and cleared her throat. "You can call me Lime."

"Lime," Ingrid said as if repeating some beautiful exotic name. "I can assure you that you will not be forced to live on the streets and that anyone who isn't an American citizen will be given the option to return home."

Lime cocked a brow. "How can you... *assure* me?"

"Through monetary compensation," Ingrid said.

Jaws dropped all around me.

"Eighty-nine million dollars was the final bid on the Death Game," she said. "The money collected will be divided between all affected individuals should you accept the sum as legal damages."

"Everyone on the island?" I asked.

She cleared her throat. "*Islands.*"

At the same time, a man with white hair, a blue button-up shirt, and shiny black leather shoes hopped out of the massive aircraft and walked toward us, a smug smile on his face.

"I highly suggest you don't accept this offer," he shouted, his voice carrying across the Village.

"And who are you?" I asked.

He extended a hand toward me. When I didn't grab it, he cleared his throat and plucked at his wrist cuffs. "Giles McCaver," he said. "I'm your attorney."

"Attorney?" I asked.

Ingrid and Giles exchanged a playful smile.

"Why don't we get everyone into the aircraft?" Ingrid said. "I believe you and Giles have a lot to discuss."

CHAPTER 17

"Three thousand dollars?" I asked, staring up at the white ceilings overhead.

This aircraft was huge. They kept referring to it as a helicopter, though it looked nothing like one.

Giles nodded, his perfectly combed hair barely moving. "Almost." He clasped his hands together, and the wind it created sent the smell of his crisp cologne up into my nostrils. "There are approximately thirty-two thousand prisoners across the different penal islands, and that's going based on the assumption that the population has dramatically dropped due to poor health and killings."

I glanced sideways at Ellie, who sat next to me in the aircraft's gray fabric chair, and at little Robin, who lay quietly in her arms. I didn't understand how she was sleeping amid all the noise around us—women came stomping down the aisle, some laughing loudly and others clapping their hands together. They reminded me of children about to go on a school trip.

Some women had decided to stay behind.

Through the small circular window on Ellie's side, I watched while the women moved away from the helicopter as the propellers kicked in. A deep rumbling filled the entire aircraft, but it wasn't loud—not like when I'd been inside the plane.

"Personally," Giles said, "I think this offer is insulting."

"Three thousand dollars is nice," Ellie said. "I'd be happy with that."

Giles smirked and shook his head. "How was your time on this island, miss? Did you enjoy it? Was it peaceful?"

Ellie looked away.

"The conditions you've been exposed to are beyond inhumane. Did you know that Mr. Milas even went as far as to request carnivorous animals be planted on this island? And the same thing was done nearly a century ago when this island was being used but not publicized? These people wanted you to die on this island. As I've said, three thousand dollars is insulting, and I urge you not to accept this offer."

"What're you proposing?" I asked.

As the words came out of my mouth, I heard how broken up my speech was. I'd never noticed it before; everyone around me spoke the same. But when Ingrid and Giles spoke, it was apparent that I'd lost some of my basic communication skills.

"Right now, the lawyers involved are proposing

splitting up the remaining portion of the funds between everyone sentenced on the islands, dead or alive. This also means that families of loved ones will be receiving some of the money, which will dramatically lower everyone's share." He leaned back into his chair and as he did, Fisher, Biggie, Coin, Rocket, Elektra, Hammer, and even Murk took up the seats around us. They leaned forward, eyes shifting left and right.

"With the severity of this situation, Miss Brone, we shouldn't even be discussing in the millions."

I stared at him. "Then what should we be discussing?"

"What I propose on going after is in the billions."

Biggie spat out what appeared to be part of a muffin—where the hell had she gotten a muffin? When I eyeballed it, she shrugged, and with her mouth still half-full, said, "What? They're offerin' some food upstairs. And what's this about billions o' dollars?"

A few other curious women leaned in closer, wanting to hear what Giles and I were discussing.

My eyes rolled toward the ceiling again. "There's an upstairs?"

Biggie nodded and shoved the rest of her muffin into her mouth.

"Look," I said, "I just wanna go home. I don't know anything about legal stuff, okay?"

"You don't have to understand it, Miss Brone. All you have to do is agree not to accept the settlement and allow me to do my job."

I didn't know what to say. There was so much running in my mind.

I felt Ellie's eyes on me, so I turned to her.

"If he says he can get more, Brone, you should listen to him."

"I need a unanimous vote on this one, Miss Brone. And from what I am told, you're in charge of these women. Everyone has to agree to take this to trial."

"Trial? Are you sure we'll even win?" I asked. "And a unanimous vote? What about the other islands?"

Giles leaned back, crossed one leg over the other, and without blinking, said, "Don't worry about the other islands—every single one is being addressed individually. And I'm the best there is, Miss Brone. While the battle may be long, you have my word that you and your women will be walking out of that courtroom with at least five million dollars."

Everyone's eyes bulged, and Ellie dug her nails into my thigh.

Coin gasped. "F-f-five—"

"Million..." Rocket whispered.

Biggie's lips stretched into a massive grin. "I could buy myself a mansion wit dat kinda money."

"Or a bunch of cars!" Hammer said.

Whispers broke out throughout the entire helicopter as word spread. I reached for Ellie's hand, and only then did I realize we'd already started flying. I'd been so caught up in my conversation with Giles that I hadn't even felt the aircraft rise. Out through the small window next to her shoulder was Kormace Island—small and alone, with nothing but ocean water surrounding it.

Would I miss it? Would it become a distant memory, or would it haunt me every night? Money would never fix what I'd lived through, but it would certainly help my people get back on their feet. I turned to the others, who stared at me with open mouths and eyes shining with excitement.

"This isn't merely about the money," Giles said. "Think about everyone involved in setting up these penal islands. They need to be held accountable for the lives they've ruined. And so does every person involved in the Game of Death."

Giles was right.

Countless people had known about the islands, and yet no one had done anything to stop it.

The road ahead wouldn't be easy; it would take a long time to adjust to living in the real world and to heal from our trauma. The legal process would probably also be tiring, but I owed it to my people to fight for our rights.

And what mattered most of all was that we had each other. I stared at my friends, feeling full of love despite their dirty faces, their matted hair, their torn skin, and their unsightly scars.

With Ellie's warm hand in mine, I kissed her cheek, and then Robin's fuzzy head. While the idea of financial freedom was attractive, what I wanted most of all was for justice to be served, and that was precisely what Giles was offering.

Breathing out through my nostrils, I smiled up at my friends—at my family.

"You guys up for the fight?"

To my surprise, everyone inside the aircraft stood up, and Giles' head turned from side to side, almost as if he was confused. Even several of the soldiers stepped forward, hands hovering over their rifles.

But my women didn't want to fight—at least, not in the physical sense.

Their eyes, full of fiery hunger as I'd once seen before, lingered on me as if I were the only person standing in the helicopter. With bowed heads, they created fists with tucked thumbs—a gesture that had once been reserved for Rainer—and slammed them into their chests.

Smiling, I turned to Giles. "We aren't the type to go down without a fight. Let's do this."

Visit **shadeowens.com** for more works by Shade Owens.